ACTIONS SPEAK
LOUDER

A Novel By
Shandra Hill

Pullen Press

Published by Pullen Press
P.O. Box 162841
Atlanta, Georgia 30321

Library of Congress Catalog Card Number: 98-91192

ISBN: 0-9662469-0-X

Revised edition

ACKNOWLEDGMENTS

For planting the seed of thought that led to this creation, for guidance and for countless blessings, I thank God.

For unyielding love, support and encouragement, I thank my parents, Willie and Betty Hill, and my sister, Shavohn.

For sharing love, friendship and writer's woes, my favorite cousin, d. l. smith (sunflowr).

For walking me through the process at a very young age, many thanks to my beloved former middle school teacher, Cynthia Anuebunwa.

For extending herself beyond the classroom time and time again, Andrea Parnell.

For being true "sister soul mates," Machelle Simmons and my associate publicist, Elayne Bowden.

For possessing a photographer's eye, Douglas Smith.

For coming into the picture at just the right time, editor Debra Ginsberg.

For their editing assistance and top-notch feedback, Blanche Richardson, Chandra Sparks, Lesley Kellas Payne and Writer's Digest's Michael Garrett and Nan Schram Williams.

For encouragement, friendship and advice, Joy Jones Keys.

For her newfound friendship and constructive criticism, Faye McDonald Smith.

For lending their talents to this project, Clarence E. Smith and Cecil Anderson.

For serving as my reading circle, Patricia Dianne Ryan, Nia Damali, Jamarva Kelsey, Denise Pines, Virginia DeBerry and Donna Grant, Angela Walton, Amanda Gordon and Christine Saunders.

For making their office my office, Lisa Johnson and the rest of the staff at Brookstone Apartments.

For you, the reader, for taking the time to join me on this journey.

Finally, for Gerald Evans, for his classic words of wisdom: "If you treat it like a full-time job, it'll pay you like a full-time job."

To my family, my strongest supporters

When people show you who they are, believe them.

Maya Angelou

Chapter One

"Come on people! Move it! I have a celebration to get to." I was determined nothing would make me late for my appointment. More important, nothing was going to dampen my mood on this Friday afternoon. Not the traffic, or the pounding rain, which, even with the wipers on high, made it nearly impossible to see the road ahead. All the more reason to get out of it, get to my destination, as quickly as possible. It was understandable how the foul weather could impact a person's driving and I, for one, believed in being safe. But this turtle-paced commuting on 285 was uncalled for.

"What are you slamming on the brakes for?" I frantically steered my Acura Integra to the left to avoid rear-ending the non-driving soul behind the wheel of a red Ford Festiva. *Not that my car's all that much bigger, but if I'd hit **that**, there's no telling how much damage would've been done.* I'd always wondered why anyone would invest in those potential safety hazards. The wheels just didn't look big enough to support the weight of the car.

"Figures!" I heard myself say as I caught a glimpse of the reckless driver before resuming my speed and passing the car via the middle lane. "It's a female! And a sister at that." I didn't have anything against women. But some of us just didn't need to get behind the wheel. In particular, those who either had a tendency to slam on the brakes or drive at maniac-like speeds. *Remember, let's not get upset,* I reminded myself, as I turned onto Fairburn Road. After all, I couldn't have been happier than I was at this very moment. If I were feeling this good, I couldn't begin to imagine what my little friend, Tiffani's, emotional state was like.

Knowing Tiffani, her face is probably beaming as bright as it was the final day of fourth grade when she took home honor ribbons in all her classes. Or she's wearing the same goofy grin as two weeks ago when she managed to trick me into getting on that silly Six Flags ride, which left us both soaked. I should've suspected something by the name, Thunder River.

Whatever the expression, I was certain it outshone the one I'd sported all day.

"Jasmine, I'm glad you could make it. And you brought gifts. Tiffani will be so surprised." Katherine Owens held the glass door—to the Department of Family and Children's Services' Southwest Atlanta office—open wide enough for me to fit through with an armful.

"Of course I made it. I wouldn't have missed this for anything. I can't thank you enough for letting me come along to do a follow-up. These are the type of stories I get the most pleasure out of."

"And they're the kind of endings I like to see. But fifteen years in this business have prepared me for reality," Katherine said, looking down at me. The forty-something mother, who never wavered from her Coretta Scott King 'do, stood at least five-feet-nine, about seven inches over me. She pushed her eyeglasses back into place, then clasped her hands in front of her big-boned body. "It's sad to say, but most of our kids may never be fortunate enough to find a stable home. Tiffani's definitely the exception. But after all that poor child's been through, she deserves it. She'll be thrilled to see you, Jazz; she simply adores you. Come along." She motioned. "She's waiting."

I followed Tiffani's caseworker to her desk near the back of the large office, passing by at least a dozen others who kept busy at their cubicles. By the time we'd made it to the middle of the room, I spotted the little girl, relaxing in Katherine's chair. I smiled.

"Jazz!" Tiffani stood and briskly headed toward me, hands held out. "Is all this for me?" asked the usually outspoken fifth grader.

"It sure is. I'm so happy for you, Tiffani." I handed Tiffani the gifts: a pair of mylar balloons, one, which read 'Congratulations;' the other, a smiley face; a stuffed three-foot Mama Panda, embracing her cub; and a jarful of the ten-year-old's favorite candy. On one of our first outings, I'd introduced Tiffani to several flavors of gourmet jelly beans sold inside the candy shop at Shannon Southpark Mall. It took no time for her taste buds to declare the winning flavor.

"Jelly beans." Tiffani studied the jar. "Bubble gum! My favorite!" She held the bears in her right arm, the candy and balloons in her left hand. Tiffani looked adorable in her red velour cardigan and matching stirrups. Her above-the-shoulder-length permed mane, pulled back in her usual ponytail, looked as if it had been freshly done, specifically for this day. A day long overdue.

Within minutes, Tiffani would finally be settling into her new home, a permanent one this time. And, to think, I had something to do with it.

Six months ago, when I wrote the feature on the thousands of children in Fulton County waiting for adoption, I'd hoped, but never fully imagined, it would bring two people—both searching for someone to love and to love them—together. Nor had I imagined just how much the handful of kids, particularly Tiffani, would grow on me. And no one could've told me I'd be here today, tagging along for the happy occasion.

Tiffani had just moved back into a DFACS shelter—for the third time in her young life—when I met her. That following her removal from foster home number three after her most recent guardian died of breast cancer. The previous sets had both fulfilled their two-year arrangements with DFACS.

Naturally, I felt proud to be able to help Tiffani. When I looked into her eyes, I saw a less fortunate version of myself, and I realized the huge difference having a loving mother *and* father at home made for me. Also, following a really traumatic experience one year ago that I didn't care to relive, I became more attached to children in general.

You've gotta stop doing this to yourself, I thought. I did my best to push the memories of that day out of my mind. I'd rehashed them a hundred times before and didn't want to do it again today.

Katherine reached inside the bottom right drawer for her purse, then grabbed her cranberry wool duffle jacket from the back of the chair. "You guys ready?"

A chill—equivalent to the one I had felt as I walked across the stage to receive my college diploma three years ago—ran through my body. "More than ever," I said. I turned to Tiffani. "And don't forget your umbrella."

She nodded and put on a big smile. Underneath the smile though, I thought I detected another emotion, a seemingly reserved one. She'd been disappointed so many times already, I wondered if she feared it happening again. I tried not to read too much into Tiffani's look and relieved her of her load by taking the balloons and candy. "This is it, kiddo," I said, as the three of us neared the door I'd walked through some ten minutes earlier.

The rain had slacked up but the clouds weighed heavily. Katherine opened the driver's side and pressed on a button, unlocking the passenger's door, so Tiffani and I could climb into her gold Pontiac Bonneville.

"Mrs. Owens! Mrs. Owens!" I heard a desperate voice shout just as I shut the door. Katherine apparently recognized the woman, who was wearing a navy coatdress and heels and appeared to be in her thirties. She pushed her door to and drew near her. The two talked a couple of yards away, as Tiffani and I remained inside.

"Where did Ms. Owens go?" Tiffani asked, a puzzled look on her round, walnut-colored face.

I didn't know what to say. I had no idea what was going on.

"She's talking to a friend right now. She should be right back."

My assurance apparently didn't satisfy Tiffani's curiosity. She stood on her knees in the back seat getting a perfect view of Katherine and the "stranger."

"Barbara!" Tiffani shouted. "That's my mommy! My new mommy!" Tiffani fidgeted in her place about as eagerly as a puppy or kitten trying to scratch its way through a closed door.

What's she doing here? I thought. *She's supposed to be at home, waiting for us.*

The corners of Tiffani's mouth dropped as the woman took off and Katherine headed in our direction. "Where's she going? Where's Barbara going? I'm over here," she said, tugging at the door handle, a defeated look on her face. The child safety lock apparently in place, she soon surrendered.

Before I could speak, Katherine poked her head in and sighed.

"There's been a change of plans, ladies," she said, looking nowhere in particular.

"What's wrong?" Tiffani insisted. "Why did Barbara leave?"

"Come on, honey." Katherine's voice broke slightly. "I'll explain when we get inside."

Back inside, Katherine's boss gave up her office to the three of us so we could have some privacy. Katherine closed the blinds draping the double glass window before taking a seat next to Tiffani, in the only other chair in the office. Plopping down in the soft leather swivel behind the executive desk, I came close to asking what was going on. But I hesitated to give Katherine time to explain. Besides, Tiffani beat us both to the punch.

"She doesn't want me, does she?" the little girl asked, looking into Katherine's eyes, then down at her small hands. "I thought she liked me." At that moment, Tiffani's strength overshadowed her pain, as she did a good job of holding back her tears. I, on the other hand, was having a hard time. But I did all I could to keep from breaking down. I had to be strong for Tiffani.

"Honey," Katherine broke in. "It's not that at all. Barbara does like you. She's crazy about you."

"She sure has a funny way of showing it," Tiffani mumbled.

"We all are," I heard myself say, inadvertently interrupting the dialogue between the two, hoping my words would somehow soothe Tiffani's aching heart.

"That's right." Katherine nodded and gave me a look that said "good answer." "It's just that Barbara has had a change of heart."

"That's no surprise," Tiffani murmered, bringing to mind that look she'd worn earlier.

That explains it. She must've known all along, intuitively, that is.

"She's just not as ready for this as she thought, as any of us thought." Katherine looked as though she wanted to say *especially me*. After all, she felt she'd made the perfect match by choosing Barbara, a thirty-one-year-old administrative assistant, over a white family in Raleigh because she believed it was best to keep Tiffani with her own.

"Remember the story Barbara told you about her first child?"

Tiffani nodded.

"Well, it seems it's gonna take her a little more time to get over that," Katherine explained. "So, sweetie, please don't think it's you.

You're not the problem. Barbara loves you, but unfortunately, the timing isn't right."

Katherine deserved a round of applause. How she was able to handle this so well, I'd never know. I never would've pulled it off. I was too busy fighting off tears.

How could anyone do this to this beautiful child after all the cards she's been dealt? What were all those visits and sleepovers for if Barbara wasn't planning to go through with this?

"So it's back to the shelter, right?" Tiffani appeared to be the strongest person in the room. Not once did her voice alter and the few tears she eventually released rested in the corners of her eyes.

Amazing. Wonder if I'll be able to handle disappointment or pain this well, when and if it strikes.

"Yes, sweetie," Katherine answered in a nasal voice.

I wished Tiffani could go with me, if only for the weekend. But I knew that wasn't possible. I was in no position, financially or emotionally, to raise a child right now. I felt so helpless.

Children should be able to look up to and depend on adults and I can't do a thing.

I left Katherine's office in worse shape than Tiffani, at least that was how the pain made me think. I couldn't believe this had happened.

I felt responsible, like I'd failed Tiffani. But no more than Barbara had by pulling out at the last minute. Unbelievable. Especially since she'd shown interest up to this point. I remembered the day she inquired about Tiffani, soon after the January issue of *Amsha* hit the stands, just like it was yesterday. Barbara immediately contacted DFACS, got the ball rolling, and within a few months, everything was in line. Finally, Tiffani had a permanent place to call home. At least we all thought.

This abandonment was perhaps as devastating as Tiffani's first, ten years ago, the particulars of which I prayed she'd never be privy to, at least not until she was older.

Far too often, thanks to Atlanta's less than hopeful daily news, I was reminded of Tiffani's painful past. Each story, sadly enough, was the same.

A newborn baby is in critical condition after she was found, wrapped in plastic, inside a Dumpster, this morning....

My reaction upon hearing each one was also consistent.

It's hard to fathom how anyone, especially a mother, could be cruel enough to toss the baby she'd carried inside for nine months into a Dumpster and leave her for dead.

That was Tiffani's story in a nutshell. Had it not been for a guardian angel, who overheard piercing cries coming from behind the Sensations Hair Salon on Tara Boulevard, there wouldn't be a happy ending. Tiffani was here today, I knew, because of that man—who was on his way to get his hair cut—and the doctors at Southern Regional Medical Center. The very first day of her stay there, hospital workers named her "Baby Tiffani." A name was the one sure thing DFACS—which immediately took custody—had in its sketchy files on the abandoned infant.

A month later, authorities had identified and arrested Tiffani's twenty-year-old mother. Soon after that, Tiffani went home with her maternal grandmother, who was in the dark throughout her youngest child's pregnancy and delivery. She stayed there for the next three years, until a stroke took a terminal toll on the forty-eight-year-old mother of three. The stress of dealing with her daughter's arrest, combined with caring for Tiffani, and worrying about her drug-dealer son, apparently "drove her to her grave." That was an old saying of my eighty-year-old great-grandmother's whenever she'd refer to someone dying from anything other than disease or natural causes.

The day of her grandmother's funeral also marked the day of Tiffani's return to foster care. After all, she had nowhere else to go, with her only known grandmother dead (Tiffani's mom wasn't sure who'd fathered the child), her uncle in and out of jail, and her aunt struggling to care for four kids of her own.

Initially, I was elated for Tiffani and proud of myself for having played a part in her escaping foster care. Now I no longer felt I'd earned the letter to the editor from DFACS praising me for my efforts.

Nor did I feel I deserved the handmade thank-you card Tiffani had created from red construction paper. She knew red was my favorite color. The first thing I'd do when I returned to work Monday would be to remove both from the partition surrounding my desk and place them in my top right drawer.

My emotions today were the complete opposite to the day Katherine called to say she'd found Tiffani a home.

"We placed Tiffani," she'd shouted on the other end of the phone one particular Tuesday afternoon. "She had a nice, easy placement. She'll be in her new home in no time."

Speaking of Katherine, she'd done a good job of beating herself up, too, after breaking the news to me and Tiffani. "I can say the right words," she'd said to me in private later. "But I myself don't understand why things like this happen, so how can I expect Tiffani to?" Little did Katherine, who'd tracked Tiffani's progress from day one, or any of us, know this would happen. All we did know was that Barbara had been burned before and she wasn't completely over her pain. Pain caused some six years ago when she was living in Rome, Georgia. There, Barbara had become a foster parent to a seven-year-old girl whom DFACS had taken from her crackhead mother. The next year, the child's aunt—her mother's sister—cut Barbara's dream of eventual adoption short when she sought custody and won.

Although Barbara had been assured there was no reason to worry about something similar happening with Tiffani, she apparently couldn't get past her fear. Overwhelming fear that landed Tiffani right back where she started and left me convinced things never worked out quite the way I imagined they would. Every time it seemed as if I'd reached the top of the mountain, I'd get knocked down, face first.

I knew I couldn't go home when I reached my exit, Memorial Drive. I had to talk to somebody. Daniel. *He'll be just as crushed as I am.* I drove north for another three exits to Lawrenceville Highway, where I'd find Daniel working at The Home Depot.

I dreaded coming in here, I thought while walking toward the automatic sliding door. Daniel's boss always gave me this look—all the while sporting a rather pleasant personality—that made me feel like one of those women who unexpectedly made it a habit to go on the job checking up on their man.

Daniel didn't care for me to drop by either. Though I never knew why, I respected his request, saw it as being strictly professional.

It had been a while since my last visit. He'd know something was wrong the minute he saw me.

A beeping noise and flashing blue light snapped me back to attention and possibly saved me from harm. I looked up to see a forklift, carrying bags of cement, heading my way.

Inside, I saw everyone else—dozens of customers, almost that many workers—*there are always new faces when I come in here*—but no Daniel.

"Plumbing—207," the desperate female voice called out over the intercom. "Plumbing—207. I need a price check, please."

That's an idea. But perhaps having Daniel paged would be a little too drastic, after all. I continued to look, passing rows of wallpaper and tile and taking in scents of lumber and sandpaper.

Closer to the tools, I spotted the back of Daniel's small head as he stacked boxes of plastic storage organizers on the display end of a shelf.

As I got closer, he began lowering himself via the step ladder, oblivious of my presence.

He's off in space or somewhere again. One day he'll follow my advice to pay more attention to his surroundings.

"Daniel," I called out softly, to prevent startling him.

He immediately turned my way and shot me a look that was a cross between "What's wrong?" and "What are you doing here?"

"What's up? What's the matter?" he asked, placing the box he now held in his hands back on top of the others.

"Everything," was all I could get out.

"What is it, Jazz?" He removed a tissue from one of the pockets on the bright orange smock he wore over knee-stained jeans and a T-shirt. With one stroke, he wiped sweat from above his right eyebrow.

"You won't believe it," I said. "What time do you get off?" I looked down at my watch. It was already a little after eight, barely two hours since I'd left Fairburn Road.

"Nine. Why? Why don't you just tell me what's wrong?"

"Tiffa—" I began, but was drowned out by the same forklift that nearly ran me over outside. More cement on its prongs, I waited until it was far enough away before I completed my thought.

"Tiffani didn't get her wish, after all."

"What are you talking about, Jazz? Come on baby, spit it out. You see I'm at work."

"Basically, the lady decided she didn't wanna go through with the adoption." Daniel's boss, Monique—wearing a short ponytail and looking as if she hadn't had a day off in weeks—stopped as she was passing by, pushing a buggy of merchandise to be shelved.

"Hi, how are you? Ja—Jasmine?" There was that look.

For a moment, I thought I was going to have to help her with my name. *Truthfully, feeling like crap.* "I'm okay. How are you?" I hadn't noticed before, but Monique wasn't much taller than me.

"Just fine. Good to see you." *If you say so.* She continued on her trail down the light bulb aisle.

"Look, this isn't the place. I'm sorry I dropped by. I hope I haven't gotten you in any trouble, but I really needed to talk about this. I'm just trying to understand." I looked away toward a long line of un-happy faces at one of the checkouts.

"I know. You don't have anything to be sorry for." Daniel used an index finger to turn my head back in his direction. "I'll be off in a few minutes. How 'bout I bring some food over to your place, we can sit down and you can tell me everything that happened then?"

"That sounds good."

"What do you have a taste for?"

"Something light." Better to be safe than sorry since I didn't think I could stomach too much of anything as it was.

"Okay. Chinese? Mexican? I know," he said snapping his fingers. "I'll pick up some of those chicken quesadillas with the black beans inside from that place down the street you like."

"Okay," I said, fingering my car key.

"See you in a minute." Daniel leaned in slightly, placing a kiss on my forehead.

"See you in a minute."

It was a good thing Daniel suggested food. I had an appetite the size of a bird but the hole in my stomach was as hollow as a whale's belly.

"School just let out what, five weeks ago. She had a new home to go to soon after." I bit into the last tortilla slice—a grilled chicken-mozzarella cheese-black bean-and-sour cream combination. "In essence, she had two good reasons to look forward to summer. Now she has none." I finished chewing, sitting Indian-style alongside Daniel on the living-room floor—our routine whenever my dining room table was covered with take-home work to be typed, written and/or edited. "Something's gonna come through. You know that." Daniel wiped his mouth with one of the napkins from the package of plastic eating utensils. No surprise—he seemed better able to swallow the news than I did.

"You're right. Katherine did say girls in general and older children with the least amount of problems—in other words, *baggage*— are easier to place. That's something else that bothers me: people who won't give a child a chance because of his or her background." We began cleaning up the mess we'd made. "Anyway, that bit of reassurance doesn't erase the fact that Tiffani has to go back to school a month from now and try to forget any of this ever happened."

"She's stronger than you think, Jazz. She'll be okay."

"I know that. I just wish it hadn't turned out this way."

"But it did and it wasn't your fault. That's what you need to realize." Daniel took the small garbage bag of empty wrappers, used napkins and crumbs and headed toward the kitchen.

"In a way, I feel like it was."

"Why?" he asked, quickly returning to my side.

"I did write the article that put Tiffani out there like bait, reeling Barbara in."

"But you didn't tell her to get cold feet, did you?" Our shoulders touched as we sat, legs stretched underneath the coffee table, our backs against the sofa. He took my left hand into his.

"Jazz, you're confused and upset right now." He began rubbing his thumb against my index finger. "Don't let that cause you to blame yourself 'cause you haven't done anything wrong. You did the right thing. This lady didn't."

"*Why* didn't she?"

"I can't speak for her, Jazz. People make choices that not only they but other people have to live with all the time. It's probably best that she backed out now, instead of later on down the road when Tiffani had settled in."

I nodded in agreement at Daniel's simple, yet compelling advice. His capacity for seeming to almost always know what to say was one reason I'd been so taken by him two years ago. Besides that, Daniel was down-to-earth, a trait we shared in common as a result of our upbringings.

"Come on, you need to get some rest." He stood, reaching for my hands to help lift me up. "No matter how long we talk about this, it won't change things."

Daniel ran a hot bath filled with bubbles. Both of us squeezed into the standard-size tub—our legs twisted together—as we'd done dozens of times before.

"Here, let me get that for you," he offered, reaching for the terrycloth hand towel. He rubbed the towel across my chest, his movements getting slower each time his hand landed on my breasts.

"Feeling better?" he asked while playing with a nipple.

"Much."

"Are you relaxed now?" His hand was now on my stomach.

"Can't you tell?" It was true. I was much more relaxed than I'd been a half-hour before. But I was far from in the mood for sex and was relieved that Daniel knew not to push that button. After helping me dry off, he tucked me into bed, before wrapping his entire body around mine. Before long, I felt light breathing brushing against the back of my neck. I lay wide awake, an unwelcome symphony of bugs, namely crickets, performing outside my window; the hopes of a better day for me and Tiffani tap dancing in my head.

Chapter Two

The more I worked, the more I understood why the typical first day of the week was dubbed "Blue Monday." It seemed as though the weekend would fly by so fast, you'd find yourself asking where all the time went. And after what happened this past Friday, I definitely needed more than two days off. Don't get me wrong—I loved my job. Who wouldn't when you're doing what you couldn't see yourself doing without? A concept my father sure didn't understand. To him, government work or work anywhere that you could devote half your life to was real work. He never knew it, but his outdated, set-in-my-ways mode of thinking was my impetus.

Another upside of the job: as with Tiffani, it gave me the opportunity to meet people, and, on occasion—when things didn't backfire—help them in one way or another. That and the fact that it provided a sense of stability made up for the low, but livable pay.

What I hated about it, or any job for that matter, were manic Monday mornings. The only good thing about Mondays was the workload, which was typically smaller in comparison to the rest of the week. Monday was one of three days Jennifer was able to lend me a helping hand, when she wasn't busy fulfilling her administrative assistant obligations. As a part-timer, she worked Mondays, Wednesdays and Fridays. She spent half the day answering phones and performing other secretarial functions; the other half, assisting me with editorial. But that wasn't always a positive thing.

When I came on board as *Amsha*'s associate editor, Jennifer was one of three people working in editorial. But she was the only part-timer and non-family member in the bunch. The owners, Malik and

Sandy Sabir, were partners in marriage and business, while switching gears to publisher/editor-in-chief and managing editor, respectively. Sandy also was in charge of making sure the bills and staff got paid on time. Then, there was Jonathan, Malik's nephew and a senior at Morehouse, who was fortunate enough to already have a full-time job as art director. My introduction to *Amsha* came roughly two years ago, during my final months of a year-long stint with *The DeKalb Sentinel,* a small weekly. Regular freelance writing assignments eventually opened other doors for me at *Amsha.* The biggest being to help relieve the couple's strain, permitting them to concentrate on their operational and managerial responsibilities. At that time, Jennifer already had two years under her belt. Prior to her tenure, Malik and Sandy were doing it all, so she certainly proved to be an asset. Needless to say, the move to fill the newly created full-time vacancy with me was a slap in the face to her.

Despite the fact that I had more experience and an English degree, Jennifer, an arts graduate with a graphic design emphasis, felt her years of dedication alone—beginning as an intern—were enough to earn her the spot. She went so far as telling me so one day as I was leaving work.

"I always thought I was just as qualified for the job as you, Jasmine," she'd said, sounding as if she were seeking retribution and compassion all in the same breath. "Plus you'd think loyalty would count for something," she'd added. *Maybe your beef should be with Jonathan, not me,* almost came out, since he had the job she'd spent four years studying for. The face-off had caught me completely off guard. But I recalled my delayed response sounding something like this: "I'm sorry you feel that way, Jennifer. But that's a bone you'll have to pick with Malik." The nerve of her, I'd thought: walking around perpetrating as this born-again Christian, in her "Sunday-go-to-meeting" dresses. That was another saying from my childhood I had picked up from my great-grandmother's lingo. Underneath Jennifer's neck-covering, near-virginal garb, though—I soon discovered—hid the biggest devil in the world. One who'd be quoting scriptures one minute and hurting your feelings the next. I got to know that part of her character through that particular incident and a couple of others prior to it. Since then, however, things had been different and I hadn't had any other encounters with Jennifer.

As a matter of fact, a year later, with that temporary but painful situation behind us, Jennifer and I had a cool, but not too cozy, relationship. It was about as close as I'd allow myself to get to a co-worker. In my short twenty-five years of living, I'd quickly learned my personal and professional lives just didn't mix. That was one of my philosophies. Another—the most important of all—*do unto others as you'd have them do unto you.* Unfortunately, not many other people in this world understood what that meant or maybe the naiveté was deliberate on their part.

Jennifer sat at her oak laminate-finish desk, only about six feet away from and parallel to mine, typing her typical seventy words per minute. I walked over and peeped around her partition. "Hi Jennifer. How's it going?"

"Oh, hi Jazz. I'm fine, thank you," Jennifer said, never taking her eyes off the computer screen.

What's that all about? I thought. *Either something's up or she's swamped.* When things were less hectic, Jennifer usually found time to chit-chat—oftentimes venting—if for no more than five minutes.

She typed her last sentence and finally let up, turning toward me. "How are you?"

Now that's more like it.

"About the same," I said. Actually, I wasn't feeling too hot. I couldn't quite put little Tiffani out of my mind. But I knew life had to go on and although I wanted to share the sad news with Jennifer, the vibes she was feeding me were telling me to wait. I took a seat and wheeled the gray swivel-back chair, which let out an annoying squeak each time I moved, up to my desk. "You look like you've got a lot on your hands. Did something happen?"

"No, everything's fine." Jennifer stood and walked over to the only other desk in the room, one occupied infrequently by interns. Stacked high was a mountain of papers about as tall as the city's business directory. "I'm just trying to knock out as much of this today that I didn't get around to on Friday." Jennifer thumbed through, then began separating the papers. "Sometimes it's hard to keep up when you're not here every day."

If my ears heard correctly, I'd swear I detected a slight sense of bitterness in Jennifer's voice. I'd admit her workload had been pretty heavy lately, what with Malik out of town on back-to-back business trips and Sandy holding down the fort singlehandedly. I even realized how difficult it had to be for Jennifer to squeeze all her responsibilities into three days without the luxury of overtime. But I also had to constantly remind myself that I wasn't responsible for things being this way. Besides, work for me—or any of us for that matter—wasn't exactly a breeze either.

Working for a small business like ours, a black-owned one at that, oftentimes required us to wear many hats. I could probably count on one hand the number of days I'd been able to focus on one thing and one thing only. My business card may have said 'associate editor,' but underneath that, it should've read 'reporter, staff writer and data processor,' to name a few. But you'd never know that by my pay. I couldn't complain though. I enjoyed what I did, was happy to have my lifelong dream come true. And, I'd have to admit, having so many responsibilities presented quite a challenge. Challenge was good. So were the opportunities provided by *Amsha,* Swahili for "to wake, to rouse"—to stir things up, if you will—which we'd developed as our mission for the black community. While the magazine featured sections on health, education, business and entertainment, among other things, it occasionally presented topics or current events—controversial at times—all germane to African Americans.

"Jennifer, feel free to let me know if you need any help. I don't have any outside assignments scheduled for today, so I'll be more than happy to help out." What I did have was enough desk work of my own to keep me busy, having left the office a little early Friday to go meet Katherine and Tiffani. Besides, the material Jennifer was finishing up was the very work I'd asked her to assist me with last week, but what the heck.

"Well, you know what I'm doing," Jennifer said, almost disgustedly. "Same 'ol. Same 'ol: editing and typing. I've completed about half of what you gave me the other day." Jennifer pointed toward the two stacks. "Here's the remaining editing pile and this is what needs to be typed."

Typing had never proven to be one of my true talents. It was no secret to me or anyone else in the office that I typed just a tad better than average speed. Still, an hour later, I wished I'd pulled work from that pile instead of the grueling editing stack. Proofing article after article was no easy task. Especially when ninety-eight percent of the time I'd find something that needed doctoring and/or rewriting in each one of the freelance submissions. Proof that *you get what you pay for,* as my mother would say, and as I came close to saying many times to Malik. First, editing proved to be engrossing. Then, little by little, it began to aggravate me, before finally becoming mundane. At those times a trip to the breakroom or bathroom would always come in handy. This time the latter was calling.

Ten minutes back at my desk, I struggled to regain momentum, unlike Jennifer who had assistance from the small radio placed on a table in between our work stations. She'd switched it on while I was temporarily out of the room.

The R & B lyrics—to a tune I couldn't make out—did nothing more than distract me. So did work at this point. I finished editing the article I'd abandoned while away at the bathroom and knocked out a pair of columns. But neither the monthly "Money Matters" nor "Ask Dr. Ruby" were receiving my full attention. My mind drifted from thoughts of Jennifer's aloofness to Tiffani's disappointment. As I searched for Katherine's number in my rolodex, I spied Tiffani's thank-you, tacked onto my partition, next to the one from DFACS. On the outside, hers read simply: *Thank you.* Inside: *Jazz, because of you I now believe that dreams do come true. I love you, Tiffani.*

I'd done more damage than I'd realized. Not only had I misled Tiffani into believing foster care was a thing of her past, I'd created this false notion that, at this moment, seemed next to impossible. I'd ruined her—at least that was the way I now felt. I also felt pretty lousy after re-reading the letter to the editor from DFACS:

Dear Jasmine Brown:

Thanks to your excellent article, Fulton County DFACS Homefinding Unit has received several inquiries regarding fostering a child. Many callers stated that before reading the article in your publication, they were unaware there was such a high number of African American children in shelters.

Hopefully, I hadn't jinxed all the kids. The inquiries may have been rolling in. For some, the paperwork was perhaps already in the works. But how many other potential parents would back out? Snap out of it, I silently told myself as the male voice broadcasting from a live remote echoed in the background. *You didn't tell her* (or anybody who does) *to get cold feet,* I reminded myself of Daniel's pep talk. Certainly if Tiffani had lost faith in anyone, it wouldn't have been me. And to prevent that from happening, I'd work at becoming the one constant—outside of Katherine—in her life.

Something about the standard on-the-job telephone greeting on the other end told me what kind of day she was having. "Adoption Services. Katherine Owens," the seemingly spirited caseworker had answered minutes earlier. I'd hoped her lively tone was an indication of something more: Tiffani's prognosis. I was partially right. The good news: Tiffani's hopes had not diminished altogether. By contrast, her list of letdowns continued to grow.

Instead of spending the remainder of the summer break adjusting to a new home, a new mom, a new life, Tiffani would find herself preparing for her third adoption fair in three years. And there was more.

"Well, the truth of the matter is, Tiff may be wise beyond her years but she's still a child," Katherine said. "As such, she's having a difficult time accepting that she won't be going shopping for back-to-school clothes, after all. That was one of the first things Barbara had promised her they'd do as a family."

I could do nothing more than let out a sigh mixed with an "ummm," the whole time trying to digest what Katherine had just said.

"So, does she have *anything* to wear?" finally came out.

"She has clothes at the shelter. Each child there has a wardrobe and from what I can tell, it's pretty 'hip,' to borrow a line from the young folks."

"Really? I never knew the shelter provided clothes for the kids. You're right. It is pretty spiffy, if what Tiffani had on Friday is an example."

"That red pants outfit? I believe that did come from her closet."

"Do they get to take the clothes with them when they leave? Do they share outfits?"

"Since I don't work out at the shelter, I really can't give you yes or no answers. I don't think they get to keep them when they move on to a foster or adoptive home. And if you're asking whether or not Tiffani could be wearing a certain dress this week and another little girl could have it on next week, I can only say that I wouldn't think it would be that way."

"What about clothes for gifts?" By nature, I'd slipped into reporter-mode, one question following another.

"Can the kids receive clothes as gifts?"

"Right."

"They're not supposed to because they have more than enough to choose from. But I would imagine if we're talking about something small, exceptions can be made."

"I'd like to take Tiffani shopping," I said, running my fingers across her card. Fortunately, Friday past was pay day. Over the weekend, I made out the checks for all my bills and got a better idea of what I'd have to work with over the next two weeks when I'd see another paycheck. "I can't afford a whole wardrobe, but I'm sure I can manage something. What does she need, in your opinion?"

"Like I said, nothing right now—not while she's in the shelter. What she wants is another story." She chuckled. "Tiffani is like a grown woman in a little girl's body, Jazz. That child loves herself some shoes."

I joined in on the laughter.

"What kind? Dress shoes? Tennis shoes?"

"All kinds," she interrupted. "If she could have every color in every pair made for her little feet, she would."

More laughter. "That's funny," I said. "I learn more and more about Tiffani each time I talk to you."

Katherine informed me the adoption fair was set for mid-August, a week before school started, almost a month away. We both agreed Tiffani could use a break from the shelter before then. I committed my upcoming Saturday to our shopping excursion. A perfect opportunity for Daniel and Tiff to meet, I'd thought, until I realized he'd be working this weekend, too. Unlike me, Daniel didn't mind losing his weekends to work. "Money is money, no matter what day of the week you make it," he'd say. Despite the truth in that, I valued my Saturdays and Sundays. It was bad enough when, occasionally, we'd have to come in here on Saturdays to complete a project that was due yesterday. Not this weekend.

Not long after ending my conversation with Katherine, I called the only other person I thought would be interested in accompanying me and Tiffani shoe shopping. More like the big brother I never had, Dave Warner stepped into my life at the start of my sophomore year at Standefer State. My Pell Grant hadn't made it in and the school's director of financial aid—I like to think of him as a lifesaver—helped me out of a major bind, pulling strings to get the money in my hands before the quarter started. He was the one who found ways to get around my two-parent-income roadblock, helping me qualify for assistance in the first place. Since, following countless talks and innocent lunch dates (his treat) at some of the city's most popular establishments, our friendship had blossomed, despite an eight-year age difference. At times, I liked to think it made it all the more better.

"What's going on?" I asked, when Dave answered by saying his full name. For two people who'd had five years to memorize the sound of each other's voice, no introduction, no formal greeting, was needed.

"What isn't? It's week one of summer quarter, or have you forgotten all about what goes on around here since you left us behind?"

"No, of course not. I won't hold you up. Just wanted to find out what you're doing this weekend."

"If I can get out of here on time, I'll be going out Friday night."

"Going out?"

"On a date."

"Whoa! Who's the lucky girl?"

"Her name is Dedra. Met her at one of my buddy's birthday parties last month. We've been on three or four dates already. Gonna check out a play and grab a bite to eat afterwards."

"Ahh, isn't that cute? Dave and Dedra."

"Don't start. I like her and all, otherwise, I wouldn't be going out with her. But I haven't been bitten by the love bug yet."

"Yet. Sounds promising, at least."

"Maybe, maybe not. That's where you ladies mess up a lot of the time, trying to turn nothing into something too soon."

"You ladies? You gentlemen sometimes give us reason to, with your smooth talking." Jennifer looked my way, a sign she was more than likely listening in, probably wishing I was in the middle of an argument with Daniel. At least I had someone to argue with.

"Jazz, by now, you should know how the saying goes, 'Actions speak louder than words.'"

"Yeah, but I still believe people shouldn't say things they don't mean. I'll take it a step further. I think everything we say we mean to say. You may only mean it at that moment, but the point is, you mean it." I hoped Jennifer was still bending an ear my way.

"It happens all the time though and men aren't the only ones guilty of it."

"Yeah, yeah, yeah. I'll get off my soapbox if you'll get off yours. I thought you had more pressing things to do."

"Yes, ma'am, I do. So what exactly is the nature of your call again," he asked in a professional tone.

"Don't try to sound all professional with me. It's not like anyone can hear you. Mr. I'm-lucky-enough-to-have-my-own-office-which-I-can-shut-the-door-to-whenever-I-please. I called to ask you about your weekend. Remember? More specifically, Saturday."

"Saturday's open," he said.

"Good. What are the chances of you and Xavier tagging along with me and Tiffani in search of new shoes?"

"New shoes for you, or for Tiffani?"

"For Tiffani, of course."

I rehashed my conversation with Katherine.

"This really is a nice gesture on your part, Jazz. It should lift her spirits some. I'll definitely be there and it shouldn't be a problem gettin' li'l man there. I'll just have to check with his mom," Dave said. "Who knows, we might find him a pair too. He has been talking about some new Jordan's."

Dave had been acting as big brother to eleven-year-old Xavier through the Big Brother/Big Sister program for three years. Another reason I had much respect for him. Their relationship reminded me, in many ways, of the one Tiffani and I shared.

Half of my weekend agenda set, I began focusing briefly on plans for tomorrow and Wednesday nights. Those were Daniel's only off days this week. With him leaving work after ten tonight, well beyond closing, there wouldn't be much for us to do besides recount our day's events before I'd have to get some shuteye. Unlike me, Daniel wasn't a morning person. He didn't mind going in as late as two in the afternoon, as long as he could still put in eight hours. But it wouldn't always be this way. A year on the job had not only earned him a slight pay increase. "Somewhere down the road," his supervisor had promised him, was a daytime-hour, one weekend-per-month schedule. Even better, hopefully, he'd be in a position to ditch customer service work for bigger, more fulfilling things, like going back to college and nurturing his artistic talents more. A self-trained artist, Daniel had developed a small following through sales at local art galleries and festivals. His unlikely tools: items such as wire and scraps of wood (supplies he was able to get on the job), even specialty-shop bargains that cost as little as a buck. His apartment, adorned with acrylic paint images on canvas and wood-carved figurines, among other things, was a showcase. Mine, with some duplicates and originals, including an embracing couple made from coat hanger wire and spray painted in black, was getting there.

The doorbell snapped me out of a light sleep. I rolled myself off the mauve sofa and let Daniel in.

"Hey, baby," he greeted me as he rushed inside.

We shared a small, lips-only kiss.

"Hey," I responded, turning the deadbolt lock.

"You feeling okay?"

"Just tired."

"Me, too." Daniel, sitting on one end of the sofa, removed his sneakers.

"Anything to eat?" He walked into the kitchen.

"I was so worn out, I heated up a frozen dinner for myself. There's plenty to choose from if you'd like one."

Daniel picked out a turkey-and-dressing combo and placed it in the microwave.

"I wanna hear about your day," he said, pouring himself a glass of cold water from a small pitcher.

"I talked to Katherine today." I raised my voice a pitch higher than usual to drown out the microwave.

"Everything okay?"

"Yeah, I guess." I repeated what I knew.

"What time did you say you're taking her shopping?"

"I didn't. We'll probably go sometime around noon or a little before. I'll have to find out what works for Dave."

"Who?" Daniel took his same seat. Light dusts of steam raised from the carton.

"Dave. My friend in financial aid at Standefer State? He's going with us. I've told you about him. Every time I say his name, you ask who he is."

"It ain't like I ever met the man, so how you expect me to remember who he is."

Daniel stretched his mouth to receive a chunk of turkey, sliding it from the clear plastic fork he was using.

"I guess the same way I'm able to keep up with friends of yours I've never seen. But I've heard plenty about them and could match their names to their stories."

"So, why haven't I ever met this dude?" The room smelled of jealousy almost as much as it did of microwave dressing.

"I don't know. There's never really been any occasion, or reason to, for that matter. Just as there hasn't been with all your friends—male and female."

He didn't back off as easily as I'd thought, or hoped. I first found his expressions of envy flattering, cute in some strange way. Now, Daniel was beginning to bug me. Surely, he wasn't accusing *me* of wronging *him,* particularly in that way. That would've been "like the pot calling the kettle black," as I'd heard many a female in my family say from time to time. I wondered what the shoe felt like on his foot. See, I didn't want to go there. But Daniel was making it hard not to.

"So, it'll be the three of you, just like a little family?"

Uh-oh. How could I tell him the "family" was one person larger than he thought? Somehow, he began making me feel guilty and sorry for him at the same time, though I had no reason to.

"No, Xavier, Dave's little brother he mentors through Big Brother/Big Sister, is coming, too. And no, we won't be like a little family, Daniel."

"Sure sounds like it," he mumbled, while scraping the remains of his meal.

"You have nothing to worry about, okay? Dave's like a big brother to me, too. I wanted you to go—still do—but you'll be working."

Finally, he came around. "I'm sorry, baby. I don't know what got into me. I ain't no jealous type now, but the thought of your woman

spending a day with another man can make any man act a little fool-
ish."

He kissed my forehead, breaking the ice for what came next. "I
understand, Daniel. I think it's sweet the way you were carrying on.
I'd feel the same way if the tables were turned." *When* the tables were
turned was more like it. But I couldn't find the strength to say it. Negative talk like that had no place within our renewed commitment, effec-
tive since the latter part of January, now going on six months.

"I know what you wanna say, Jazz." Daniel temporarily placed
the now-empty box on the coffee table.

"But I won't."

He played with my fingers.

"I wouldn't be mad if you did."

"There's no room for that here. Remember our vows?"

"You're too much," he said. "I'm still trying to figure out what I
did to deserve you."

The week traveled faster than a rumor in Smithsville, my small
Florida hometown I made every effort to distance myself from. Saturday had arrived, bringing with it feelings of anxiety. I was nervous for
two reasons: Would this be the setback to ignite a drastic change in
Tiffani's behavior? Would she have a hard time opening up to Xavier
and Dave?

No surprise to me or Katherine, Tiffani was more reserved, a lot
quieter than usual. Getting back to her old self would take time, I
knew. Getting her to again trust and open up to people would take
work. That included me.

"Tiffani, what have you been up to?" I asked, as we drove away
from the DFACS parking lot, minutes after Katherine had placed Tiffani
in my care for much of the day.

"Nothing." She focused her attention outside the passenger's window.

"Nothing? You can't spend all your time doing nothing. Have you
made any new friends lately?"

"No." She maintained her stare. "This new girl and her little brother
moved in this week," she said, almost as an afterthought.

"What's their names?" We were five minutes from the shoe shop.

"Gloria and Jacob. She's ten like me. He's eight."

"Oh." I didn't know what more to say. I tiptoed around touchy topics like how the siblings had ended up in the shelter or where their parents were. Did foster kids even talk about things like that or was that subject matter off-limits?

"Their daddy shot their mama in the head right in front of them," Tiffani volunteered. "She's in heaven. He's in jail."

How did she know all this? Each child took a different path, told a different story, but had the same tragic ending, nonetheless. If Tiffani knew other children's histories, how much did she know about her own? I was under the impression that Katherine had been hush-hush up to now. *She'll be better off finding out when she moves into a permanent setting* was Katherine's belief. Even so, what was an appropriate age to tell a child they'd been abandoned by their natural parents?

"Who told you that?" I asked, parking.

"Gloria."

"And what did you tell Gloria about yourself?" I couldn't resist. No better time to ask than now, I figured. As I turned the car off, she began, "I told her I didn't have a mama or daddy either. Ms. Owens and the other ladies took me from them when I was a baby 'cause they knew there was somebody else who could watch over me better." Not one variation from the story I'd written in the article until, "'But I'm not in as bad shape as you and Jacob,' I told her, 'because at least I never knew 'em.'"

My eyes, slightly watery, settled on Tiffani for the next thirty seconds. No words, no sounds, broke the silence.

Finally, "let's go inside. Dave and Xavier are probably waiting."

I'd been told the month leading up to the start of school was the busiest for back-to-school shopping. A stampede of parents, stepping over dozens of scattered shoe matches to get to the bright-red, for-sale signs, validated the advisory.

Commands of "Mama, look at this!" echoed throughout the free-standing store.

"I'm not buying you anymore white shoes!" I overheard one put-out mother say as Tiffani and I made our way to the adult sizes. Hard as it was to believe, Tiffani, almost as tall as me, was already wearing a woman's seven.

"You wanna see if there's anything you like while I look for the guys?"

Just as Tiffani gave me the nod to take off, I felt a tap on my shoulder.

"Hey, lady," Dave said as I turned to face him.

I looked up to a welcome smile beaming down on me and returned the greeting before looking over Xavier's way. Tiffani joined us in a small circle.

"Xavier, how are you?" I offered.

"Fine," he said. It was his usual response.

"This must be Tiffani." The words came from Dave's lips before I had a chance to go through with the formalities.

"Yes, this is Tiffani." I placed my hand across her shoulder. "Tiffani, this is my good friend, Dave, and his little brother, Xavier." I'd told her all about them before we left the office.

"Young lady, I've heard a lot of good things about you," Dave offered, causing Tiffani to blush.

Dave stood straight and addressed me. "So, how've you been?"

"Good," I answered, "and you?"

"Blessed. How's Daniel treating you?"

"No complaints."

"Well, if you don't have anything bad to say, you oughta at least have something good to talk about."

"We're fine, Dave. We'll be celebrating six months of being back together at the end of next week."

"Congratulations. Long as I know you're happy, I'm happy."

"Thank you. So, how was last night?"

"It was okay. The play was excellent."

"The entertainment was more entertaining than the date? That's not good."

"I mean, I'm not saying I didn't have a good time with her. It's just—well, it seems there were more sparks flying in the beginning. The first day we met, we talked for hours on the phone."

"That's normal in any relationship, isn't it? One week you're on cloud nine, the next, you're back to reality."

He shrugged.

"I guess." By now, Tiffani and Xavier had grown tired of listening and had wandered off to their prospective corners.

"We'll talk," Dave said. "Right now, it's their ball game."

We decided to split up in pairs for a short time: me and Tiffani on one end; Dave and Xavier on another.

The plan was to find one pair of shoes—dressy or casual—for Tiffani. It was her choice. I started with what I thought were good picks.

"What do you think of this?" The first contender was a white Nike cheerleader sneaker that allowed you to change the color of the familiar symbol every day if you wanted.

I knew the answer before she spoke a word. The half-frown on her face gave it away.

I switched to sandals, beginning with a flat, simple, toe-revealing leather model with straps. "What about these?"

No luck there either.

"What's wrong with these shoes?" I asked, truly out of curiosity and not hurt.

"They're not me." *How do you know what's you,* I wanted to ask. *You're only ten.* Then, I realized, she did have a mind of her own.

"Okay, you've got a point. You are the one who has to wear them. See, *I'd* wear something like this." I held up a more formal, low-pump pair, a cute silver design across the top. Tiffani giggled, a sign my third attempt had also struck out.

"Your turn."

Without blinking, Tiffani pointed to a flashy something that I was sure had been part of my mother's, if not my grandmother's, wardrobe at some point.

"That's what you like?"

You have to remember, that 60's/70's look is back in, I thought. Bell bottoms and platforms were the in-thing around the time I was born.

Tiffani nodded.

I had to be honest. "I don't. You don't see anything else?" We walked to the end of the long row, before moving over to the other side. Sale items were mixed in with the regular-priced bunch. The cycle continued: Everything I liked, she didn't, and vice versa. I didn't realize we'd been inside for more than an hour—nowhere close to a consensus—until Dave and Xavier returned from their side of the store.

"We're ready," Dave said.

"Really?"

"Yeah," Xavier said, sounding as if he'd just bought up the whole store.

"What do you expect, Jazz? We men don't take all day like you women."

Here he goes again with his men versus women crap. I won't even acknowledge it.

"Anyway." I shifted my focus to Xavier. "What did you find?"

"A pair of Jordan's." He removed the lid from the box to reveal a white sneaker with a familiar black-and-red emblem of basketball legend Michael Jordan leaping into the air.

"Nice." With guys, there were two adjectives I'd learned from Daniel and Dave not to use: "sweet" and "pretty." Xavier smiled as if he'd designed the shoe.

"So, what have you two found?"

"Not much," I answered.

"Uh-huh," Tiffani said, sounding her age for a change. It was true: Tiffani had the spirit of an older soul, but she was indeed still a kid.

She picked up a bubble-like style, taking me back some more years.

"Cool," was all Dave could say. And somehow he sounded convincing. He took the match from Tiffani and examined it more. "I can deal with this. This is what all the young ladies at school are wearing."

"That's because you're at a university, not an elementary school."

Tiffani joined in. "All the girls wear them at my school," she said, defending her pick.

"Mine, too," offered Xavier. I guess he figured, 'If I can have what I want, why can't she?' "They're tight," he said, using a term I'd been hearing from middle to high schoolers a lot lately. "I like 'em."

Tiffani smiled, as she apparently awaited my approval.

"Ahh, come on, Jazz," I heard Dave say before a voice inside my head spoke: *What happened to 'She's the one who has to wear them?'* *They're on sale,* it continued.

"Okay." My own words surprised me.

Tiffani was grinning from cheek to cheek. "All right. Thank you, Jazz." She grabbed the box from the rack.

"You haven't even tried them on, Tiff."

"I already checked. They're the right size." Excitement trembled in her voice.

"They may be, but you still need to try them on. Every shoe fits differently."

She spotted the nearest chair and rushed to remove the sandals she wore with a simple short outfit.

"Walk over there," I instructed Tiffani once she had the shoes on. "How do they feel?"

"Good."

Of course.

It was settled, with some compromising on my part. Tiffani was again happy. I'd done a good deed and we'd all had a good time.

Chapter Three

Daniel wasn't big on surprises. But that didn't stifle his creativity one bit. When he really wanted to, he could concoct a simple evening of romance sure to impress most any woman—almost without effort. Tonight was proof. The evening got off to a perfect start with Daniel giving me a handmade symbol of our love: a wood-carved humming-bird resting on a perch. "It represents our love taking flight again," he'd said. In celebration of our six-month reunion, Daniel and I then strolled downtown, our arms keeping each other close. Quite the way it had seven years ago, during my college-scouting days, the skyline worked its magic. The city's attractiveness was the first magnet.

"I still can't believe it," Daniel said out of nowhere.

"What's that?"

"You, me. Almost two years. Tonight."

"Yeah, I know." We stopped on the corner of Marietta Street, waiting for the "Walk" signal to cross over to Peachtree.

"I'm not just talkin' about all the stuff we've been through, breakin' up, gettin' back together," he explained, squeezing my right side. "I'm thinkin' back to how it all started and how if it had been left up to you, it never would have."

Here we go. No matter how much time passed or how much reassuring I did, Daniel never failed to remind me of my initial disinterest in him back then.

"Why do you always have to bring that up?"

"I was just thinking, that's all."

"Can't you reflect on more pleasant times?" I said, as we relaxed on the marble encasing a decorative fountain.

I regretted reliving the memories of the day we met about as much as I regretted my actions. That Saturday was as clear as tonight's dazzling sky. Graduation had come and gone, I was starting a new job, my first, and with all that came a move from the apartment I'd shared with the same roommate for two years into my own place, another first. Since Standefer State was mostly a commuter school, there were no on-campus requirements. No loss to me. I hated the thought alone of dormitory living: tiny quarters that placed you a few steps away from the stranger or strangers you were somehow "matched" with, and overcrowded restroom space you shared with even more strangers down the hall.

Four years and two different roomies later, I was ready to step out on my own. To save money on moving expenses, my parents and sisters, Justice and Marlo, made the trek to the city to help me get settled. Once here, my dad rented a truck and filled it to capacity. Whatever couldn't fit inside made it into my car or the family van. Even with a moving van, we made I don't know how many trips back and forth, picking up and dropping off. I didn't realize how much I actually owned until I'd had it all boxed up.

It wasn't until one of my final deliveries that I bumped into Daniel.

"This must be my lucky day," he'd said as I entered my new apartment across the hall from the one he was exiting.

"And why is that," I asked, wearing a frown, all the while using my foot to open the door to my new place.

If that's his idea of a pickup line, he could use some help, I'd thought, hands full with the medium-size box I was carrying.

"Because," he went on to explain, placing the bookshelf he was holding by his side, "I should be halfway across town right about now, on another move. Instead, I'm here, in the company of a beautiful woman, all because I got pulled off that one at the last minute. I'd call that luck, wouldn't you?"

I didn't recall saying anything. Rather, I caught a glimpse of the logo on the shirt Daniel wore, before easing my way inside. Rude, I could now admit. But it was the first thing I thought to do. After all, I wasn't impressed with Daniel's come-on or his line of work at the time. Sure, he had good looks—smooth "brown sugar" skin, sexy, one-inch thick eyebrows and a goatee. But, he was after all, a moving man.

Wrong as it was, I assumed anyone getting paid to risk throwing his back out daily couldn't have anything more than a high school diploma. That wasn't enough for a recent college grad like myself. I later realized how horrible I was for thinking that. Though Daniel didn't have a college degree, he did have three years' worth of courses under his belt. Forty-five hours was all he lacked to having a bachelor's in business.

And none of that should've mattered anyway. The fact was, Daniel was a nice guy. He deserved as much of a chance as anyone—degree or not.

"Yeah, you tried to play all tough and everything, like you didn't need nobody. Then when you broke that lamp in the parking lot..."

"How many times you gonna tell this story?" I interrupted. "When I broke the lamp, you came running down, too eager to help me clean it up. *That's* what happened."

"Ahh, Jazz, you know if I hadn't helped you, you would've been out there all day. Plus, it was ninety degrees outside. You know you would've melted."

"I had to admit, the way you handled things was interesting, kind of cute."

"I know how to work it, baby. Like when I finished helping you clean up the lamp—remember what I said?"

I sighed. "Yes, Daniel."

"'You know you owe me, right.'" Daniel repeated the classic line. "That was smooth."

"It sure was," I said, giving him a verbal pat on the back.

"You worked your charm, baby." Pat, pat.

I leaned into his arm.

"Just like you did on our first date."

Our first date, two years ago, was like no other. We spent five hours together, doing the two things guaranteed to win my heart. First, there was the picnic in Piedmont Park on a gorgeous fall day, the October sun slightly piercing through the evening breeze. Later, the sparkle from the romantic combination of a full moon and stars—much like tonight—set the mood for a midnight walk. The entire time, we were talking, about everything from our jobs to music to past relationships.

Although we clicked that night and on many other dates following that one, the possibility of a relationship was still a long shot. While Daniel was persistent, I held back, thanks to my college sweetheart, whom I wasn't completely over, some two years later. I knew Patrick and I weren't going to get back together after I'd somewhat regrettably broken off things with him. Not because he wasn't loving me right. But because Patrick slowly developed into a slacker and a moocher. In no time, he lost the desire to pursue his dream of becoming a musician. Sometimes I felt Patrick's only purpose in life was loving me. So I cut him loose. Still, months after the breakup, I was holding on to the love a little bit, and holding back on others. I never was one for dating on the rebound, and always believed in giving myself sufficient time away from a relationship before jumping into a new one. Eventually, however, Daniel's persistence paid off. Before long, six months had passed, then a year, then two years. For the most part, we'd had an on-again, off-again relationship but we never stayed apart for long, until last fall, when we lost three months over some drama. This January turned it all around for us, though.

"...and you're still working it," I continued. "I know you can agree that things have been a hundred percent better since we started over."

"They have, haven't they? I'm glad we had a second chance, baby. Thank you for giving me one."

In all the time I'd been with Daniel, not once had I initiated sex. In thirty-one years, Daniel had gotten around, I'd assumed, and anything I did couldn't quite measure up to what some of his more experienced lovers—the kind you don't take home to mama—had to offer. But tonight, for the first time, I felt a little more comfortable with my sexuality, more relaxed, less self-conscious, for some reason. So relaxed, not only did I come on to Daniel, I added a touch of creativity.

Back from our walk, Daniel headed straight for the shower.

"I'll be in in a minute," I yelled from the bedroom as I removed a below-the-knee length, canary sundress.

I lit every candle in the room—a dozen short, tall, thin, round ones, some scented, all a different color. Music from a local jazz station completed the scene. To Daniel, small touches like these made all the difference.

I soon joined Daniel, a little nervous, but also excited.

"Wash my back," he asked in a gentle tone, while handing me a bar of soap and his washcloth. Daniel returned the favor before I rushed out, to prevent giving him time enough to make the first move. Tonight, I was in control, for once.

Daniel's penchant for taking half-hour showers gave me time to dry off, make it to the bedroom and slip into a red hot, G-string teddy. I'd been saving it for a time like this for months. Finally, after a little under thirty minutes, the water stopped.

Sliding the towel along his shoulders and back, Daniel said nothing. He simply wore a smile.

"What's all this?" he asked, looking around the room.

I remained slightly under the floral, flat sheet, the top half of my sexy getup revealed.

"I'll finish this for you," I said, crawling from under the covers and stepping off the bed. I took the towel from Daniel's hands. His smile grew, as did the look in his eyes.

"Ummh. Where'd you get this?" he asked, running his finger across the lace design circling my breasts.

"I've had it for a little while now," I said, slowly spinning around for him. "You like it?"

"Love it." Daniel's hands cupped my butt.

I wiped a couple of spots on his back before dropping the towel to the floor.

Again, I turned to face him, pushing Daniel's body onto the bed. I kissed his chest, his face, his lips, as Daniel caressed, glided and gripped. Next thing I knew, I was sitting on top of him. Daniel continued to squeeze my hips as I took one of his hands and placed it on my breast. The more he grabbed and squeezed, the more I squirmed and sighed until finally, "Take it off, baby," came from my lips.

All of this was so out of my character, but it felt good, physically and mentally. As Daniel unsnapped the seat of my nightie, I slid my hand underneath one of the pillows where I'd tucked away a condom.

Daniel and I rocked together, our bodies becoming one. At times, Daniel slowed the pace, his eyes locked with mine.

"I love you, baby," he'd whispered twice, making me feel desired and loved, all at once.

"What got into you?" Daniel asked as we later snuggled.

"What do you mean?"

"You've never done anything like that before." All the candles were out by now but I could tell Daniel was beaming. I was pleased.

"There's a first time for everything, isn't there?" I stroked his chest. "You're not complaining, are you?"

"No, hell no. That was good, baby. Great."

I lit up.

The banner greeting us as we neared the hub of activity simply and appropriately set the stage:

"Every child deserves a home. Think adoption."

Daniel had made sure to request this Saturday off far in advance to attend the August adoption fair with me. Even better, he'd convinced his boss to come, too. Monique and her fiancé, Marcus were considering adoption because doctors had warned her she couldn't have children.

I soon learned Monique wasn't alone. Many of the potential parents here shared the same sad story. There were also those big-hearted couples who didn't mind extending an already four- to five-family household by as many as six or seven. Single females—no male prospects in sight, or no time on their side for childbearing—completed the group.

"Nice crowd, huh?" Daniel asked when we entered a large conference area inside the Grayland Grimes Recreation Center. The boxing great and Atlanta resident, orphaned at birth, was one of the main sponsors of the event.

"Sure is." I'd never attended an adoption fair before but Katherine had given me an idea of what to expect.

There had to be a thousand people here. A young ballet troupe performed on stage for a few hundred spectators. Pizza, chips and sodas attracted another mass to a makeshift dining hall while others flipped through the pages of dozens of photo albums, displaying the résumés and faces of deprived children. The remainder conducted on-the-spot interviews with the lucky few who were chosen to be in the flesh.

"Preston, Cameron and Chastiny," I overheard one lady say to a man standing alongside her as she pointed to a picture. "Says here they prefer to be kept together."

I had mixed feelings about this fair. While I knew it was for a good cause, I was bothered by the appearance of these unquestionably well-meaning folks shopping for kids.

"I don't know if I like this," I told Daniel, as I read over the bio for a four-year-old boy named DeMario.

"Like what?"

"It's like a meat market." Daniel studied another scrapbook.

"I see what you mean," he said. "Think of it this way though, there are people here who, if nothin' else, will get to see these kids up close. Maybe that'll make a big difference."

"That's true." Always the right words. And always so plainly, but well put.

The two of us were on our fourth album when we spotted Monique and Marcus who stood across the long table examining their own set of snapshots.

"How long have you guys been here?" I asked, following Monique's brief introduction of Marcus to me. I felt awkward, but at least this time, I wasn't getting the look.

"About two hours," Monique answered, looking at her watch.

"What do you think?" The question was lame, I admit, almost as bad as 'See anything you like?' but I didn't know any other way to put it.

"We're glad we came."

"Yeah," Marcus interjected, "they should have these more often. We didn't realize there were so many black foster children."

"It's definitely a benefit to us, since, you know..."

I nodded. Then a terrible thought that I'd attempted to bury so many times before came to me: And here I am killing mine. Having an abortion was the most difficult decision I ever had to make. That horrible image was still painfully clear: my legs placed into the steel stirrups as the sucking of a machine snatched out what had been grow-ing inside for six weeks. Daniel, not quite financially stable in my opinion, wasn't ready for the responsibility of being a father. And my low-paying, albeit, gratifying career was just starting to pick up steam.

It couldn't be: Jasmine Brown pregnant out of wedlock. Jasmine Brown pregnant at twenty-four by a man she'd been involved with just short of a year. Boy, would my daddy have loved that. *What did we send you to college for?* I could hear him say. *Told you you didn't bit mo' need to move to no damn Atlanta.*

Though Daniel was very supportive—*whatever you choose to do, I'm with you*—and actually beamed at the thought of becoming a father, especially if the baby had been a boy, I couldn't go through with the pregnancy. Too much emotional pressure from home and not enough combined pay between me and Daniel made for a big mess, I'd concluded.

"But I firmly believe those doctors are wrong," Marcus said, taking over. "Ain't nothin' wrong with Monique or me. My God has told me that." A spiritual man. I liked that.

"Marcus." Monique wore a "not-again" look. "I believe in miracles too, honey, but we've gone to so many doctors already," she said, apparently more for my and Daniel's ears. "We've gotta do something. That's why we're here."

Within our first hour, we bumped into Katherine who led us downstairs to a play area where we found even more adults and kids, including Tiffani. She was nearly drowned by a sea of colorful plastic play balls inside a tent-like structure.

Katherine motioned for her to come out. After slipping her shoes back on, Tiffani was escorted by Katherine in our direction.

"Here she comes," I warned Daniel. I sensed he was a little nervous, considering he had very little experience with children.

Wonder what it would be like if we'd had the baby.

"You okay, Tiffani?" I detected something was wrong.

"Yes."

"You having fun?" Daniel asked her, in an attempt to break the ice.

"Yes."

For reasons unknown, she wasn't opening up, not even to me. Maybe she was bothered by this whole arrangement, too. After all, it had only been her third adoption fair.

I wish I could remove her from all this. Give her a stable life. Love her. Protect her from fear or harm.

Daniel, standing a few inches over me and Tiffani both, probed a little harder. "Are you always this quiet?"

"Not really."

It was a lost cause, I sensed him surmising.

"I'm gonna go get something to eat. You want something?"

I didn't have an appetite.

"Tiffani, want something to eat?" It was his final try.

"No, thanks."

"Tiffani, are you sure nothing's wrong?" I asked, as Daniel walked away.

She shrugged.

"What is it?"

"What's up with *him?*

"Who?"

"Your friend," she said. "I liked that other guy, Dave, better. He was much cooler."

Look, missy, I thought, what would you know? Could the fact that he sided with you when we bought those ugly shoes have something to do with it?

"That may be true, Tiffani. But Daniel's not as used to being around children as Dave is. That doesn't mean he's not a nice guy."

"I didn't say he wasn't nice. He just doesn't look like he would be too much fun."

"He *can* be fun. Maybe the three of us can do something together one day."

"Maybe," she said before being called off by Katherine to go talk to a lady I'd noticed had been watching us for a short while.

School started the next week. A month went by before I saw Tiffani again. Following Daniel's suggestion, the three of us checked out what was considered the world's only black circus.

Tiffani warmed up this time, but whatever reservations she had were registered in her head. What it would take to remove them I didn't know. Even still, something wouldn't let me brush her thoughts off altogether. Was it possible she was onto something?

What was even more perplexing was why I'd let her opinion bother me in the first place. She was just a child. What did she know?

Chapter Four

I'd been craving a break practically ever since I got to work. At the back of the office, the small, unoccupied break area—not much bigger than the dining space in my one-bedroom Decatur apartment—was the perfect relaxation spot. Other than lunch, most times one person would have the space all to himself. I poured myself a medium-size cupful of coffee, stirring in plenty of sugar and my favorite hazelnut creamer. One of three chairs surrounding the round table became my comfort zone, long enough for me to take a handful of sips, before being reminded of all the work awaiting me when I heard Jennifer's slight southern accent come across the PA.

"Jasmine Brown, you have a phone call holding in editorial."

Who is it now? I thought. *I'm not in the mood to talk to another PR person.* Seemed as though every public relations director and their mama had something to sell: *the* story that just *had* to be covered. *Just wanted to make sure you got the fax we sent about tomorrow's ribbon-cutting*, she'd say (most times, it would be a female). *The mayor and other city officials are going to be there*, she'd continue in a customary flighty, southern voice, making you wonder how she got the job in the first place. Made me wanna ask, 'What have *you,* or the mayor, done for *me* lately?' Sometimes they'd be worth listening to, especially if a free lunch or dinner was part of the deal. But the chances were usually pretty slim. And right now, I just didn't have the luxury time it would take to find out.

On second thought, it could be my sweetheart, Daniel. I hadn't talked to him since about three hours ago, when he left my apartment for work. He did say he'd call me later on. And when Daniel made a promise like that, he rarely let me down. I walked through the door just as Jennifer was about to page me again.

"I'm here. I was walking as fast as this coffee would allow." Before picking up the line, I got another swallow or two of what had become one of my favorite beverages. The java was on the nose—the color of cocoa, with the right amount of cream and sugar, giving it a sweet enough taste that didn't take away from its strong, invigorating flavor. The fact that it was in one of those Styrofoam cups I despised drinking coffee from didn't bother me at all. I hoped this call wouldn't take too long. I didn't want a good thing to go to waste.

"This is Jasmine," I answered in my professional, but just-in-case-it's-somebody-I-don't-wanna-be-bothered-with voice.

"Hi, Jasmine. This is Denise Jackson. How are you?"

What a surprise! It was actually somebody I wanted to hear from.

"Denise, hi. I'm fine, thank you. How are you?"

"Wonderful. How are things going over there for my number one alum?" Denise sounded as perky as always. Her animated personality was quite fitting for her role as director of Standefer's Alumni and Career Services Department. During my senior year, one of the most taxing times in my life, Denise had helped keep me focused and optimistic. She had also kept me informed of job openings throughout the city. We'd inevitably developed a friendship in the process.

"Good," I said. "Busy, of course."

"Well, hang in there. You know we're always rooting for you."

"Why thank you, Denise." I picked up the cup, and got in three more sips, hoping to finish off the coffee in between responses.

"We're proud of you. I've told you that before. It's not every day a student graduates into a job doing what they love most. That's why I'd like for you to speak at our upcoming job fair. You could help reassure other students that the same can happen for them."

Someone's asking for something that will benefit me for a change?

"Wow, I'm flattered," I said, placing the now one-quarter cupful of joe next to the phone. "I'd love to do it. When is the fair?"

"Friday, October 21st at noon."

The 21st. The 21st. There was something about that date. I looked at my poster-size desktop calendar to see if I already had something penciled in. Just as I'd suspected: a prior eleven o'clock engagement.

One I couldn't afford to reschedule.

"You won't believe this."

"Oh, don't tell me you can't make it," Denise said, disappointedly.

"I really wish I could. I'm honored that you even asked. You have no idea how much I'd love to be able to come back on campus to speak at such a significant event. But that Friday I have to interview Andy Young. I've had the appointment scheduled for about three months now. As a black publication, we feel it's our duty to give him his props for his role with the '96 Olympic Games. As you might imagine, he's a hard man to track down. Matter of fact, when you call his office, you rarely get a human voice; most correspondence is by way of faxes."

"I understand, Jasmine. I'm disappointed, but I do understand. And I think the story is a wonderful idea."

"Again, I apologize, Denise. I really regret having to say no. But since I can't make it, may I suggest a substitute?"

"Sure, that would be great."

"How about my boss, Malik Sabir?"

"Tell me about him," Denise said.

"Malik's success story is truly inspiring. His first job out of college was in the mailroom of a small circulated newspaper. He later became publisher and editor-in-chief of *Amsha,* which, you know, is based here. What you didn't know is, he and his wife started it in the basement of their home six years ago. Today, it has a circulation of around 50,000."

"That's wonderful. The only thing is, he's not a Standefer State alumni," Denise said, sounding as if she were really hoping to show off her own.

"Yeah, I know. I'm really sorry about this."

"Stop apologizing. It's not a big problem. We'll have to take what we can get, with just a little over a week's notice. And don't you worry, there will always be other job fairs, for which, of course, you'll be the first I'll call."

"Thank you. I'll discuss this with Malik and get back to you. If anybody has to fill my shoes, I'd rather it be him. I'm sure he'd be honored, if he can find the time." Finding the time wouldn't be a problem. Malik and I had a wonderful rapport; he'd try to make the speaking engagement if for no other reason than to oblige me.

I was thrilled to recommend Malik, a man who'd been such a relief from my first editor, who was a couple of years from retirement, grumpy with old age, and quick to lay blame. Malik, who'd just celebrated his fortieth birthday, was quite the opposite.

If anybody deserved recognition, he did. He worked hard, put his all into his business. "You work harder for yourself than you do for anybody else," he'd said, time and time again. But "there's nothing like being your own boss," he always added.

Not only was he committed to his business, he was a family man. From where I was sitting, he and Sandy, who'd met during an entrepreneurial workshop, had a great relationship. Although they're quick to tell you, they've had their moments, especially early on. "Marriage, relationships, it's all work," Sandy had advised me during one of my episodes with Daniel. "Both people have to be willing to accept that." They were good people and I considered it a blessing that they were part of my life.

Even with the perfect backup plan, it hurt me to have to turn down an invitation to speak at my alma mater. That invite was just what I needed to help me feel better about what happened with Tiffani. Plus opportunities like that didn't come knocking every day. Not only had I reached my goal of becoming a full-time journalist in a major market, I had the chance to share my story—in the hopes of making a difference—with other aspiring students.

The very next day, I got an answer from Malik, although, intuitively, I'd known what it was all along. Once he said yes, I got on the horn with Denise. What she said when I gave her the news almost knocked me out of my seat.

"Jasmine, there must be some confusion. Your colleague, Jennifer Mitchell, has volunteered to take your place. I thought you knew that. I was about to call you and say 'thanks.'"

I was nearly speechless. "I don't understand, Denise. As I told you yesterday, Malik was my choice for a replacement."

"I'm sorry, Jasmine. Obviously there's a misunderstanding. Jennifer said you asked her to give me a call because your boss wouldn't be able to make it. She mentioned she has a degree in graphic design, but assists with both the technical and editorial ends of the publication.

Therefore, she says she could talk to students about how to make themselves more marketable in the workplace."

"Right." I didn't know what else to say. I looked over at Jennifer's desk, wishing today weren't an off day for her so I could get to the bottom of this.

"Jasmine, if there's a problem, let me know. I'm sure we can work something out."

"No, everything's fine. Jennifer, it is," I said, feeling a slight headache coming on from all the confusion. What in the world was going on here? Why would Jennifer do something like this? When did she have time to call Denise? Where did she get her number?

Thinking back to yesterday, when Denise called, I had noticed Jennifer's typing slowed significantly. She went from her normal above average speed to literally pecking, but I'd just assumed she was giving her fingers a rest as a safety measure to keep herself carpal tunnel syndrome-free. Instead, Jennifer must have been listening in on my conversation, which she'd done before—like the day I'd made shopping plans with Dave. It wasn't hard to do in such a small room. I'd always hated the close-knit environment of this work space. Too close for comfort was how I described it. The snugness made it impossible to carry on private conversations—such as personal phone calls or those to and from bill collectors—because you never knew when someone was eavesdropping. But who would've thought a conversation like the one I'd had with Denise could be of interest to anyone?

I had no idea what triggered Jennifer to do this. I honestly thought she'd put what happened a year ago behind her; I thought she'd accepted the fact that Malik chose me for the full-time position. It really hurt, knowing I'd spent much of Monday helping her with her workload. And this was the payback I got? I'd had about enough of helping folks. From friends and family members alike, the result would generally be the same. They'd come out on top while I'd get little or no appreciation.

My first cousin, Tamara—one of about a dozen relatives in the city, including aunts, uncles and other cousins—still owed me the fifty bucks I let her borrow three months ago when her car was in need of a tune-up. Still, that didn't stop her from calling me every chance she got to put in her request for my unused or unwanted media passes to a particular event. In fact, that was about the only time I heard from Tamara. She didn't even think enough of me to pick up the phone just to see how I was doing.

Then, there was my cousin, Saudia, also on my mother's side, who'd borrowed my boom box-style stereo with the six-disc changer. The one that I got back *broken*. Listening to a CD just wasn't the same anymore. The song would play halfway through and either get stuck, sounding like a scratched forty-five, or it would skip back to the very beginning. No longer could I enjoy my Anita Baker *Rhythm of Love* CD, Mary J. Blige's *My Life,* or even TLC's *CrazySexyCool,* which used to get me going most mornings. Saudia said she'd give me the money to get it fixed, but I hadn't seen a dime yet.

Speaking of money, my ex-boyfriend, Patrick, hadn't repaid me either. He owed me big time and I had many a credit card statement to prove it. A cash advance here. A shirt or pair of pants there. Even a car battery and tire. You name it; my love took up the slack many times for what his wallet lacked. *I promise you, baby, you'll get it all back and then some,* he'd said. In just one year, Patrick maxed me out, first financially, then emotionally. That was when I knew it was time to call it quits. After Patrick, I decided no more major financial favors for anyone, especially a man. Daniel could attest to that.

I just hadn't quite learned how to say no when it came to most everything else. Only because I believed I'd one day reap the benefits that mattered the most: the many blessings of all my kindheartedness.

Good thing all this happened toward the end of the day. My only regret was that Malik had taken off before I could tell him. I'd gotten so caught up in the madness, I almost forgot the significance of this day, even with the sweet little reminders Daniel had delivered earlier to my job. Today marked yet another anniversary for me and Daniel. In three months, we'd celebrated two separate milestones: Back in July, six months of being back together; now, the two-year anniversary of our first date.

Besides sending me two dozen red roses with a card that read "Invitation Only" attached to one set, he'd made plans for us to celebrate in some way. Around this time last year, we didn't have reason to. Daniel and I broke things off the very day before—I'd never forget that Sunday—October 10th. That morning, we'd attended the eleven o'clock service at New Birth Missionary Baptist Church, not far from my place, off Snapfinger Road. Afterwards, Daniel hurried home to catch the final moments of the Green Bay Packers-Kansas City Chiefs game. Later that eve, he'd said, he was expecting a houseful of guys, namely his closest friends Miles, Joe and Dex—short for Dexter—to come over to watch game two, now that their wives were *letting them out of the shackles for a few hours*. I still couldn't understand why Daniel—the oldest—was also the only unwed one in the foursome.

Being the big-hearted person that I am, I thought it might be a nice gesture to take the guys some "grub." I packed up some of my home-cooked sweet potatoes, baked pork chops, rice and broccoli and cheese, leaving myself enough for dinner that night and lunch the next day. Pulling into Daniel's yard, I expected to find a sea of cars. Instead, I spotted one—an unrecognizable ocean-blue Chevy Cavalier—alongside his. As I parked my car—blocking in Daniel's—I noticed him climbing the steps leading to his back door. In front of him was a fairly plump, red-headed white chick.

I watched from the car, debating whether to leave or get out. Before I knew it, I was inside. From my living room view, I saw the young woman—dressed in an oversized charcoal sweatshirt and black jeans—sitting comfortably on Daniel's bed, watching TV. Obviously, she had been there before. As I questioned Daniel from the living room, I kept my eyes focused on her. For the next few minutes, he went back and forth from the living room—where I paced the floor—to the bedroom, apparently in an effort to keep us both entertained. Eventually, Daniel introduced his guest as Becky, when, on her way out, she showed her face for the first time all night. Now, looking back, I couldn't begin to tell you why I'd refrained from making a scene, or even why I'd stayed. I guess I figured since I was the girlfriend, I didn't have to go. Granted, Daniel wasn't expecting me to come over, but there shouldn't have been any reason for another woman to be there. In his bedroom for that matter. His alibi: *She's just a friend, Jazz.* More specifically, a friend who just happened to drop by.

That particular October night, I made a decision I'd forever regret. I stayed with Daniel. In my own stupid little way of thinking back then, I believed spending the night would confirm I was special in

Daniel's eyes and Becky was not. That there really wasn't anything happening between them. In essence, what I did was place myself in a precarious position. Daniel was extra horny; I wasn't in the mood, mainly because I hadn't completely bought his story. But, for whatever reason, he wouldn't let up, despite my constant pushes and pleas. A fifteen-minute struggle under the covers with Daniel left *me* weak and yielding, and *him* victorious as he forced his way inside, no condom in sight, which was far from the norm on my part. Exhausted from pleading and pushing, I lay there motionless, eyes closed, praying for it to end soon as Daniel—one hundred eighty-five pounds and all—selfishly satisfied his own desires and worked toward his main goal: an orgasm. I fought back tears and prayed that an end was near. It felt like—from what I'd always understood the definition to be—a case of date rape.

From that night on, I wanted nothing more to do with Daniel. I never thought I'd forgive him. But somehow, three months later, he mended the wounds. Only because, for a number of reasons, particularly the fact that I discovered I was pregnant with his child shortly after that incident, I had a stronger attachment to Daniel than anyone I'd ever loved. I couldn't explain it, but something about knowing I was carrying his baby—even if only for a short time—automatically drew me closer to him. After that, I better understood why my childhood pal, Miko, hadn't lost all her feelings for her son's father, Elliott.

No sad thoughts, remember? I reminded myself. This was supposed to be a happy time and Jennifer had already done her best to try to change all that. But I refused to let her, or negative thoughts, get in the way.

Upon leaving work, I made a quick stop by my apartment to pack an overnight bag, drop off the roses and telephone my mother. I wanted her to know about my day at work. After all, I considered Mama one of my best friends—my childhood pal, Miko, being the other—and would call her up nearly eight hours away in my small hometown of Smithsville, Florida, whenever there was a problem or I was feeling under the weather. As I'd anticipated, Dorothy Mae Brown knew just the right thing to say.

"Jazz, what do I always tell you when you call me about these lowdown folks who've hurt you? Put their name in the Bible. Just write her name on a small piece of paper, fold it up and place it any-where in the Bible. Psalms and Proverbs are good choices."

"I know Mama, but..." The cordless nearly slipped from my left shoulder, as I removed the Pear-scented Victoria's Secret body lotion and splash from the wicker wall rack, where I kept all my pampering toiletries. I stuffed those two items, along with my toothbrush and tartar control Crest into a black duffel bag.

"No *but*," Mama interrupted. "What's her name? I'll do it if you won't. I've told you, you can't worry about these backstabbers; they're everywhere. Let God handle them. Put it in His hands."

My mother had always been big on three things: letting go and letting God, keeping the faith and forgiving people. I credited her for many of my good-natured ways. But I wasn't so sure I always agreed with her philosophy of letting things go.

"Another thing, Jazz," she said. "You really have one of two op-tions here. You can one, stoop down to this young lady's level; or two, bring her up to yours. It's that simple."

Feeling ninety-five percent better, I headed for Daniel's to see what he had up his sleeve for the night. When I walked in, I couldn't believe my eyes. I almost felt like turning around and reentering. Perhaps that would give some credence to the proverb *seeing is believing*. Daniel's hardwood floors had an astonishing luster to them that never before had I noticed. And *no* sign of the slew of dustballs which occasionally found refuge in the cracks and corners, before Daniel would get the energy to sweep them away.

It was such a drastic improvement from the norm, it even stood out in the dark—the only glow radiating from votive candles. I counted six on the glass-top dining table: three to each side, all lined up, a couple of inches apart, inside individual glass candle holders. Three more were in the living room, with the final two surrounding Daniel's headboard. Total: eleven for our anniversary date.

Every single candle was white, which I found so romantic. On the table: a white tablecloth adorned with a crystal centerpiece. Inside: a dozen white roses. Even more romantic. Where on Earth did he find these? Daniel watched my reaction from the sideline.

"Daniel, this is so sweet of you. You went through all this trouble...."

"It wasn't any trouble," he interrupted, hands in pockets, still leaning against the wall connected to the dining room bar. "Don't you even think that." He walked toward me, eyes making contact with mine the whole time. "Anyway, you deserve it. You deserve more than this."

Daniel was starting to sound like a new person, one I was falling in love with all over again. Facing me, he looked pretty irresistible. His low-cut hairstyle had a just-trimmed look to it, while his goatee appeared to be freshly groomed, too. Daniel even donned a dress shirt, blazer and slacks for the special occasion.

"Come here, baby. You look like you could use a hug. Tell me, how was your day?" As Daniel pulled me to him, I caught a whiff of his favorite body oil, a soft, sweet herbal mixture of myrrh and chamomile.

Nice, I thought. Not too much, not too little. He began swaying from side to side.

"You don't wanna know." I pressed my forehead into Daniel's chest and rested my hands on his lower back.

Daniel stopped the slow-dance-like motion and took two of his right fingers to raise my head by the chin. "Yes, I do or I wouldn't have asked." He wore a troubled look on his face.

I pulled away from the embrace and walked toward the kitchen. Daniel followed my lead, and the two of us began setting the table. Knowing exactly what he'd say once I was done, I quickly gave him a rundown, beginning with yesterday.

"Jazz, you're too nice. You can't let people run over you like that. You're always doing for other folks, puttin' their needs before yours. I've told you time and time again, you need to start thinkin' 'bout cha damn self," he said.

"I know, Daniel. But I wanna believe not everybody is out to hurt or use me. Are you saying I shouldn't extend myself to anyone anymore?" With two medium casserole dishes in hand—one containing pasta, the other, meatless spaghetti sauce—I trailed Daniel to the dining room. A man who couldn't live without his meat, Daniel carried a separate bowl of the latter with his preference: beef.

"No, but everybody don't think like you, Jazz. And you need to realize that."

Everybody doesn't, the editor in me wanted to say. But I knew it was best to separate work from pleasure. Besides, Daniel had talked that way ever since I'd known him and if it hadn't presented a problem before, why should it now?

Daniel took the food from my hands and placed it on the table.

"What you need to be doing is figuring out how you're gonna handle this," he said, looking and sounding more like my father than my lover. "You need to put ol' girl in her place."

"What do you mean?"

"I mean, handle your business, Jazz. Let the bitch know that you know what she did and I bet she won't mess with you again."

"I *was* planning to say something. I would've done it today, but Jennifer doesn't come in on Tuesdays." I crossed my arms over the back of one of the dining chairs, as Daniel took a seat.

"All you have to say is that you found out about what she did from your friend—what's her name? Denise? That's all you'll have to do."

"But she has to know I was gonna find out. She obviously didn't care if I did or not."

Daniel motioned for me to sit.

"Hell yeah, she knows. But lettin' her know you do means she won't exactly get away with this bullshit. Make her worry a little bit, trying to figure out what you're gonna do."

How romantic, I thought, as I halfheartedly listened to Daniel. I was still disappointed that he didn't even think to get out of his seat and help me into mine.

Just because we've been together all this time doesn't mean you can stop doing the things you did to get me, I wanted to say, while taking a seat. But I didn't feel like ending one serious conversation only to dive into another nor did I want to spoil the mood.

"Anyway," I broke in, now slightly perturbed. "Let's not ruin the evening talking about this all night." At that point, the tomato sauce sitting in the middle of the table was not only demanding, but winning, my attention. "I hear what you have to say and I do plan to take it into consideration. But right now, I wanna know how your day was."

He may not always remember to be thoughtful, but that doesn't mean I have to follow in his tracks. Besides, the chair thing is minor, considering how he went out of his way to make tonight memorable.

"Good. I've been busy ever since I got home from work gettin' ready for tonight." Daniel used a fork to scoop portions of pasta onto my plate. Aside from his dishes, his lack of silverware was yet another sign of his bachelorhood.

"Guess what?" he continued, giving me no time to respond. "I went shopping, to the grocery store of all places. I picked up a little somethin'-somethin' to cook for us for dinner and even bought some things to go in the fridge, since you always complaining about me not havin' any food."

"I'm proud of you." I leaned toward Daniel and planted a kiss on his lips.

"One more," I said, just as Daniel started to serve himself. "So, what made you choose pasta for dinner?" I twirled my fork around several strands. "And you even used angel hair instead of that old thick spaghetti."

"Baby, I know what you like. Plus, it was something simple. You know I'm no chef. But I did want to cook for you, so I stuck with something I knew I couldn't go wrong with."

Daniel and I were opposites when it came to food. While my plate was loaded with angel hair and very little sauce, his was so covered with sauce you could barely see the pasta. And while I tried to eat as little beef as possible, Daniel could not resist the temptation to indulge and had heaped his plate with meat.

I wasn't exactly sure what had gotten into Daniel, but it wasn't like him to cook for me. This dinner, complete with wine, breadsticks and cheesecake (never mind that it was store-bought), really stood out more than any of the handful of others he'd thrown together in the past.

"Daniel, that was so good. What are you trying to do, impress me or something?" I jokingly asked.

"You liked that?" Daniel donned a look of pride.

"Sure did."

"I'm glad, baby. I just wanna make you happy, that's all. Think you can stand one more glass of wine?" Daniel answered his own question, as he began pouring my third glass, filling it halfway.

"I guess I don't have a choice in the matter, huh? Why would you want me to have another drink, Daniel, when you know about two is all I can handle before I start feeling a buzz." The Zinfandel circled the stemware, as I rotated my wrist, as I'd been instructed during a wine-tasting event Daniel and I had attended earlier this year.

"I know. I like it when you get a little tipsy, though." A devilish grin appeared on his face.

"Why is that?" I asked, taking a sip of the wine. "Could it be because you know a little buzz makes me a little horny?"

"You said it. I didn't."

Our lips locked for what felt like hours. Daniel lifted me up into his arms, and carried me into the bedroom. I hadn't noticed earlier, but his queen-size bed was a sea of rose petals. Daniel had ripped every petal off most of the thorny stems, and tossed them onto the white satin sheets. The scene was romantic. The scent in the room, aromatic.

As inviting as it was, though, we slid right past it, into the bathroom, where Daniel and I took a quick, warm shower together, before crawling underneath the covers. Daniel smelled sensational as always, even without a trace of cologne or oil on his bare skin. *Nothing but Irish Spring deodorant soap, baby,* he'd boasted, as he curled up with me, underneath the black-and-white zebra print comforter. Whatever it was, it was quite a turn-on. To have the fresh scent of Daniel's bare skin next to those parts of mine, exposed through the black satin chemise I'd slipped into upon getting out of the shower. The skin-to-skin contact generated a welcome warmness between us. Sure, I knew it wouldn't be long before it would come back off. But that was another thrill: to have Daniel work his way through to the prize.

"You okay, baby?" Daniel softly asked, as he removed my nightie and planted tender kisses on my nose, lips and neck. Daniel pulled me close and rolled over, placing my "buck-o-five" (as he oftentimes described my weight) on top of his slightly muscular frame. With help from the radiance of the pair of burning candles, Daniel's glossy black eyes followed his hands as he massaged, cupped, and then tasted my breasts. I was always convinced this man's soft, sweet lips were made for kissing.

"Oh, yes." During our twenty-one months together, the lovemaking between me and Daniel had always been good, with the exception of a few "quickies," which only satisfied him and left me to hang dry, literally. Things changed, however, the first time I suspected Daniel of stepping out on me. Those suspicions—mostly a result of numerous phone calls, visits and letters from females—had never been confirmed, i.e., I'd never caught Daniel in the act. Still, it was enough to put me on guard. But I'd made a promise to him and myself not to let those particular incidents interfere with our present or future. After all, I'd made the decision to forgive and move on, and lately, I hadn't regretted it the least bit. Things between Daniel and me were much better. The phone calls had dropped to an all-time low, we'd rediscovered the meaning of friendship and we were having the time of our lives right about now.

"Hold me tight," I whispered, my head resting on Daniel's hairless chest, my arms gripping his coffee bean-colored shoulders. My legs began to shiver, as Daniel suddenly killed the romance by asking, "How many is that, baby?"

Enough, I thought, which was the best answer I could come up with. Surely Daniel didn't think I'd kept count of the number of orgasms I'd had tonight. Did men really believe women took mental notes on those kinds of things? And why was the number so important to them anyway?

I woke the next morning with the memories from the night before fresh on my mind. However, the feeling was fleeting, particularly once I realized I'd have to go to work and face Jennifer. The advice Daniel had given was priceless and insightful as usual, coming from a man six years my senior. He wasn't always right, but more times than not, convincing. On the other hand, my mother, who had several years on Daniel, was also persuasive and most times I felt God was speaking to me through her. Still, I wasn't clear on what route I'd choose. I trusted that was something I wouldn't know until I was face to face with my co-worker.

Chapter Five

Stoop down to her level or bring her up to yours.
Handle your business, Jazz. Let the bitch know you know what she did...

My mother's advice vs. Daniel's. Both kept ringing in my head as I neared the office, where I'd have to face Jennifer. The more I thought about it, seemed as if they were saying the same thing, for the most part. I could make Jennifer aware that I knew how she'd seized the moment on my level, or, if I put it another way, by following my modus operandi.

Confronting her didn't mean we had to lock horns. That wasn't called for, nor was it my nature. Saying something, I believed, would suffice. I had to at least do that much. After all, I was tired of taking crap from people. Tired of having a better handle on my professional life than I did on my personal.

I exhaled twice before turning the knob to the walnut-colored door leading to the outside reception area. I walked in and was immediately swept away by the enhanced ambience. Apparently, overnight, Malik and Sandy decorated the office with some more paintings, doubling their black art collection.

More than likely a trade for advertising, I thought.

Not a bad trade, though. Not bad at all. Particularly the framed painting of a black man's upper anatomy extending a brawny arm to support another's weight through the grasp of his hand. Even more compelling: the caption underneath, which read, "He's not heavy. He's my brother."

Entering the editorial department, I soon found the walls weren't the only thing to receive a facelift. At first glance, I didn't even recognize Jennifer, who stood before a filing cabinet near my desk, a pair of manila folders in her right hand. Seemed she'd finally put an end to all the talk and gotten those extensions (braids to be exact) she'd been raving about for weeks. With them, Jennifer resembled teenage R & B rising star Brandy to a small degree.

"Good morning, Jennifer," I said, while placing my briefcase on the floor beside my desk.

"Morning." Jennifer slightly turned her head my way as a show of acknowledgment, her synthetic hair stiffly swinging with the movement.

As I'd expected, a rather dry response and negative visual contact. Still, I refused to lower my standards in order to fit in.

...bring her up to yours.

"Jennifer, when you get a second I need to ask you something."

"Shoot," she responded, still not giving me her full attention.

"It's pretty important. I'd rather wait till you're done." I leaned against my desk, arms folded—my way of showing Jennifer I meant that literally. Seemingly feeling my presence behind her, Jennifer shut the cabinet door and turned to face me.

"What's up?"

What's up? Is that what she just asked me? As if she doesn't know what I need to talk to her about. I get it, that's just part of her I'd-better-play-dumb act.

I'd had plenty of time to think of exactly what to say by now, but, for some reason, I wasn't sure where to start. *Just cut to the chase, already,* I told myself.

"I understand you'll be speaking at my alma mater next Friday. I'm just curious as to how that came about."

"I don't know what you mean by how it came about." She said the last part in a voice I gathered was intended to be an imitation of mine.

Smart aleck, I thought, but probably wouldn't have been able to get the words out of my mouth had it come down to it.

"I mean, how did you end up finagling your way into the speaking engagement?" *Now—is that language you understand?* "From what I'm guessing, you had to hear much of my conversation with Denise last week. I also assume it wasn't hard for you to figure out what day we were discussing, since everyone around here knows when my interview with Andy Young takes place. And if you heard all that, you should've also heard me say that Malik was to stand in for me."

I'm on a roll.

"The part I haven't quite figured out is, why you supposedly told Denise that Malik wouldn't be able to make it. That was far from the truth. Malik was actually very excited about the opportunity." I added that tidbit of information in an attempt to play on her emotions. But the numb expression on her face never faded.

"I'm also coming up blank with answers to some other questions," I continued. "Like how you knew how to reach Denise in the first place and why this happened at all."

Your turn. Now what do you have to say for yourself?

Jennifer walked away from the filing cabinet toward her desk, moving for the first time since we started talking. For a minute, she looked as if she weren't planning to say anything.

"I don't know what it is you want from me, Jasmine. All I can say is I'm sorry. But I really don't feel that I owe you an apology. You couldn't speak at the school; I could. Basically, I did you a favor."

"You did me a favor?" I said as calmly as I could.

"That's right. They were in need of someone to do the job. The show had to go on with or without you."

"That may be true, but it wasn't left up to you to decide. The *show* was supposed to go on with Malik, not you."

What's gotten into this heifer? Why can't she just admit she's wrong and move on.

"When I hung up with Denise Monday, she was under the impression that Malik would take my place. And he agreed to do it, but before I got the chance to let Denise know that, you'd already tracked her down and stolen the spotlight." The longer I talked to Jennifer, the more irritated I became.

"Yeah, I did. Why did Malik need to do it, anyway? You, too. You're both in the limelight enough as it is. It's about time an underdog got his, don't you think?"

"No, I don't think anybody should get theirs if it's done underhandedly. If you were interested in the speaking engagement, you should've said so. But, more important, you had no right listening to my conversation in the first place. And I still wanna know where you got Denise's number from."

"You can thank Malik for that."

What is she talking about? This is too crazy. Surely Malik's not in on this. I'm starting to get a headache.

"Do you care to explain what you just said?"

"Malik is the one who had the old call return added to the lines, isn't he?"

I'd forgotten about that ridiculous *69 service. I didn't even know why Malik and Sandy were paying for it in the first place. They were always complaining about having to cut back on expenses, but they could afford to pay three to four dollars a month, or whatever it was, for a telephone feature nobody needed? This, if nothing else, was proof that it served no positive purpose. Now I was mad at Malik, although I realized he couldn't have known investing in a phone service nearly every American household had by now would be such a bad thing.

"I admit, it wasn't a very professional thing to do, Jasmine, but what you have to realize is, it's not work-related."

That's not exactly what I expected to hear, Malik. Why do you always have to be so calm about things? I wanted to ask, while standing across from Malik's desk, where I'd just informed him of Jennifer's manipulative ways. Sitting, he continued to stuff his briefcase with press kits and other presentation materials for an afternoon meeting with an advertiser he was trying to woo.

"I guess it really bothers me because this isn't the first time I've had problems with Jennifer. I just never mentioned them to you."

"Well, I wasn't aware there was static between you two," Malik said in his native Virgin Islands accent, which I found to be somewhat sexy, calming to listen to.

"It doesn't seem to interfere with your work or hers," he added.

"No, it hasn't gotten that out of hand."

"So, what's there to worry about?" Malik took his eyes off me, long enough to lock the attaché. "You see, Jazz," he said, lifting himself from his leather seat, "sometimes conflict is good. It keeps you on your toes."

Good point.

"When your time at *Amsha* is up—which I hope is never—could you remember to carry one thing with you? It'll prove to be a lifesaver in the long run." Malik removed his beige, waist-length jacket from a rack next to his desk and began walking toward the door.

"What's that?"

He buried his right, followed by his left, arm into the jacket's sleeves.

"Always know—no matter where you go—no matter how good or bad you are as a person or a professional, there will always be jealous people. You could spend all day and night trying to determine why someone envies you and still never know. That's because it's about them, not you. Always."

Powerful words. Too powerful for me to ever forget.

Malik never ceased to amaze me. The man was full of knowledge.

Guess that's what living does to you. Blesses you with wisdom and clarity. My only fear is not knowing what it'll take for me to earn mine.

"You can make love to me whenever the mood hits you, whether it be in the middle of the night or first thing in the morning. You can wake up just in time enough to watch football on Sunday. But you can't get dressed to go to church with me?" At that moment, Daniel Kevlon Wood (whenever I got mad at him, I'd refer to him by his full name) fit the description of the hackneyed expression "couch potato" to a tee. From the bed, he'd gone straight to the toilet, then the fridge for a glass of water and now the living room sofa. In a matter of five days, he'd gone from being Mr. Loverman to Mr. Lackadaisical.

"Jazz, don't start. I told you, I didn't bring anything over here to wear to church." Daniel—dressed, for the first time, in nothing but the bottoms to the hunter green flannels his mom gave him last year for Christmas—leaned over to retrieve the remote control from the coffee table.

"That's no excuse. We could've gotten up early enough to swing by your place so you could throw something on." I plopped down on Daniel's lap, wrapping my arms around him.

"Baby, please don't nag." He sighed. "I'm not in the mood." Daniel wore a look that appeared to say, *I wish I could go back into the bedroom and place a "do not disturb" sign on the door.* The current expression was a complete contrast to the euphoric one he'd donned in the silver-framed 5" x 7" photo sitting on an end table to the right of him. We'd taken it together six months ago at the wedding for his closest friend, Miles, and his wife, Nina. The best man looked like a million bucks in his black tux, while, I must admit, I mirrored twice that amount in my silk and linen pastel yellow dress.

"Daniel, I'm not nagging. I'm just making a point."

"Point well taken. I just wanna relax and watch the games today. We can go to church next Sunday."

"Next Sunday, it'll be the same thing. The only difference is, there will be two new sets of teams for you to watch."

"I'll just have to miss some of the first game. I promise you, we will go."

I'll believe it when I see it. Getting Daniel to go to church was almost as difficult as persuading him to fly. He'd never even set foot on a piece of aircraft and always vowed he never would. He had been inside a church before, although since his childhood, the majority of the times he'd gone was with me and always at my urging. That was my pet peeve with Daniel. He was a good person, and undoubtedly, believed in God. Still, he always seemed to have some excuse about why he couldn't make it to church. *I don't have anything to wear. I only have one suit and I wear it every time.* It was understandable that Daniel's present-day attendance, compared to that of his adolescent days, had tremendously declined. That was the case for many adults nowadays, with professional, social and family lives to balance, and Mama no longer around to watch over and either make you go or escort you there. But all this excuse-giving was getting old.

Daniel dampened my mood, so I ended up playing hookie. Frustrated, I decided to throw on some sweats and keep myself busy by cleaning during the first quarter of the Falcons-Cowboys game. It was a game which slightly piqued my interest, only because the home team was playing Deion, Emmitt and the rest of the Dallas crew. Honestly, I really didn't care to see the Falcons, who'd been billed as "lousy" up to this point. That was the only reason Daniel had agreed to watch the game at my place. Had there been a more competitive match on TV, he would've gone home or camped out with some of his boys.

I left Daniel alone for about fifteen minutes. Long enough for me to drive to a nearby convenience store, half a mile away, to get three dollars' worth of quarters in change. *It makes no sense that none of these one-bedroom apartments have washer-dryer hookups. I'm paying enough rent to have a complete laundry area. Better yet, a house.*

Once I started my two loads of clothes in the laundry room adjacent to the rental office and weight area, I returned to find Daniel glued to the 19" screen. The Cowboys had a 14-7 lead over the Falcons when I decided to tune in with him. Besides a black rodeo, he loved no other sport more than football.

I also liked it, had since my high school days, during which I cheered on the Burke County Bulldogs for four years. I just couldn't sit through an entire game watching any two teams matched up, as most guys could. It wasn't until I got to college that I realized I truly enjoyed the sport. The very diverse Standefer State, believe it or not, had no football team. Imagine that: a major college with a student population of more than 20,000—in the heart of Atlanta—minus one of the two key sports.

Good thing Daniel played wide receiver at the all-black Brenard State for three years. Years later, Daniel, who'd dropped out for financial reasons, was still loyal to his alma mater. Each season, he tried to make every home game the Wildcats played. He even traveled out of town for a couple of matches, sometimes with me right by his side.

Watching the players on the field in their close-fitting uniforms and protective head gear, I forced an image of Daniel in his retired blue and gold jersey, proudly sporting the number forty-two—*an even number brings more luck than an odd,* he'd say, showing off his college scrapbook. Since then, Daniel—no longer bench pressing three times a week—had trimmed down slightly, especially below the waist. At five feet eleven, he was still fairly muscular, with a medium build; in many ways his frame resembled that of a former athlete, a quarterback in particular. Another physical sign of Daniel's nostalgic football days: a scar—the likeness of a bullet wound—on his back, near the right shoulder blade. Each time I'd run my fingers across it, I was thankful my sweetie didn't suffer any worse injuries, as many athletes in the sport do.

The Falcons lost by almost thirty points. Daniel just had to watch every minute of the boring and upsetting defeat. I, on the other hand, was relieved when the game was over.

"Daniel, I need to ask you something," I said, turning down the volume to an inaudible level.

"What is it?" Daniel kept his eyes focused on the screen, appearing to lip-read through the Budweiser, Pizza Hut and Wrigley's Spearmint gum commercials.

"Do you love me?" I leaned in closer, hoping to become his center of attention.

"Jazz, I don't even know why you're asking me that," he said, finally looking my way. "You know I love you. I tell you that all the time."

"So, what do you plan to do—"

"There you go, asking questions," he interrupted. "You can't just let us have a nice moment without having to ask a bunch of questions, can you? We've talked about this over and over, Jazz." Daniel simultaneously slapped the outside of his right hand into his left palm, as if to drive his point home. "My answer is still the same. You know I wanna be with you, forever if possible. You're the best thing that's ever happened to me, but you already knew that."

"That's what you say, but then I can't help but wonder why you're not doing anything to prove that to me."

"Like marriage." It sounded more like a comment than a question.

"Yes, like marriage."

"Jazz, let me tell you something." He gestured with both hands. "Naw, better yet, I'll say this. Yesterday I read your horoscope. You didn't know this, but sometimes I check out your horoscope when I'm reading mine. Yours said something like 'stop trying to move a mountain that's not ready to be moved.'"

"I take it you're the mountain and you don't want to be moved right now, perhaps not ever."

"See, there you go puttin' words in my mouth. What I said was the horoscope read, 'stop trying to move a mountain that ain't *ready* to be moved.'"

"And again, *you're* the mountain, right?"

He shrugged. "I guess so. But that doesn't mean I'll never be ready. Just not now, baby."

I felt a pain in my heart. "Why not? That's not what you said earlier this year when we got back together."

"Oh, that. I did mean everything I said...then. Now, I feel a little different. I don't feel I'm ready. Not now." Daniel stood and started walking toward the door. I didn't move an inch.

"I'll call you when I get in," he said, making his way back to the sofa. He leaned over and kissed me on the lips, before giving me one of his lazy "grandma" hugs, the kind that said "I know I'll see you later, so let's not get too mushy."

"Where are you going? That's so rude of you, Daniel. We were in the middle of a conversation."

"A conversation headed nowhere," he said, standing over me. "Jazz, we can talk about this until we're both blue in the face. That doesn't mean we'll come to any conclusion. We never do. I've told you time and time again how I feel about you. Can't that be enough for now?"

I can't believe him. This is not the same romantic, loving, attentive Daniel I spent a memorable anniversary night with just last week. He's running from the simple word commitment, *much less the act.*

Daniel wore a look that said, "Now, can I please go?" I didn't say a word. A few seconds later, he was out the door. No more than sixty seconds after that, I was right behind him, on the way to retrieve my fresh laundry from the dryer.

I'm not gonna let him upset me. Either he'll come around or he won't. Anyway, he said he's just not ready yet. *He didn't say never.*

I hated to see Daniel go. I felt he'd left me hanging, the issue unresolved.

As I took flight down the steps leading to the parking lot, I saw Daniel's car go full circle below. *What could he have forgotten?* I heard myself ask. I quickly went through the list of possibilities. But I couldn't come up with anything: He didn't bring a change of clothes; he was wearing the blue and gold Brenard State sweatshirt and blue jeans he'd worn over yesterday, with his pajama bottoms underneath. I remembered seeing him put his covered toothbrush inside his jacket pocket and, as always, he'd brushed his short, lowcut hair into place with the hard-bristled brush I'd ordered from an Avon catalog when I was a junior in high school.

By the time I reached the bottom of the steps, Daniel's sparkling silver 280Z was slowly approaching my building, building F, but suddenly went past it, making a stop in front of the unit to the right of mine.

What's he doing? Who could Daniel know in the complex besides me?

He apparently was acquainted with the Hispanic-looking chick he was flagging down. Following the wave of Daniel's right hand, the female cautiously drew near the car, as Daniel—oblivious to the fact that I was watching—reached across the passenger's seat to let down the window.

What is going on? He has to know I would see him.

The dialogue between the two continued while I was getting into my car. Instead of exiting in the opposite direction, I deliberately pulled up next to Daniel, with my young neighbor sandwiched in between. She looked no older than twenty—the average of my sisters' ages—at least a decade younger than Daniel. I recognized her from a couple of brief encounters at the mailbox. Daniel looked beyond her, his eyes making contact with mine. As I sat there, window lowered, the car idling the entire time, I saw his lips moving. Seconds later, she walked away. Not a word was exchanged between Daniel and me before I drove off first. My mission—to make him aware that I saw him—was accomplished. What I refrained from doing was pointing the finger or jumping to conclusions, as I had in the past, although my gut feeling told me Daniel was undoubtedly hitting on the girl next door.

Turning the corner to the laundry room, I noticed Daniel's sporty, two-door, two-seater Nissan—the last make put out by the Japanese automakers and the one Daniel had vowed never to get rid of—in my rearview mirror. Once his car was no longer within view, I decided to make a U-turn, heading back in the direction of the apartment, hoping to find my neighbor still standing in the same spot. *If so, what would I do?* I thought. *How would she respond?* Maybe she did exchange numbers with Daniel after all, unaware that he was involved with someone in the adjacent building. And why was I going after her anyway? Daniel was the one I needed to confront.

Still, I pulled into the first space I came to. I guess in a way, I wanted to torture myself by seeing closeup what Neighbor looked like. I jumped out of the car, moving as quickly as I could to catch up with her, as she proceeded to her car. In no time, I was facing Neighbor, questioning her as though she were an interviewee for an assignment.

"Excuse me, could I ask you something?"

She nodded, a look of concern written all over her face.

"I was just wondering..." I felt a stutter coming on, but managed to keep it at bay. "Did that guy just hit on you?" There. Straight to the point always had been and always would be the best route to take, I thought.

Neighbor ran her fingers through her silky, auburn-tinted hair and tilted her head to the side. She was very cute, very petite, very young looking. I could see how Daniel would be attracted to her.

"Yeah," she answered liberally, her big brown eyes appearing to offer a look of sympathy. "He asked me for my number."

My heart sank. "Did you give it to him?"

"No." Her answer may have been somewhat alleviating, but the fact that she was even faced with the request from my boyfriend was indeed something I could not stomach.

"Thank you," I said, walking away, my head slightly drooping.

I couldn't bring myself to fold a piece of the laundered clothing, now piled in a corner on my bedroom floor. Instead, I sunk in the middle of the bundle, my right knee covered by part of a baby blue fitted sheet. Sitting there, I opted to mull over this afternoon's parking lot episode, which, hours later, still astounded me. I couldn't believe it had happened. *How could Daniel do this—right in my neighborhood— not a half mile down the road at the Chevron convenience store, but right outside my door, right within a clear-cut view from my bedroom window? The gall of him.*

In the two years that I'd known Daniel, I'd never felt so disrespected as now. It hurt as much as, if not more, than when I found out about the fling with his previous girlfriend, Terry ("T," as he'd called her), during the very early stages of our relationship. A pair of love letters I'd run across one day while removing a blouse from Daniel's closet gave it away. What was Daniel thinking today? Obviously he wasn't, or was it that he wanted to make some kind of statement? Was this his way of *showing* me the mountain wasn't yet ready to be moved? Well he did just that and more. He not only did the unthinkable right before my eyes; he did it with someone twice as good-looking as I. My short, permed haircut, which required weekly upkeep, couldn't compare to Neighbor's naturally straight, thick-textured tresses. And her earth-toned, makeup-free skin was absolutely flawless. By contrast, my eight-glass-a-day-drinking-water deficiency would result in an occasional facial pimple or two on my golden complexion, usually made over with pressed translucent amber face powder by Fashion Fair. As for weight and height, Ms. Nameless had nothing on me; in fact, we were equals in that sense. Still, overall, I felt in Daniel's eyes, she was a ten, while I missed the mark by several points. At least that was the way I felt at that moment.

The first ring of the cordless telephone in my bedroom abruptly brought me out of my trance. Three rings later, the machine picked up. I didn't move an inch, as I heard Daniel's voice coming through.

"Jazz, it's me. Pick up the phone. Baby, I know you're there. Would you please just pick up the phone?"

I was tempted to answer just so I could lash out at Daniel with a few choice words, but profanity was seldom a part of my vocabulary. Most times when I'd attempt to use an expletive or two, I'd usually only get as far as the first syllable, or when it came to those four-letter words, the first letter. It wasn't that I considered myself holier-than-thou, nor did it bother me one bit that for Daniel and some of my friends, every other word would sometimes be a "cuss word." But for me to curse, I had to be real angry, burning mad. At those times, somehow, the language would come out with ease.

It wasn't ten minutes later before another call came in. This one also from the jerk. "Jazz, baby, where are you? Give me a call when you get this message."

I waited a while before I broke down and returned Daniel's calls.

"Hello," he answered, sounding as if he were out of breath.

"What do you want?"

"I was just calling."

"What are you calling me for? You didn't have any trouble getting my neighbor's number today, did you? Why don't you use it? Or have you already?"

"I don't know what you're talkin' 'bout, Jazz. I didn't, and wasn't tryin' to get nobody's number," he said in his most convincing tone.

"Is that so?"

"Yes, it is."

"So you didn't try to get her number? Is that what you said?"

"Sure didn't. See, this is the kinda shit I'm talking about. I can't handle you and your accusations. While you're jumping to conclusions, I recognized that girl from somewhere else. I met her one night when she came into the store."

The old turn-the-blame-on-you trick. I'm not falling for it. Wrong is wrong.

"So you met her on your job?"

"Yeah, I helped her pick out some new tile for her bathroom."

Daniel was lying, I knew. That excuse about meeting this girl at work was probably the quickest thing he could think of; maybe he'd conjured up the story during his drive home or the time I spent dodging him.

How I ended up at Daniel's duplex, I'd never know. Somehow during the course of the phone conversation, he convinced me to drive ten minutes away to Stone Mountain so we could talk. Daniel let me in to a dim living room; the only light inside came from a white candle burning in the center of his coffee table. *Probably one of the candles from our anniversary celebration, the last beautiful moment we spent together.* A Sade CD was playing, the volume relatively low. I sat to the right of Daniel, giving him a look that he instantly read.

"I know you're wondering why I asked you to come over," he began. "First, let me say this. Right before you got here, I said a prayer. I asked God to work on me, to make a change in my life. I don't know what's wrong with me, Jazz, but I've been like this since I was in college. I messed things up with Celethia fuckin' around with some other girl and by never really being able to be faithful to her. Since Celethia, you're the only other woman I can honestly say I've loved, and how many times have I screwed up with you? Too many to count. I'm surprised you haven't kicked my ass to the curb for good by now. I don't deserve you. You're too good for me."

I refused to look at Daniel, simply because I'd heard a similar speech before.

"Jazz, I have a confession to make. Today, you were right. I did ask that girl for her number. Basically I lied to you."

For a moment, I stopped breathing.

"I don't know why I did what I did; I know why I lied though, 'cause I didn't want to hurt you again. But I don't know what made me go up to that girl, especially right in your complex. Maybe I have a problem. It's not that I can't control it; I think I can. It's not that I have to hit on every woman that comes along, but..."

"Then why do you do it?" I interrupted Daniel's meaningless rambling, internally recounting some of his past mistakes which had caused me plenty of heartache.

"I don't know, Jazz. It doesn't happen every day. What happened today even caught me off guard. Sometimes I'll ask for a number just to see if I can get it and I'll never even use it."

"But you shouldn't be collecting any other numbers. You're in a relationship."

"You're right. And I'm very happy to be with you. You're the best thing that's ever happened to me, baby. I mean that."

"So, what is the problem?"

Suddenly, I was reminded of what Malik had said about jealous people.

It's about them, not you.

That's it. Has to be. Daniel's philandering ways are about him, not me.

"I don't know; sometimes I wonder if I'm afraid of commitment."

Daniel wasn't making much sense to me and I don't think even he was buying what he was saying. I felt a headache coming on, a common occurrence whenever I'd get upset. I massaged my temples as Daniel continued talking nonsense.

"Jazz, I love you and I wanna be with you. I can even say I want to marry you. One day. You're a good woman, a damn good woman, and I'd be a fool to let you go. I just have some kinks to work out within myself. But I don't wanna lose you. I need you by my side. I'm sorry I've ever hurt you, but please don't give up on me. I want this to work and I believe it can."

Chapter Six

One day I was going to learn to pay more attention to my first thought. I knew, before I'd even made it out of bed this morning, that coming to work wasn't a smart thing. That unexplainable ill feeling I noticed earlier hadn't let up by lunchtime. To make matters worse, it was a Monday. But at least one thing was no longer troubling me—this situation with Jennifer.

All morning long, we'd been two busy little bees. The usual tension between us had evaporated, perhaps, in large part to Malik's noteworthy advice last week. Or maybe it was because I wasn't feeling well. I wanted to chalk it up to being tired. But this felt like much more than fatigue.

I had an unrelenting migraine and no sign of an appetite. Skipping breakfast hadn't been such a good idea, after all. Maybe some herbal tea and a pack of wheat and cheese crackers would help, I thought, as I headed toward the breakroom. On the way there, I made my third stop within the past hour by the restroom.

Too much coffee this morning, I remembered.

The minute I turned the corner, my knees caved in and my legs felt as if they were going to give out on me. *Maybe I do need to eat something.* Surprisingly, I managed to maintain my balance and was able to make it down the long hallway to the three-stall restroom we shared with the other small businesses renting space on the Equitable Building's fourth floor. Luckily, the center one was empty. I rushed inside and fumbled for a minute or two with the latch before successfully getting the door to lock.

I didn't realize just how long I'd put off this much-needed visit until I was behind closed doors. By the time I'd silently counted to fifty and the other two ladies had washed their hands and left, a stream of pee was still rushing out. It was the most aggravating feeling, thanks to excruciating abdominal spasms and a burning sensation I experienced while relieving myself. It felt as painful as the day I slipped off the monkey bar in fourth grade and my tiny, fragile pelvic bone slammed onto cold, hard metal. This was more than just hunger pains, I thought. Something else had to be wrong. But what, I didn't know. I promised myself to get to a doctor as soon as possible to find out.

Whenever I felt the slightest unfamiliar pain, I'd head straight to the doctor's office. *That's what you have insurance for,* Dorothy Mae would remind me. I wasn't like a lot of my people who would avoid medical treatment like the plague. I had my own personal gynecologist and family doctor. I couldn't quite figure out what it was about black folks that made them dread hospitals, doctors and the like. Not me. I wanted to know what was wrong with me. Probably because I'd always assume it had to be the worst possible thing imaginable. Of course, I'd always assume wrong.

Aside from the discomfort between my legs, I felt feverish and feeble. I wanted to lower myself to the floor and rest there for a moment. Better yet, I longed to crawl under the covers of my bed. But with only four hours left in the workday, I decided to hold out and endure the pain for the remainder of my time here. After all, if I gave off any vibes that something was wrong, I'd have everyone in my business, and that was something I just didn't need right about now.

As the days passed, the pains only worsened. Thursday night, while taking a bath, I noticed six blisters on my vagina. *No more waiting to see a doctor,* I'd said while counting them. Dr. Smith's booked calendar was the only thing preventing me from having gone so far. Her first available opening was at least two weeks away. Since I couldn't wait that long, urgent care would have to do for now.

Just gotta get through the interview tomorrow. I'd either go after that, or first thing Saturday morning, I promised myself.

I didn't know how I'd made it to the end of the work week without breaking down. Emotionally or physically. But, thanks to the Andrew Young interview, I had to get through at least the first half of Friday.

As it turned out, today's appointment was a blessing in disguise; speaking before hundreds of students about my "wonderful life" was something I didn't feel up to.

Throughout the two-and-a-half-hour-long meeting, I felt miserable—warm all over, and my whole body ached. Almost like I had the flu. But October wasn't exactly what I'd call flu season. Once that was out of the way, I got permission from Malik to leave early. "I'm just not feeling well," I'd told him. "I could be getting a virus or something." I could only hope it was something that simple; but deep down, I knew it was much more serious.

Fear rocked my body. I didn't know what was going on. I'd never felt this way before. I'd come close though. The one time in my life that I was brave enough to get a flu shot, my temperature shot up to a hundred and three degrees. I was confined to my bed for twenty-four hours. This time around, my body felt just as hot. And these lesions. I'd never seen anything like them. They started out looking like blisters, and within days, developed into open sores. Talk about painful. It even hurt when I walked, but what bothered me most was the stinging sensation caused by urine oozing into the tender spots.

Intuition kicked in the minute I arrived at my apartment. I dropped everything—my black rawhide briefcase, pecan leather purse and the junk mail I'd just gotten out of the box—at the front door and scurried to the bathroom, nearly knocking over a bowl of lavendar floating candles that rested on an end table. First stop—the medicine cabinet. Nothing. Aside from the Alka Seltzer Plus Cold Medicine, daytime cherry Nyquil and other just-in-case pain and cold goodies Mama encouraged me to keep on hand.

Next—the cabinet underneath the sink. Nothing there either. *It's gotta be in here somewhere*, I said, pushing a bottle of Lysol and a can of Pledge furniture polish out of my way. By the time I'd finished ransacking my neatly-kept lavatory, I found what I was so desperately looking for: my Massingill douche, stashed away in one of the bathroom drawers. Tucked inside the box was the answer to all my concerns: a health insert that contained information on sexually transmitted diseases.

After reading the first few lines, I ran across the description that matched my visible and physical symptoms. It couldn't be. Not me.

When? Why? How? Oh, I knew how—trusting Daniel enough not to insist on a condom every time. Of course, he had me convinced I had no reason to. What do you have to say for yourself, now Daniel? I shouted out loud. Would he come clean or try to blame it on me? Blame me for trusting him? For giving him chance after chance?

Guilt came over me: I should've had the baby. If I had, I wouldn't be in this mess. Instead, I would've been pregnant up until two months ago—surely, I wouldn't have been too sexually active. There was one other way of looking at this: Was Daniel totally to blame?

Did he know he was infected?

I fell to my knees, dropping my head on the cold toilet seat cover. I lay there motionless, watching tears bounce off the white porcelain onto the hardwood floor. For a brief moment, I couldn't feel myself breathing, and a certain part of me actually wanted that to be the case.

For the umpteenth time during all this madness, I thought of calling Daniel but again decided against it. *Not right now,* I told myself. Although I needed to, and a certain part of me wanted to let him know how I was feeling, I couldn't bring myself to do it. I still hadn't forgiven him from this past weekend. That was why each time he'd called since, I'd found a way to get out of spending some quality time on the phone with him.

I know it'll have to happen sooner or later. Just not right now.

Midday Saturday, I opened my eyes to the cool fall light beaming through the closed blinds hanging from the window beside my bed. And to all the pandemonium a city like Atlanta brings on a daily basis. Still I didn't want to get up. It was already two-thirty in the afternoon, but the longer I could stay under the covers, the longer I could shield myself from reality. This was one of those rare times I didn't want to hear what the doctor had to say because I was almost certain my assumption would be right.

About a half-hour and an empty box of Kleenex later, I forced myself out of bed, into the car and downtown to the Temple QuikCare Emergency Center. My regular gynecologist, Dr. Smith, didn't have weekend hours, and I knew I couldn't afford to put this visit off another day.

Walking into the waiting area, I felt a twinge of nervousness shoot through my body. That feeling intensified once I made it back to the examination room.

"Scoot down until you're almost about to fall off the table," Dr. Martinez said, standing near my feet, which rested on the exam table.

"Place the ball of your feet here." She touched the tips of the stirrups, as I followed her orders. I couldn't comfortably rest my feet in place, though, because the metal was too cold and the position I was lying in felt too awkward. On top of that, Dr. Martinez, rather Dr. Impersonal, wasn't making me feel any better.

"That's definitely what it looks like," she said, scraping my vagina with a cotton swab. The stroke of her hand, protected by a latex glove, felt about as rough as the tone of her voice. Her piercing eyes delivered an even harsher telepathic message: *You wouldn't be in this mess if you hadn't been sleeping around.*

Dr. Smith never would've responded that way. The sistuh probably would've broken down and cried with me. But, unfortunately for me, she had to have some time off, which meant I had no choice but to come here. Where, I guess, I got what I paid for. A callous brunette with a Hispanic name, but not the first sign of Spanish blood.

"You're gonna feel my hand first, then the speculum," she said, talking to my bottom. I stared at the ceiling and tightened my muscles. The room became suddenly silent, with the exception of a baby's screams next door. *Poor thing must have gotten a shot.*

As she'd promised, I felt fingers first, then the sharp, even colder—than the stirrups or Martinez' personality—speculum with a force so strong I could feel it in my stomach.

"You've got a few more blisters inside," she said. "This culture, which we'll send off to the lab, will confirm what it is. We should have the results by Wednesday."

She picked up a tube of K-Y Jelly and squeezed a palm-size amount onto her fingers. "We will call you if it's positive," she said, applying the lubricant. "If it's negative, we won't call. Or you can call us if you're curious," she added.

If, I thought. *If I weren't curious, I wouldn't be here in the first place, stupid lady.*

Finally, she pulled her hand away.

Thank you.

"You can get dressed now." She removed the gloves and began washing her hands. "Will you be needing an AIDS test today?"

An AIDS test? I hadn't even thought about it. What if I have AIDS, too?

"You need some time to think about it?" the doctor asked.

"No, I think I'll wait." For the first time, I could empathize with my brothers and sisters whom I'd criticized before for dodging doctors. I wasn't prepared to take an AIDS test. I'd never had one before and hated needles with a passion. Besides, I'd received enough bad news in one day.

"That's fine," the doctor said, lifting a small tray. "Again, give us about three or four days on this."

In the meantime, I lay in bed. No food. No real sleep for forty-eight hours straight, playing hookie from work on Monday, but reluctantly returning the following day. Midweek I made the call since I hadn't heard from anyone at Temple. A nurse, who probably could teach her boss a lesson or two about compassion, broke the news to me.

"I'm sorry, Ms. Brown, your test results came back positive."

The results didn't come as a complete surprise. With that critical information in hand, there was only one thing left to do: tell the man I loved. The very person I still wasn't ready to deal with, and the one who, without a doubt, was responsible for all this.

Take a deep breath, Jazz, I told myself as Daniel made me a warm mug of the Swiss Miss white chocolate I'd introduced him to this past winter. I needed it after the short walk from my car to Daniel's apartment door; the temperature outside had fallen to forty-three degrees. But inside, I felt as if my blood pressure had nearly doubled. I didn't know what to say. Didn't know where to start. As delicate a topic as it was, I decided it was best to just be frank.

"Daniel, I have herpes." I placed the mug on his coffee table and waited for a response.

Before speaking, Daniel bit his upper lip and leaned forward, resting his elbows on his knees. "Will it go away?" Daniel looked upward as if the ceiling might hold good news. His tone reflected absolutely no sign of denial. He knew this lifelong curse couldn't have come from anyone else.

"No, it can recur at any time."

We sat on his black leather couch motionless. Finally he looked directly at me. "So," I could hear a slight tremble in his voice, "how do you know?"

"Well, at first I was having body aches. Now blisters, which make it painful to use the bathroom. This morning, my lab results came back, and the doctor's office, where I was tested on Saturday, confirmed what's behind it all."

"You didn't tell me you were sick. You mean you were *that* mad that you couldn't talk to me about something this serious, Jazz?"

"It wasn't so much that I was mad. I just wanted to find out exactly what was going on with me before I said anything."

"Well, I haven't been having *any* problems," he said, as if he were vindicated, the sympathy in his voice dissipating by the minute. "I hadn't noticed any of those blisters you're talkin' 'bout. What do they look like?"

Is that all you have to say? How about a little compassion?

"First of all, let me say this." My voice raised a pitch or two. "You probably haven't noticed anything because you can have the virus and not even know it. So it would be wise for you to get checked out, too. To answer your question, the blisters look like *blisters*. And after a few days, they start crusting over so they can heal. When that happens, you have painful, open sores, almost like gashes in the infected area."

"So, what do you have to do if it doesn't go away?"

"*We've* gotta take medicine. Forty pills to be exact, to get rid of the symptoms. But the virus remains in the nervous system forever. And an outbreak can happen at any time. Once. Twice. Even *four* times a year. With no warning whatsoever." I tried to sound as firm as possible. But before long, I was drenched in tears. "Daniel, why couldn't you tell me? Why couldn't you tell me I wasn't the only one? I asked you if there was anyone else. You always said no."

"Look, don't lay the blame on me. You found out about T and came back. You would'a kept doin' the same shit over and over again. You know you would'a just kept comin' back," he said.

So this is my fault? He sleeps around, lies about the fact that he is and I'm the one at fault? And where did that come from, anyway. Daniel sounded like a monster, rather than the man I'd foolishly come to believe was my soul mate. The look on his face was indifferent. I wanted to slap it right off. Slap him until his cheeks bruised. It was hard enough dealing with the situation. I didn't need insults from a man who clearly had no remorse.

"'Comin' back'? You begged me back. Begged for a second chance. Or did you forget that part? You told me there was nothin' to those letters and like a fool I believed you."

Now I *really* knew what Daniel meant when he'd said, *People make choices that not only they but other people have to live with all the time.*

An even harder pill to swallow came a couple of days later, after I hopped off yet another urgent care exam table. "I can look at one of these right now for chlamydia," the doctor had said. "And like I said, the other we'll have to send off to the lab." Turns out the love of my life had given me two gifts for the price of one. This time, not blisters, but what appeared to be some kind of growths, clumped in a cauliflower-like shape. All the signs of one more non-curable but painless disease: condyloma, or genital warts.

Daniel was about as apathetic this time as before. "I know there's not anything positive about all this, but look at it this way. We're not the only ones with it and there are plenty more people in the world going through something worse than us," he said.

I didn't want to sound selfish or anything, but I wasn't concerned one damn bit about everybody else. In fact, at that moment, I was thinking of no one but myself—the victim—who'd trusted this man with my heart, possibly even my life. One that Daniel's lies and infidelity had changed forever. I knew then it was over between us and nearly two years of my love and devotion were down the drain.

Chapter Seven

I just washed down the second pill with a glass of water, with three more to go before I was done for the day. For the next eight days, I had to take five colossal capsules a day of Zovirax. If I could stand it. Not only did the pills leave me with a migraine headache, they made me want to throw up. The liquid medication for the warts wasn't any better. Each time I applied it, it felt as if I'd lit a fire between my legs.

I'd also spent much of this past weekend with my head buried in books and other reading materials such as pamphlets. According to all I'd read, some 40 million people—500,000 each year—had some form of the herpes simplex virus. What was worse, I found, was that the disease could be passed from mother to infant, with serious, sometimes even fatal, consequences. *One in six babies who gets the virus won't survive,* one brochure read. *It can have damaging effects on a baby's eyes and brain and lead to retardation.*

I may never have children with these type risks, I thought. *That means adoption may be my only option. If so, I'd choose Tiffani.* It wasn't like the thought hadn't crossed my mind before. According to Katherine, I met the legal age requirement. If Marcus and Monique could consider becoming parents while they were still newlyweds, I didn't have any excuse. Sure, it would be two of them compared to one of me, but their lives wouldn't be all that much simpler.

It was a noble idea, which was exactly what I'd told Daniel a few months back, the day he'd suggested *we* care for Tiffani. "Maybe one day soon we'll be able to take her in," he'd said, and like a sucker, I'd believed him.

How were we going to make a major decision such as adopting a child when Daniel wasn't moving in any direction toward marriage?

I couldn't help but wonder if these diseases were my punishment for not giving birth. In many ways, I felt the choice I'd made eleven months ago was about as bad as the one Tiffani's mom made a decade before.

From this day forward, I vow to say a daily prayer for my baby boy or girl, who's now in Heaven, and for Tiffani, who's been through a living hell at such a young age. If only I could learn to be as strong as her.

I'd spent the past two days doing nothing more than resting, reading and beating up on myself. I now knew first-hand what that oldies singer Mama used to listen to while cooking and cleaning meant when he said, *If I could turn back the hands of time.* Tyrone Davis, I believe was his name. I didn't know why *he* wanted to turn back the clock, but whatever the reason, I understood his pain.

I couldn't believe this was happening to *me.* A twenty-five-year-old educated, professional black woman. A diligent worker who, after maintaining a 4.0 GPA throughout high school *and* college, landed herself a job in her field long before graduation. The one most everyone back in my small hometown expressed having great pride in. Skinny little Jazz. The product of, to put it mildly, a strict upbringing. The one who'd vowed never to have sex before marriage, and who grew up with not one, but *two*, parents in the home. But that didn't count for much, considering I received more love and attention from my mother.

While hoping death would become my saving grace, I longed for the next best thing: comfort. But I had no one to turn to. I couldn't tell my parents for two separate reasons. For one thing, I didn't want to disappoint them, especially not my mom; I knew the news would crush her. Nor did I want to give my father, the critic, yet another reason to say *I told you so* or another opportunity to remind me that I really didn't know what I was doing. On top of that, there were practically no secrets in my family, particularly among parent and child. So, it would be automatic that my two sisters would soon find out. *And what kind of role model would I be then?*

I wasn't prepared to confide in my small circle of friends either. I was certain my best friend, Miko, and Dave would be understanding as they'd always been. But this was too embarrassing to tell them about at the time. And I sure couldn't talk to Daniel. Not unless I wanted to hear more reasons why *I* was responsible for this. *You would'a just kept comin' back.*

Daniel had actually said those words. The same Daniel I'd been having the time of my life with lately. The same Daniel who had never taken a tone like that with me before and who'd gone out of his way in the beginning to win me over. But once he did, I had to remind myself, it wasn't long before I began regretting it.

Homecoming two years ago was the first time I'd gone to Brenard State with Daniel. After sitting through four hours of a game that ended in a last-minute loss for the Wildcats, Daniel and I crashed at his place. That's when I discovered the man I grew to love wasn't talented just on the field. He had a voice out of this world. As we cuddled in his bedroom, Daniel serenaded me with one of my favorite Isley Brothers' tunes, "Don't Say Goodnight." In no time, I was out, still fully clothed, but wrapped in his big brown arms. That is until the knock at the back door.

"Yeah, what's up?" I'd heard in the background.

"You said it was okay to drop by to see you," a female voice murmured.

"Yeah, I know, but I have company."

"Why would you tell me I could come over if you already had company, Daniel?" She snapped.

"You said you *and* your girls might stop by for a few after the game. So what's the big deal?"

By this time, I'd made my way into the living room entrance, where Daniel and his visitor stood talking in the dimly lit doorway. The screeching melody from the hardwood floors tipped him off.

"Jazz, this is Wanda." He motioned for me to come closer. "Wanda, Jasmine. So, what's up?"

You've asked that already, I wanted to say to Daniel, as I gave Wanda a quick once-over. The first thing I noticed was the stupefied look on her long, horse-like face, which made her dark brown skin crinkle slightly. She sported a short, layered haircut similar to mine and a rose tattoo, about the size of a live flower, above her right breast. It was easy to see, thanks to the low-cut neckline on her short, skin-tight black dress.

"So *which* one of your girlfriends is this, Daniel?" She asked, while slightly rolling her neck, like a sistuh sometimes does when she means business. "Number one, two or three?" She held up a finger for each number, her acrylic nails painted with designs that had become increasingly popular thanks to FloJo.

Talk about a fashion statement. All I could do was stand and stare in disbelief.

"Anyway, I don't know what you're talkin' 'bout," Daniel said, his facial features reminding me of Bleek, Denzel Washington's gigolo-like character in Spike Lee's *Mo' Better Blues.*

"Sure you don't. I guess *I'll* come back when you don't have your hands full."

When Wanda left, I didn't ask any questions. Didn't want to. In some ways it didn't matter. I was in a position where I could cut things loose without any hard feelings, without being hurt. I guess Daniel must have realized that.

"Jazz, in case you're wondering, Wanda is just a friend. She was just dropping by. We're not dating or anything, and I don't have any interest in her. So I don't know why she was trippin' like that."

I'd wanted to believe him, but for some reason I had doubts. Maybe they came from the betrayed look I detected on Wanda's face. She seemed to be let down. Like there was some reason for her to be hurt by finding me at Daniel's duplex. Walking out of his bedroom. I didn't ponder over it too long. But from that night on, a hidden, numbing feeling settled in my stomach.

"You two aren't committed yet, right? So, just enjoy him."

I probably never would've continued seeing Daniel had it not been for advice like that from Dave. That was one of my main problems, listening to too many people. Most times I'd end up feeling my friends' opinions were ones I was better off without. But Dave was a little different.

I took the advice. I didn't stop seeing Daniel, but I was cautious. And with reason. That same paralyzing feeling I'd gotten the time Wanda *dropped by* reappeared, during an evening out for dinner and drinks. Daniel and I had gone to Malone's in Riverdale—one of our favorite bar and grill joints—for chicken fingers and fries. That was something we had in common. We both loved eating out. Two

Heinekens and a pair of fuzzy navels later, we headed back to his place. We'd been there all of five minutes, and I swear the phone had rung a handful of times. During each conversation, I could tell he wasn't talking to any of the guys.

"What's up?" He'd responded during the last call. "Me, I'm just hangin'. Probably by the weekend, I'll be gettin' into something. Hey look, I still got your number. I'm gon' have to get back with you later a'ight."

Each call left me feeling the way I'd felt the night after the game. At least that night I'd gotten as far as an introduction. This time, on the phone, he couldn't even admit he was already busy, with his *girlfriend*. These things were my very first warning signs. Forewarnings which weighed me down on one shoulder, while Dave's "words of wisdom," as I sometimes called them, hung over the other.

Nevertheless, I spent that night with Daniel. We didn't have sex or anything, but it got close. If he'd been really insistent, I probably would've given in. Instead, we spent the night mostly holding one another. Daniel rubbed his fingers through my hair, and kissed my breasts, both big turn-ons for me. He didn't even try to get between my legs. Still I knew something was wrong. I couldn't stop thinking about the phone calls or the visit.

"What's wrong baby?" Daniel had asked as he ran his hand across my stomach. No matter how much of a bulge I'd have before going to bed, the next day I'd always wake with a flat belly.

"I was just thinking about something, that's all."

"Something like what?"

"Oh, nothing really." I didn't feel comfortable letting him know I was already feeling suspicious, when we'd just recently committed to each other.

"I'm glad you stayed. Feels so good having you in my arms. I love your breasts. They're so soft."

I almost melted. Without thinking, I placed Daniel's hand on my breast. We kissed as his hand moved from the right to left. Until he had to remove it completely when the phone rang. Again.

This conversation had the same ingredients, and ended just as all the others, "Let me holler back at you later, okay?"

I turned over, with my back toward him.

"Baby, what is it?" Daniel sat up in bed, leaned over and tapped my shoulder.

I couldn't hold back any longer. "Daniel, you get a lot of phone calls. Are you sure you're not seeing someone?"

"No, I'm not. I mean, yeah. I am sure. I'm not seeing anybody else. That's not how I operate, baby. You're the only person I'm spending time with. You're the only one I want. I wouldn't be spending this much time with you if there was somebody else."

He sounded convincing, and I wanted to believe him. But it was obvious, in too many ways, Daniel's actions were speaking much louder than his words. And silly little me who believed all people had some good in them—they just sometimes made bad choices—wanted to give him the benefit of the doubt.

A thought hit me: Wonder if Monique always gave me that look because she knew something. Did other women drop by the store to see Daniel, too?

I counted at least two dozen kids getting off the school bus, as I sat, trapped by the red stop sign, just a block away from Daniel's. To my surprise, I was actually going through with this. But, unable to accept these horrible gifts as my due somehow, I was in search of some answers. I felt I deserved that much. Even if it meant confronting Daniel on his turf. Slightly in sync, the last group of kids crossed the street to their apartment complex facing the road. The bus finally moved forward, with me not too far behind.

I never thought I'd set foot in this place again. It hasn't changed at all, I thought, as I entered Daniel's apartment. It was the same bachelor's pad it was two weeks ago, and more than likely always would be.

The living room was filled to capacity with Daniel's precious black leather sofa, now covered with a leopard throw; and his entertainment center, where you'd find some of his favorite toys. A 19-inch color TV with stereo sound system, and hundreds of CDs. Oh, and let's not forget, Daniel's pride and joy: all his handmade art. The paintings and other figurines were probably the most tasteful decorations you'd find here. Unlike that poster hanging inside his bedroom closet. It was far from refined. Three raunchy women, each with their derrieres—far bigger than mine, mind you—hanging out of G-string bikinis. No matter how much I pleaded, I never could get Daniel to part with it. *They ain't got nothing on you, baby*, he'd said. *So, you don't have anything to worry about.* Despite Daniel's attempt at reassurance, I could only imagine how he must have lusted over those swimwear models in private.

"So, how have you been?" he asked, widening the door so I could walk in. His question reminded me that it had been a couple of weeks since we'd last seen each other. Although we'd talked a few times since then, each conversation never exceeded five minutes.

"I'd have to say I'm about as well as can be expected, Daniel. How are you?"

"I can't complain."

Of course not, I thought.

"What is it you wanna talk about?" Daniel stopped in the middle of the living room, alongside the coffee table.

"Could we at least sit first?"

"Yeah, come on in here."

Daniel, in his favorite cotton pajamas, headed toward his bedroom.

"Why can't we just talk out here?" I insisted.

"I was doing something in the other room, and I wanna finish it up, while listening to you at the same time. You don't mind, do you?"

Despite my concern, I followed behind, only because I wanted to get a look at Daniel's "love fortress" one last time. I guess deep down inside I was curious to see if there were any clues that someone new had been there this soon.

"So, what's on your mind?" He asked, while placing an armful of fresh socks and underwear inside a drawer. Daniel had just finished folding a basketful of clothes. But the stench of deviled eggs he was stuffing his face with smothered the fresh scent of fabric softener coming from his laundry.

"I just wanted to talk to you about a few things."

"Like what?" He began walking toward me, as I gave him the take-a-good-guess look and rested at the foot of his bed.

"So you wanna talk about *that* again?" Daniel said, looking as foul as the smell coming from the paper plate sitting atop his dresser. He sat beside me, leaving just enough room for another size five person like myself to fit in between us.

"Is that a problem? Anyway, what did you expect?"

He didn't say anything.

"For one thing, I was wondering if you still haven't spotted any symptoms," I said, looking straight ahead.

"No, I haven't. But down at the health department, they did find some that I wouldn't be able to see no matter how hard I tried. So what you told me is true."

"Is the medicine giving you any problems?"

"Not at all. Is it bothering you?"

"Yes, it causes a few side effects, like nausea and headaches. As a matter of fact, I feel one coming on now. Do you have anything I can take?"

Soon as Daniel returned with two Advil and a glass of water in his hand, I caught him off guard with my final, and most important question.

"Daniel." I lowered my head and started playing with my fingernails. "I was wondering, if you knew where—if you had any idea— where you got this from."

"No, I don't." He sighed. "I really don't."

Disappointed with his response, I raised my voice. "You don't have *any* idea?"

He didn't answer.

But I had a few hunches. A carousel of faces danced through my head. From Wanda. To the white chick Daniel had over that Sunday night. To Terry. The only one I knew for certain he'd messed around with. All thanks to a pair of her love notes. Daniel had mentioned the old girlfriend a few times. And I'd seen the letters early on in our relationship. Although the two of them had broken up and started seeing other people, Terry couldn't let go, Daniel had said. Or maybe it was just that he gave her reason to hang on.

I ran across the first letter one day while looking for a shirt I'd left behind at Daniel's. *I truly enjoyed you last night, Daniel. You felt so good inside.* After reading those words, there was no doubt in my mind he'd cheated, but I never made a big deal out of it. I guess I never really accepted it either. I just didn't see how it could be possible, when we were always together. Another, which came months before that one, read, *I just wanted to let you know I was carrying your baby, but I miscarried the other day.*

Afraid of confronting reality, I never said anything about the first letter. And when I asked about the pregnancy, Daniel brushed it off, saying Terry was never pregnant. (*No way in Hell she could be by me,* he'd said). He said she was just using the pregnancy ploy to get some attention, and ultimately a commitment. Like a fool, I bought his alibi. Only because I'd psyched myself up to believe Daniel would change, that I was good enough for him to want to. More than that, I believed somehow I'd be able to change him.

Sitting here on the edge of his queen-size love nest, I wondered how I ever could've thought that. There was no telling how much Daniel did and was able to cover up and get away with. Even right here in this *very* bed. One which we made love in time and time again. I got sick to my stomach each time I imagined how many other bodies substituted for mine when I wasn't around. And when I thought about what it was like with them or Terry. I often wondered if he did the same things with her as he did with me.

Had he held her in his arms the way he did me? Did he kiss her breasts with the same passion? Did he find her eyes as beautiful as mine? Did he kiss her lips? Did he enjoy touching her as much? All these thoughts started making me sick. What they did couldn't truly be called making love. She was the other woman, the one to whom— according to Daniel—he'd never even said the words, *I love you.* For the most part, a day didn't go by without his saying that to me. In fact, he was the first one to express those feelings.

It was last year on Valentine's Day, four months after we'd started dating. That day, Daniel sent me a big balloon, which read "Thinking of you," and a large card, with the words "I love cuddling with you." Later that night after work, he came over, we ate the dinner I'd prepared, made love, and did exactly what the card said. I'd never forget the way the words "I love you Jazz" fell from his lips.

I was a little surprised, even though I knew the feelings were there. I could sense them in Daniel's touch, see them in his smile. He seemed so happy to be around me, and he was always around. Even if we just watched TV or took a nap together, we were inseparable. That's why it was hard for me to understand why things turned out this way. Or why

I'd find that one letter in particular, dated March 12th. Less than a full month after Daniel poured his heart out to me.

I truly enjoyed you last night. You felt so good inside. Those words played over and over in my head, followed by the ones at the end of the letter, *Love, Terry.* How could I have been so stupid not to say anything? How could he not say anything? Why did he lie to me?

Terry and I are just friends. We dated over a year ago. We've been friends ever since. That's it. Just friends. Of course they were. Friends who also happened to be lovers. A friend Daniel could apparently sneak to see anytime of the day or night (no questions asked), and screw as much as he wanted.

Staring into Daniel's eyes, it was hard for me to understand how I'd fallen so hard for him. From the beginning, I'd known he really wasn't my type. I guess you could say we were opposites. The perfect date for me could be anything from a picnic in the park to camping out in a cabin for a weekend. Daniel considered a walk through the mall, showcasing me to his friends, or curling up on his or my sofa night after night romantic get-togethers. I enjoyed swimming at the beach, relaxing on the sand. Daniel hated the water and that entire atmosphere.

If nothing else, it was Daniel's charm and artistic flair that eventually nabbed me. I also loved his supportive qualities, demonstrated most recently throughout the drama with Jennifer, and, before that, my disappointment over Tiffani's letdown. With a little more drive (from me, I thought), I really could see Daniel going places. Especially since he always talked about going back to college to complete his bachelor's in business, once he got his finances straightened out.

Daniel had been financially set back since his first job in high school. Back then he had to set aside so much for his mom, the only guardian in his household. Daniel's father passed away when he was but two years old. To this day, I wondered if he knew exactly what happened; he'd been told so many stories up to this point, including the one of his daddy being shot to death over a gambling bet.

Daniel's mother, toughing out her bout with insulin-dependent diabetes, heavily depended on her baby to help her out, since she couldn't hold down a demanding job, and because she couldn't count on her oldest, the kleptomaniac, to do anything for her. She and Daniel spent most of their time and money bailing thirty-five-year-old Raymond out of jail. In many ways, I felt sorry for Daniel. He never had a father figure around and his big brother was a far cry from a male role model. So were the other womanizing men in his life—uncles and such—which Daniel claimed actually *encouraged* him, beginning in his teens, "to be a player." Daniel never admitted it, but I felt that misguidance influenced his intimate relationships to this day. Yet, instead of throwing in the towel all the other times, I'd wanted to help him see the beauty in love and how it was possible to be happy with one person.

The sound of a basketball against the sidewalk and the voices of children playing outside Daniel's bedroom window, followed by his, interrupted my reverie.

"Look Jazz," Daniel said. "I really don't have any answers for you, but I do wanna apologize. I'm really sorry. I'm really sorry I did this to you. I know I may not have any right asking this, but please don't let this be the end of us. This wasn't intentional, I promise. I was just as surprised about it all as you."

Talk about a shocker. He's actually man enough to acknowledge his wrongdoing. Still, that didn't make things better. An apology couldn't take the place of anything Daniel had said to hurt my feelings before now. Especially his reaction when I first told him about both diseases.

I appreciated his small effort displayed here tonight, but at the same time, I was thankful for those painful words that came straight from his heart two weeks ago. *You would'a just kept comin' back.* I knew they'd make me a stronger person, make it easier for me to get through this. They also enabled me to see Daniel's true colors more clearly. But more important, I was willing to open my eyes a little wider and witness each one of my necessary lessons unfold. No matter how painful.

Chapter Eight

It was hard to believe how quickly the Thanksgiving holiday came. I had a feeling it was going to be the worst one yet. A year ago, following the abortion, I recalled saying, "This is the worst year of my life." However, this one, particularly toward the end, disproved that statement. The last four weeks were a true test of faith. A few times I broke down, letting depression get the best of me. But, for the most part, I managed to hold up fairly well. During the holiday, for my family's sake, I knew I had to do the same.

They'd driven all the way from Smithsville to spend a few days with me. The small, predominantly black town, population 8,000, was just east of Orlando, about eight hours by car from here.

I was proud to have grown up there. But at the same time, glad I got away when I did. For one thing, it was one of the few places that I knew of where the junior/senior prom was *still* segregated. Plus, everybody knew everybody. As in most small towns, your business (fabricated or not) quickly became public information. It usually amounted to news about your neighbor's husband or wife screwing around, because, as some would say, "they ain't got nothin' better to do with their time." In many cases, *both* were having affairs. On top of that, no matter how unhappy they were, most always stayed together in what was nothing more than a marriage of convenience. And no one was ever lucky enough to escape the rumors. My own family fell victim to them a time or two.

In fact, that scuttlebutt somehow made its way into my high school on several occasions. One particular time during my junior year stands out the most. The day Bridget Dugger confronted me outside my locker on my way to trigonometry. *Jasmine Brown,* she'd said, calling my name like she was getting ready to pick a fight. *I hear your daddy's creeping in and out of my auntie's trailer every other Friday night.* I stood there, speechless, hoping that dingy gray carpet would turn to quicksand. I didn't know how to respond. And even if I'd known what to say, I wouldn't have been able to move my lips. More than anything, I was shocked, hurt and embarrassed.

All those emotions eventually turned into one—anger—against my father. Although I never had any proof to validate such malicious claims, I assumed they had to be true. Smithsville was too small, too close-knit. Most times when you heard trash about one of your neighbors, you were ninety percent guaranteed it wasn't made up. I figured that formula also applied to a loved one, particularly when the whereabouts of that individual, who had only a couple of friends and no hobbies whatsoever, couldn't always be accounted for.

Thinking back, I could recall a number of what I'd dubbed suspicious nights, nights when I would hear the sound of Daddy's engine, followed by the turning of the doorknob. Those were occasions when he'd be coming home real late from work, always with an alibi (in that way, Daniel reminded me of my father). Like the Saturday Daddy's supervisor at the car assembly plant had called him in to fill in for someone on second shift. He was supposed to get off around eleven, but didn't make it in until about five the next morning, in time enough to get a little shuteye before he had to get dressed for church. Daddy kept us all up worrying until about three that morning, when he called to say the pickup had broken down. He'd told us not to worry about coming out to help. *Women don't need to be out this late,* he'd advised. *It's not safe. I can take care of it. Everything will be all right.*

We all bought his story. Until this rolling in during the wee hours thing developed into a bad habit he obviously didn't want to break and compelled Mama to discover a needless, time-consuming custom of her own: tracking her husband's moves. Arguments and divorce threats ensued. And by no choice of my own, I had to admit, a slight grudge developed on my part.

Still, considering all that, and the fact that both he and my mom had to drive over half an hour to Orlando to work every day anyway, my father refused to move to the city. Thomas Lee Brown (Tommie

Lee to his peers) loved the country life.

Better place to raise your family, he'd say. *Mama brought me up in the country and I turned out fine. I've got a good family, a car, a nice home and a good job. Couple years, I'll be retiring.*

It felt good to know I eventually broke away from my little nest, got away from such sheltered mindsets and all the negativity and made something out of myself. That was a lot more appealing than falling into the same trap as many of my classmates, who wound up staying and either having a baby every other year and/or settling for low wages at a dead-end job. Working the graveyard shift at the local mill wasn't exactly my idea of a career. Hotlanta, what I considered a black visionary's paradise, was *the* place to be for a young lady, or man for that matter, with big dreams like mine.

Its diversity, combined with the many opportunities it provided, made it the perfect getaway. Sure, Orlando had its share of pluses, too. But from all I'd heard, for my people, Atlanta offered ten times as many.

Still, I sometimes missed being surrounded by my family and friends. So it was always nice when I got to go home. Or when they paid a visit to me.

My folks planned to stay three days. My only hope was that their visit would help take my mind off everything, as long as my daddy didn't add to the stress I was already enduring. He was always good (for reasons only he could comprehend) for putting a strain on our already messed-up relationship by faultfinding and saying things that were uncalled for. Criticism that made me strive harder, only to feel I was never doing enough. As always, I tried to be optimistic, hopeful that finally things were changing. I couldn't handle any additional stress right now.

"Okay, Mama, this is the year for me to learn how to roast a turkey and make dressing." I walked into my tiny kitchen to find Mama unloading a bag of groceries.

"You haven't bothered for twenty-five years. Why start now?" She gripped the Butterball turkey with both hands and dropped it over into the sink.

"Just in case I ever get married. Anyway, you know I've never had time before now. When I lived at home, I was always too busy with school, all my after-school functions and the part-time job at Magic Kingdom. From there, I leaped right into college, and on into the workforce full-time."

"Well, bring your narrow tail on in here and pay attention. Just don't expect immediate results," she said, rinsing the turkey.

"I'm not in *any* hurry, Mama. I don't have any reason to be."

"What about Daniel? How is he?"

I had a feeling that one was coming. "He's doing fine." I didn't mean to answer in such a curt manner, but I couldn't force myself to tell her the truth. That I couldn't care less how Daniel was doing. That we were no longer together. That he'd given her daughter two venereal diseases.

"Is he coming over for Thanksgiving dinner?"

What's up with all these questions? You've never really been crazy about Daniel, and to this day, neither you nor me knows why.

"No, he has a family, too, Mama." I guess my tone was a little harsh, 'cause she didn't ask any more questions.

"Okay, well. There's not much to cooking the Butterball. Let's go ahead and get it in the oven." She tugged at something. "First, you have to pull what's inside here out." I wanted to turn my head at the sight of what she was holding in her hand. "This is what you use to make your giblet gravy," she said, pulling out more parts, the only recognizable one to me being a liver.

"Next, sprinkle on your seasonings like salt and pepper. Finally, here's the secret to giving your turkey its smooth, shiny coating. Reach your hand underneath the skin like this, and rub it down with margarine." She gently glided her hand, careful not to tear the turkey's skin. "Now it's ready to go in here for the next three to four hours."

That left the dressing, giblet gravy and dessert. I got stuck with chopping two of the key ingredients for the stuffing: the celery and onions. I loved the strong smell, even the unremitting taste of onions. What I didn't care for was what they were good at doing to the eyes. Within minutes, they had me in tears.

Memories of past Thanksgivings spent at home surfaced as I watched Mama blending the ingredients for three sweet potato pies and a coconut cake. She said she wanted to send Justice back on campus with a week's worth of goodies. Things hadn't changed at all since my college days.

Preparing Thanksgiving dinner wasn't all that bad, since Justice and my baby sister, Marlo, jumped in and helped out. It felt so good to have them around. It reminded me of the good ol' days when we were all home. Now the only one left behind was Marlo. Even she wouldn't be there much longer. She and Justice had made me so proud. Justice, who was spending the Thanksgiving break at home, was a freshman at Clark Atlanta University, majoring in English, with plans to later attend graduate school. And Marlo, the budding entrepreneur, would be graduating from high school in six months. She already had everything lined up either to join Justice here in Atlanta or to move out to D.C. to go to Howard. We both encouraged her to come here. That way we'd all be together again, and I'd have my second go-round at playing big sister. My first issue at hand with both would be talking to them about safe sex. I wanted to believe neither one of them was sexually active. But some of my friends believed I was being naive, "'cause, girlfriend, times have changed," Miko once said.

After the four of us finished making a mess in the kitchen, we all set the table, while my dad sat and channel-surfed with the remote control to the 19" Zenith. It was his way of passing time until his plate was served. Something, I suppose, after twenty-seven years, my mother had gotten used to doing. Just as we pulled up to the dinner table, the phone rang.

"Happy Turkey Day!" It was the last voice I wanted to hear. "How are you?"

"I'm okay. How are you? And Happy Thanksgiving to you, too."

I really didn't mean it. I just returned the greeting out of mere courtesy.

"Thank you, thankyouverymuch," Daniel said in a jovial tone. For whatever reason he sounded too happy, which pissed me off. "I'm doing good. Hanging out with my folks and the fellas. Did your family drive up?"

"Yeah, they're here now. We were about to eat dinner." *What do you care?* was what I really wanted to say. *You've got some nerve, Daniel Wood.*

"Well, tell everybody I said hello. By the way, Miles said, 'What's up?' We're about to go bum some food out of somebody else. We already ate at home, but that wasn't enough. You know me, I can eat. Anyway, you have fun and take care, okay?"

"Yeah, whatever," I said, not sure where the words came from. "Do me and yourself a favor, Daniel, and lose my number."

"What did you just say?"

"You heard me. There's nothing else to be had between us." My face was soon covered with tears. "You have no need to call me, anymore. I'm tired. Tired," I repeated, recalling something I'd read somewhere recently, saying that once you'd had enough of something, you'd know. "I can't put up with your crap anymore; I just can't."

"Jazz, don't do this. Come on, now, don't do this. Why don't we just take some time away from each other. Just a little space."

"I'm giving you plenty of space." It became more and more difficult to talk to him. "I've gotta go now. You take care," I said, crying.

The nerve of Daniel and his little devil-may-care attitude. I couldn't believe how happy he was sounding. How could he be? Here I was, practically miserable, and he sounded like he'd just won the lottery. It just wasn't fair. He nearly ruined my life by giving me two diseases and crushing my heart. Meanwhile, he was having a good time hanging with his family and best friend; his life was going great. I wished I could tell them all about this secret, so they could see him for who, rather what, he truly was.

"Jazz, what's wrong?" My mother hit me with a series of questions when I returned from the living to the adjoining dining room. "You're barely touching your food. Who was that on the phone?" Dorothy Mae Brown had always been good for interrogating. And, like radar, she picked up on signals. I always credited that to being a trait all mothers possessed.

"I'm fine, Mama. I must have eaten too much breakfast earlier. Now I don't have room for anything else."

"Was that Daniel? What did he say to upset you?"

How did she do it? What the older generation says about an intuitive connection between God and mothers must be true.

"Like I said, I'm fine. I just don't feel like eating anymore. But I'll take care of this later. Right now, I'm gonna go take a nap. I promise, I'll eat some more when I wake up."

"Just a waste of damn food," my father grumbled. "That's why she doesn't have any meat on her bones now. Starving herself to death for some man." He nodded and slammed his fork down onto his plate.

"You're such a critic, and you're never gonna change, are you?"

Why'd you have to say anything? I asked myself, knowing I'd opened up a can of worms.

"You don't worry about me, young lady. I've lived my life. You just need to concern yourself with living yours. Let's see if you can hold down a job and take care of a family for as many years as I've been able to." He slid his chair away from the table and stormed off.

For a minute I turned away from my father and directed my attention to my two sisters, who actually looked like older, taller, even bustier, versions of me. I wondered what they were thinking. None of us ever could understand why our daddy had always been such a cynic. We always assumed he was just being the overprotective, but genuinely loving, father. The sad part was, he had his own definition of the word *love,* which looked like this: *Keep a roof over their heads, food in their stomachs and clothes on their backs.* The emotional aspect was never factored into the equation.

Jazz, don't say anything else, I told myself. *Come on, just get up and walk away.* I ran to my bedroom for solace, shutting and wanting to lock the door behind me. Curled up to a pillow, I lay on my black ironpost bed, staring at the still room. I couldn't believe how successful Daddy always had been at upsetting me.

Nor could I get over Daniel, the way he sounded on the phone, like nothing was bothering him. Didn't sound at all like he was pretending either. *Must be nice when all I feel like doing is running away. Running away from the problems and the pain.* But I couldn't. I had to live through every miserable moment, by myself, with no one to turn or talk to.

I wanted so badly to tell my mama. I wanted to tell her about the abortion and diseases, so she could wrap me in her arms and wipe the tears from my eyes. She'd always been able to cheer me up, make me stronger. Now was a time when I really needed her to do that. But I couldn't tell her *this.* I was too embarrassed. I felt I'd let her, my younger sisters, even my father, down. All because I'd slept with one too many people.

The third lover for me definitely was not the charm. *Three lovers later and I'm scarred for eternity. How could this be?* I'd never been promiscuous, had never engaged in casual sex, and loved every man I'd been intimate with.

I lost my virginity with Derrick—who was nothing more than my first love—at twenty and was only with him one other time during the six months we dated. Both times we'd used protection. Patrick and I were together almost five months before we made love; our relationship lasted another seven. After that I went a year and a half plus with no relationship, no sex, mainly because I couldn't get Patrick out of my heart.

Then I met Daniel, who didn't have any easier of a time getting into my pants, either. We didn't make love until we'd been committed for three months. During the early part of the relationship, using a condom wasn't a choice, but a prerequisite.

That first time I was so nervous.

Daniel and I had just finished off the bottle of wine Miko had given us for our first Christmas together two years ago. It was exactly two weeks before the holiday when we popped the cork. *Jazz, baby, I wanna make a toast for many more times like this together, and I hope they just keep getting better and better*, he'd said.

After we toasted, Daniel reached for my lips. I knew what was about to happen. He took my hand, and led me into the bedroom, where I lit two candles on the nightstand next to my bed. Then he slowly laid me down, caressed my face, shoulders and breasts. His tongue felt warm up against my right breast. Daniel's hands discovered practically every part of my body. As he touched me, I began to shiver. I'd already had an orgasm before he made his way inside. Two more followed as he kissed my thighs. After that, I stopped counting. Although I enjoyed being with Daniel, initially, we didn't make love that often. Maybe that was why things turned out this way. I guess he felt he wasn't getting enough loving at home.

"Jazz, are you okay in there?"

I knew I couldn't be out of my mother's sight for more than thirty minutes before she'd have to check on me.

"Come on in, Mama." She slowly pushed the door forward and stuck her head in through the crack, before completely entering my bedroom.

"Are you okay, sweetie?"

"I'm fine, really." I couldn't stand to look into my mother's doe-size brown eyes, which I'd inherited. I knew she'd be able to see I wasn't exactly telling the truth. Whenever I glanced up at her beautifully middle-aged face, I wanted to break down and tell it all. I felt like one of those troubled teens she'd drive over to Orlando every day to counsel at the McBride Center. Youths who'd had some hard times, ranging from problems with drug abuse, to child molestation and physical abuse. They'd had an even harder time expressing themselves.

Like them, I wanted to release all the baggage, but I had to keep telling myself to be strong. I didn't want Mama to feel responsible, feel that while she was helping put other children's lives back in order, her own daughter's (the one who was supposed to have it all together) was nearly in shambles.

"Jazz, this isn't like you. Are you sure everything's okay?" she asked from the right side of the bed.

"Yes, Mama. Please stop worrying."

"That's my job, honey. At least I'm asking. Your daddy, on the other hand, said if Daniel did hurt you, you probably brought it on yourself. I know he didn't mean it, though. Jazz, you and I both know, if anybody hurts Tommie Lee Brown's babies, he'll take care of them."

That may be true, but why did Daddy always have to make negative comments like that? How could he think the worst of his own child? And why is she always defending him?

Unlike my mom, my father never went to college, but you'd think he'd earned a degree in criticism. That was one reason why, besides our little tiff, I'd exchanged few words with him since he got here. Sometimes I felt like I was walking on eggshells when he was around.

"Mama, you all don't have to worry about hurting anyone, 'cause no one's hurt me," I lied and turned over on my stomach.

"Well, what is it, Jazz? Is it SAD? You know, seasonal affective disorder. A lot of people go through it during the holidays, especially around Thanksgiving and Christmas."

"I don't think that's it." I tried to say it with as much doubt as possible, so she'd convince herself to believe otherwise.

"Well, you just may wanna get checked. You wanna go see a doctor?"

Little did she know, I'd been to enough doctors already. I couldn't stand any more visits.

"No, I don't need to right now. I think I could just use some rest. You know, I really haven't had any time off since I went from freelancer to full-time."

"Yeah, you're probably right. I'll leave you alone." She pulled the sheet a little more over my shoulders. "Go on back to sleep," she said, before kissing me on the forehead. "I've put your food in the fridge."

"Okay. Like I said, I'll finish it later."

I couldn't believe I pulled that one off. Soon as my mother shut the door, the tears overflowed. Finally, as I'd done just about every night now, I cried myself to sleep.

Chapter Nine

If I had to interview another freakin' couple, I was going to scream. In two days—for next year's Valentine's Day spread—I'd already talked to probably two of the most blissful duos you'd find in the capitol city. Possibly in the entire Peach State. One couple, even after five years of marriage, couldn't keep their hands off each other. And their nick-names! *Mookie and Boopie!* I couldn't stand it. How could they be so happy and in love when every day, I had to work hard to keep from sinking into my miserable, lonely and brokenhearted state? It was hard enough just returning to work after a holiday, getting back into the groove of things. Tacked onto that, I had these daily reminders of the anguish Daniel caused slapping me in the face. The one thing that kept me going was the deadline pressure, along with peaceful memo-ries of moments spent with Tiffani, whom I'd regrettably seen a lot less lately (almost two months) during these times of disarray.

Just bear with me, Tiffani. I'll make it up to you soon.

"Good morning, Jasmine. How was your holiday?"

Excuse me? I wanted to say. *Are my ears playing tricks on me or did I just hear Jennifer speak—in a pleasant voice on top of that.*

"It was okay," I responded, turning to face Jennifer. "You know, the usual. Family, friends, too much food."

"You ain't never lied, girlfriend," Jennifer said in striking south-west Atlanta vernacular. She brushed her hands across her petite waist-line. "I'm gonna have to fast for two weeks to work all this off."

What's up with all this small talk? You haven't exactly gone out of your way to carry on a conversation with me in the past. Besides, don't you have enough common sense to know I am still pissed at you.

Jennifer couldn't be any bigger than me. She may have tipped the scale at around a hundred twenty-five pounds, but here she was talking about losing weight, with *me* of all people.

"So, Jazz, I hear you're working on something pretty interesting this week," she said, changing the topic.

"Oh really? I haven't heard yet."

"Well, I was in on the morning meeting, and Malik said you'll be working on a feature article about this couple."

Oh, did he? I wanted to ask, but instead, decided to play along. *Who knows, she may be onto something.*

"Another couple, huh?" I asked in the most nonchalant tone. "What's so special about *this* one?"

"He's black. She's white."

"You mean *jungle fever?*"

"Yep. *Jungle fever,*" Jennifer said with a disdainful look on her face.

That's what I get for being late this morning. I've gotta get out of this depressed state, before it starts hurting my work even more.

"I can't do it. Won't."

"Girlfriend, I don't blame you. I wouldn't wanna do it either. But look at it this way, it'll give you the chance to give that man a look at a *real* woman."

Girlfriend? What's gotten into you and why are you telling me all this, anyway?

It was almost as if I were talking to another person. Still, I continued to play Jennifer's little game.

"Obviously he's no *real* man if he's selling out like that. If he was raised by a sistuh, he should already know what a *real* woman is. So why are we even wasting time doing this article?"

"I'm not exactly sure. Malik says it has something to do with another article scheduled to appear in the next issue. But don't quote me on that."

"Don't worry. I won't. I guess I should be talking to him, anyway, huh?"

"To be honest, I really don't think it'll do any good. But you can give it a try. Good luck, girl. Remember what I said, it could be a golden opportunity."

"Not for me, it won't be. Or for any of us for that matter. This man is obviously with the woman he wants to be with."

It was a good thing I ran into Jennifer when I did. I appreciated her looking out for me. But I also had to wonder why. Could she be feeling guilty? Or was this her way of trying to redeem herself without admitting that she was wrong? Whatever the reason, I couldn't help but be glad for the warning but I just knew Jennifer had to be joking.

After all, why would Malik even have an interest in something like this? Is this couple part of the Sweetheart's Day layout, too? Sure, many of our articles focused on relationships and other social issues, but this was so unlike him. Mr. Pro-Black everything. From his dreadlocks to his kente cloth garb to his better half.

"Greetings, my sister. Why the sullen look on your face?" Malik walked over to my desk, handing me a 5" x 7" piece of paper with directions to an address in Marietta, an affluent suburb north of Atlanta. I assumed it was the address for my latest pair of interviewees.

"Hello, Malik. I just got wind of this." I looked down at the note I now held in my right hand.

"Oh, so you've already heard about your interview with Joseph White and Shelly Gabors? Good. This sheet of paper I just gave you will come in handy."

"So, it is true?"

"I don't understand what you mean, Jazz."

"I mean, is it true I'll be doing an article on interracial dating?"

"Yes, that is so."

"Why? Why are we even doing this piece? More important, why am *I* having to do it?"

"To answer your first two questions Jazz, we're doing it for balance."

"What do you mean?"

"Well, in our January issue, we'll be featuring an in-depth interview with author and renowned orator starr knowles. As you know, she's always been a critic of interracial dating."

"Yeah, she sure is. I've always admired her work. She never compromises her opinions."

"So you should know what to expect from her. Although we may agree with some of what she has to say, it doesn't have to show in our work, our publication as a whole. To answer your last question, this is your area of concentration. Always has been. The only difference this time is you're writing about something you don't feel comfortable about."

If only he knew. I had very good reasons for feeling uncomfortable. Malik let me go home a little early, since I'd completed my assignment for the day, and so I could rest up for the dreaded task I'd take on the next day. As I left downtown, and turned onto the I-20 East ramp to Decatur, I couldn't help but reminisce about that Sunday night in October a year ago, when I pulled up to find Daniel with that heifer.

There was absolutely no way I could interview this couple. I couldn't imagine sitting there listening to this Joseph guy talk about why he'd chosen to be with white Shelly. *Well, you know, since black women don't know how to treat a brotha, I decided I'd give someone like Shelly a chance. Sistuhs are always wantin' something, and you can never please them. And then they just nag you to death. See, Shelly doesn't ask for much. Anything I do makes her happy. On top of that, she goes out of her way to please me, without complaining. It's just a lot easier, less pressure.*

I couldn't stand to hear it. I'd heard the same bull too many times before from other brothers who sold out.

The next day, I arrived at work twenty minutes early so I could catch Malik before the morning editorial meeting. He was sitting behind his desk, completing a phone conversation when I walked into his office.

"Malik, do you have a minute?"

"Sure Jazz, but if it's about the assignment..."

"Please Malik, just hear me out."

"No, Jazz, *you* listen. I heard what you had to say yesterday, and I understand. Believe me, I do. But I also believe you're perfect for this job. Not only that, it's an opportunity for you."

"An *opportunity?* For what?"

"Well, I don't expect you to change your beliefs, but perhaps it can help you reevaluate them."

I finally backed down. I knew this wasn't going anywhere. At least not in my favor. Anyway, Malik had already called and set up the interview with Joseph and Shelly. All I had to do was show up, and try to leave my attitude behind.

As I turned into the Hill Street driveway, I immediately saw why this chick was with this brotha. At the end of the driveway, a double garage was attached to the brotha's two-story lakeside home, which displayed a beautiful bay window near the front door.

On the other side of it stood probably reason number one. Joseph was fine. He had beautiful brown skin, the color of a Mars candy bar, jet black eyes and wavy hair. Just as I'd expected, *hers*—straight and shoulder-length—was dyed blonde, the naturally brunette roots starting to show.

"Hi, I'm Jasmine Brown from *Amsha* magazine," I said, now standing in the foyer.

"Hello there, I'm Joseph White. *Amsha*, that's Swahili, isn't it?"

Hmmm, the brotha knows something cultural.

"Right, honey," a female voice yelled from behind. "We learned that in the continuing ed class we took together last semester." I assumed she said it more for my benefit than for his. "It's good to see you aren't slacking off."

He actually took a Swahili class with this chick?

"What you are slacking off on are your manners," she said, walking toward the door. "You haven't even introduced me to Ms. Brown." She stopped alongside Joseph and extended her hand. "Hi, I'm Shelly Gabors. Please, excuse Joseph. Sometimes he wanders off into his own little world."

"I'm sorry, sweetie. I hadn't forgotten you," he said, rubbing her back. "I was going to get around to it. I just got caught up in the name. *Amsha*," he repeated. "That's interesting."

"Thank you. The name is representative of our work, our magazine as a whole. We believe it's our responsibility to wake up the black community, to stir things up when necessary."

Like you for example, my brotha. You could use an awakening right now.

"You do a nice job. I've picked up a few copies in the past at the Bruno's around the corner. You're still fairly new, aren't you?"

"The first issue came out six years ago, and we've done extremely well since." So had I, I thought, moving from freelancer to full-time staff member in no time.

"Well, Ms. Brown, before Shelly gets onto me about my manners again, please come in, and have a seat."

Joseph and Shelly led the way into the nearby sunroom. Its decor took my breath away: oak-colored hardwood floors, quaint wicker furniture, a handful of throw pillows, and larger-than-life windows, offering nothing short of a picturesque view of the nearby lake. Nothing fancy, just cozy. For a brief moment, I felt a twinge of envy and actually wanted to trade places with Shelly. Even more, I wanted these same things with my soul mate. I'd never dreamed of being rich, just happy with what I was doing (which I was) and comfortable. Making enough to pay my bills and enjoy life at the same time, without something called a budget holding me back.

Since I didn't want to be here in the first place, I wasted no time getting to the interview. "So, I guess the best place to start would be with this question: How long have you two lovebirds..." Just as I tried to get the words out, I felt something run across the back of my legs, causing me to flinch slightly.

"Oh, I'm sorry," Shelly said, bent toward my feet, lifting a round, very hairy gray cat into her arms. "He's such a friendly little thing."

Where did that fat rascal come from? I hate cats. Worse, I hate them rubbing up against me.

"Pierre, who told you to come out?" Shelly carefully lowered herself next to Joseph and rubbed the stupid cat, excuse me, *Pierre,* as she answered questions.

"What I was about to ask was..."

"How long we've been dating?" Shelly smiled.

Interrupted again! My patience is already short enough, people.

"Eleven months, eighteen days, and..."

"Shelly, honey, she doesn't need you to be that meticulous," Joseph cut in.

"I'm sorry, it's just that I'm so proud of our love."

"So am I, baby. But let's not bore the woman."

Too late for that. Still I pretended it didn't bother me. "That's okay," I lied and continued the momentum.

"On to the next question. How did you meet?"

"We've probably told this story a million times now, haven't we honey?" Shelly asked, turning toward Joseph. The two sat on a wicker love seat, which was facing the matching chair I was in. "Joseph and I were taking a class together, an American Lit class," she continued. "We were both English majors at the University of Georgia in Athens. I really didn't notice him in the beginning. There were at least a hundred students in there. But then one day we met with a study group from class. That's when I got to know my sweetie a little better."

"That's also when I knew I had to ask Shelly out. She was so intelligent and she knew her stuff. But I could tell she wasn't just brains. Her spirit and smile won my heart. She has this grin that resembles a baby's when they're being tickled, and the biggest dimples I've ever seen. I'm telling you when she raised her head from that book and looked at me with those big blue eyes, the way she's looking at me now, I couldn't resist."

I wanted to say *thanks* and just walk away. They were actually sitting here gazing at each other, feeding me this fairy tale. Not that I didn't believe in true love or anything. I just couldn't see why he was so in love with *her*.

"It's obvious you two are in love." *The thought alone makes me want to throw up*, was what I wanted to say next. "But I know it wasn't easy getting here. What type of pressures have you encountered?"

"Well, as you know, even though it's the nineties, some people still look at interracial dating in a negative light. We still get those stares, you know, when we're out in public. What bothers us most, though, are the so-called friends and family who refuse to accept our relationship. Many of my friends don't care for Shelly, simply because she's white."

"And vice versa. Some of my friends don't feel I should be dating someone outside of my race. But Joseph and I love each other, and that's all that matters. We don't see color."

"That's one of the things that immediately attracted me to Shelly. I never felt like I was a *black man* with her. I felt like a man, with no color at all. That's because she treats me that way. A lot of women I've dated didn't know how to treat me. They always expected something out of me but weren't willing to reciprocate. Shelly knows how to love, and she is not demanding. She makes me happy, and I believe

I do the same for her. It bothers me that some people, mostly females, have a problem with that. They feel I should be with one of them, or any black woman for that matter. I believe I should be with whoever makes me happy, which just happens to be Shelly."

Joseph reached for Shelly's hand; the cat now rested in between the two. He whispered the words *I love you,* and leaned toward her to plant one of his sellout kisses on her lips.

"I've had it just as bad as Joseph. At first, a lot of my girlfriends couldn't believe we were dating. Some have even said the only reason I'm dating Joseph is to peak my sexual curiosity." She sounded as if she were angered by the thought alone.

"I've been accused of the same thing. But the truth is, sex wasn't even on my mind. I was attracted, still am, to Shelly the person. I mean, I'm thirty years old, and I've dated several women before her. Most of them black. But with a lot of sisters, I found trying to get close wasn't exactly the easiest thing. I was having to deal with a lot of factors outside of my control. By the time I'd worked through all that, I was tired."

That did it. Just as I got this feeling things were about to get out of hand, they did.

"What exactly do you mean?" I asked in a not-so-professional tone.

Watch it, Jazz, I told myself. *Let's see what Mr. White—talk about a name—has to say.*

"What I meant was, many of our sisters have been burned and they've built up these walls. Walls that don't necessarily make it easy for a brother to break through. A lot of 'em are just carrying around a lot of baggage."

"Do we not *all* have some kind of baggage in our lives?" I asked, defensively. "Everyone's been burned a time or two, wouldn't you say? That includes you, too."

"You're right. But there comes a time when you just have to let that stuff go, you know, unpack the baggage. None of us can afford to go around making others pay for the pain someone else caused. What kind of world would this be if we all did that?"

He had a point, although I didn't want to admit it.

"Don't misunderstand me," Joseph continued. "I'm not saying I woke up one day and declared to never date another black woman. That's not what happened at all. It just turns out, the ones I did date up to the point when I met Shelly were ones I realized I really couldn't have anything significant with."

"Meaning?"

"Well, no matter what I did, no matter how supportive or loving I may have been, it wasn't enough to bandage their scars. I did my best to try to show them what good loving was. I tried to show them that black men do know how to love and not all of us are bad. But I just wasn't getting anywhere. I soon realized I wasn't responsible for their happiness. There was no way I'd make a difference until they were willing to—excuse me for being redundant—unpack."

Unpack the baggage. I'd never quite heard it put that way before.

Boy was he making sense. I hadn't expected to actually be enlightened by this brother. Malik was right. But I wasn't sure I wanted him to know that either.

Driving back to the office, I couldn't take my mind off the things Joseph had said. *There comes a time when you just have to let that stuff go.* It was time for me to let go, unpack my baggage. But doing so wouldn't be easy and I now realized it was probably something I wouldn't be able to do alone.

I headed straight for Malik's office when I got back. Not sure of what I'd say, besides thanks.

"Knock, knock."

Malik was sitting at his desk, sorting through some papers.

"Jazz, come on in."

"So, aren't you the least bit curious as to how it went?" I stopped in front of his desk, standing over him.

"I'm sorry, Jasmine—"

"My interview with the couple," I said, suddenly remembering Malik didn't have the best memory.

"Oh, yeah. How'd it go?"

There was that accent. It really came on thick whenever Malik got excited.

"It was fine. I'm actually glad I went."

"Great! See, Jazz. I told you. So how do you feel now?"

"Well, I'll be honest. The interview didn't change the way I feel about interracial dating. But I do plan to reconsider the way I look at some other things."

"As long as you got something out of it, I'm pleased. By the way, Jazz, I've been meaning to ask you something."

"Yes?"

"Are you okay? Lately, you haven't seemed like yourself."

"I didn't realize it was noticeable, Malik. You're right, I haven't been myself. To be honest, right about now, I don't know who Jasmine is."

"Sure you do. Don't talk like that."

"I mean it, Malik. This is probably one of the lowest points of my life."

I couldn't believe I was being so candid with Malik, not because I couldn't trust him, but because I'd always been private about my personal life. But for some reason, I felt completely comfortable with him. Besides, I was tired of holding everything in. As Joseph had said, it was time to let go.

"Well, if that's the case, I recommend you take some time off. I want you to be at your best, and right now, it's obvious you're going through something. I'll give you as long as it takes to get yourself together, Jazz, but I can only afford to pay you for one week. During that time, I'd like for you to complete the write-up on the couple and get it in here to me by next Friday."

What! Talk about generous and considerate. Time off and a week's worth of pay for one article. To top it off, I could take all the time I needed. I never could have expected anything like this if I were working for *them*. Or any big business for that matter. Because *Amsha*'s staff was small, Malik and Sandy could afford to be flexible. But at the same time, financially, could they afford this and what would it mean for their and Jennifer's workload?

"Malik, I truly appreciate it. I think that would help. The pay isn't even that big a deal. But, you're right, I could use a break. I'd even thought about asking you for some time off, but my pride wouldn't let me."

"Never feel you can't come to me with something like this, Jazz. Sure, we'll be in a crunch without you around. But you won't do us much good here if you're not together. Besides, you've earned this.

Not only are you a hard worker, you're one of the best editors and writers I've met during my career. You're dependable and I don't have to watch over you. You go and take care of yourself, and be sure to bring back the old Jazz."

Chapter Ten

Thank goodness for the 70 mph speed limit, I thought, passing a Georgia state trooper, armed with his radar gun, some twenty minutes from the Alabama state line.

I've been fortunate enough to only have gotten one ticket in my life. I don't need any more than that.

The trip up I-20 West to Birmingham usually took me about two hours tops. With cruise control set at about 80, that is. Mountains of trees with fall leaves, along with miles of interstate traveled by hundreds of vehicles, particularly 18-wheelers, was all the scenery I had to enjoy. The cloudy skies weighed heavily with signs of rain, but there was none coming down. It was the kind of trip that forced you to have plenty of good music nearby to keep you singing or humming along. Or plenty of shit on your mind to worry yourself to death about. And right about now, in my life, this visit to Miko was just what the doctor ordered.

If anyone can help bring me out of this funk, it's Miko. She'll know just what to say to get my screwed-up life back on track.

"Un-tie Jazz!" Christopher hopped off his rocking elephant and sprinted toward me. As always, he called me *auntie,* rather, his best fifteen-month-old pronunciation of the word. That was actually a substitute for godmother. Miko and I knew that would be something he'd have trouble saying for a little while.

"Hey, Chris! Umh. Umh. Thank you for the hug. Now give your auntie a kiss." The curly, bushy-haired, cocoa butter-complected toddler puckered up as if he knew the game of kissing all too well.

"Girl, what have you been letting your son watch on TV? How long has he been kissing like this?"

Miko let out her usual silly laugh.

"Jazz, I don't know where he got that from. He doesn't give you just a little peck. He practically sucks your face!"

"Shhh. Don't talk that way in front of him. There's no telling how much he's able to take in now. See, look at him. He's got a smile on his face, like he's scheming or something."

We both doubled over with laughter. Christopher jumped back onto his elephant and rocked away. The thick carpet in the living room restricted him from going very fast, so it was off to the smooth race-track of kitchen linoleum.

"I sure hope he doesn't turn out to be like his sorry daddy, Miko," I said, sliding Christopher into the new spot.

"Girl, me either. Don't jinx my child."

Miko only heard from Christopher's so-called father on one condition. When he was feeling guilty. Guilty that he had not checked on his son in a whole month. Thank God, Miko was taking him to court for child support. I hated to say it, but sometimes I envied her. Elliott may have dropped her the minute he found out she was pregnant. But at least he left her with something positive. A beautiful, healthy child. Not some dreaded, filthy diseases. And at least she could do something about her problem. Like make him go before a judge. I couldn't do anything to pay Daniel back by hurting him the way he'd hurt me. Making him feel the pain I felt. But I'd thought of a few things that just might be considered the proper nemesis. Like running over his ass with a car. Or doing the Lorena Bobbitt on him. But I couldn't. Unlike him, I wasn't cruel enough to hurt another human being. Or anything living for that matter.

"So, what brings you this way, Jazz?" Miko asked, moving toward the sofa. "Over the phone, you said you had something you need to talk about?"

"Yeah, I do." I sat beside Miko. "But I really just wanted to get away for a couple of days."

I hated the drive to Birmingham, but I enjoyed visiting my best friend. She had a nice, cozy, three-bedroom home—perfect for her and Christopher, who even had his own room. Of course, it was crammed with stuffed animals, sporty play cars and train sets, all toys which eventually wound up in every other room of the house. But when they were in their proper place, the rest of the home's decor shone through, thanks to a few knickknacks, here and there. Most were flea market bargains, some of which Miko refurbished herself. My favorite had always been Ms. Essie's old rocker, which was passed down to Miko two years ago when her grandmother died of cancer. It was where I made my first stop whenever I stayed over. I also loved the smell of Miko's house. Every room contained either a basket of potpourri or a scented candle. That was the one thing that reminded me of my own place.

"So, what's up? Are you okay?"

"So-so. I could definitely be better."

"To be honest, so could I. Girl, Elliott is at it again."

"You go first, Miko. What is it this time? No, let me guess. He still doesn't want to pay child support?"

"You got it. He actually thinks what he's doing now is enough."

"You mean chipping in a few bucks about once a month and picking Chris up on the weekends he feels like being bothered?"

"Basically. He loves to cry he doesn't make enough money, he's doing the best he can. He's doing a hell of a lot better than me. Last count, Mr. Computer Programmer made at least forty-five thousand dollars; that's about fifteen more than what I'm bringing home. Shit, you, just like everybody else, know teachers don't get paid the big bucks. Never mind that we have to put up with tons of bad-ass kids every day—many of which are latchkey and we wind up playing Mom to. Fourth grade is no joke." She nodded. "Anyway, I barely have enough to live off. After I pay the house and car notes, insurance, electricity, water, phone, my student loan, these freakin' credit cards, buy baby supplies, food, and pay for day care. After all that, I'm broke. I can't even afford to get my hair done or pamper myself at all. That's why it's usually brushed back in a bun like it is today." She played with some of the strands flowing from the black bow holding her hair into place. "One of the few positive things about my job are the hours. Seven to three. It may be wrong, but I waste no time gettin' out of there so I can pick Chris up from day care, make it home in time enough to feed him and eat myself, before starting on lesson plans for the next day. Then I'm left with a few decent hours to get some rest. So I can get up bright and early and do it all over again. Meanwhile, his damn daddy doesn't have any time or money for him, but he has enough of both to spend on these heffas he's dating."

"Miko, you're right. You are still taking him to court, aren't you?"

"You know I am. I don't have much of a choice. I've already gotten an attorney. We're supposed to meet with her at the end of the month. But that's where the problem comes in. Elliott has threatened not to show up. He thinks I'm just being mean. That I'm trying to get back at him for all he's done by making him pay child support. I'll be honest, that just may be five percent of my motive. But the number one reason is because I truly need help." Her voice dropped. She looked at Christopher, who had abandoned his ride and was now kill-ing time with a set of blocks. "It's hard trying to take care of *our* baby by myself. I have to take care of him one hundred percent emotionally *and* financially. It might not be so bad if he were spending quality time with Chris, but he doesn't even do that much. I mean he sees his son about twice a month at the most. That's not enough. Sometimes I wonder if the baby even knows Elliott is his daddy. He probably thinks he's an uncle or cousin, since they're around him more. Jazz, he's probably closer to *you* than to his own daddy."

"That's a shame. But you know, he'll get his." It was so funny how I easily gave advice, but never followed my own. "You just can't do people wrong and expect to get away with it."

"Sure can't. 'Cause what goes around definitely comes around. Anyway, so much for me and my headaches. What's bothering you?"

Amazing. Miko was so strong. Despite everything Elliott put her through, despite the fact he couldn't give her the family life she wanted, because he had to make sure she was *the one,* she stayed strong. She was as tough as the kid I grew up with.

Since the day we met in Ms. Emerson's first grade class, Miko Fields and I had been tight. We graduated from elementary school together. Helped one another get over our individual fears of moving on to middle school and, later in high school, we taught each other lessons on how to develop into a young woman. We'd been through thick and thin together. Whenever I needed her to, Miko would fight my battles for me, and I'd do the same for her. She was there to wipe away the tears on my thirteenth birthday, the day I stood up from the toilet seat and discovered the bowlful of blood that colored the water. Beating my mother to the punch, Miko was the one who later told me everything I needed to know about my period. She even helped me understand why I had to be cursed with the monthly headache in the first place.

I couldn't say there was anyone who knew everything about me, but Miko sure came close. She was one of the few people I confided in when, unlike my peers, I made the decision to hold out on the guys in high school. In fact, by the time I was even introduced to sex, everybody else had been doing it for years. Without a doubt, she was my best friend. The only thing that separated us was distance. But it didn't keep our spirits apart. We had a bond that was interminable. One which grew even stronger when we went our separate ways after high school. *Always remember, success is getting what you want; happiness is wanting what you get,* Miko had written in my senior-year annual. With those unforgettable words in mind, I took off for Standefer State, while Miko took off for the University of Alabama at Birmingham. *I refuse to stay here and throw my life away,* I recalled Miko saying the day she mailed her application to UAB. We had big ambitions. The professional ones we'd accomplished. The personal life goals were a different story. I never expected to be the victim of a pair of STDs, while graduating from college into single parenthood wasn't exactly on Miko's list of must-dos. So, naturally, I couldn't help but hurt for her. She was like a sister; I hated to see her going through this. For that reason, I almost felt guilty for sharing my pain with her. At the same time, I couldn't help but admire her strength, and even wish some of it would rub off on me.

"Jazz, I know you're hurting right now," Miko said as she returned from the kitchen with two glasses of sweet tea in her hands. "But the pain won't last forever. As Mama always says, 'this too shall pass.' Look at it this way, you're better off finding out who Daniel really is now, than somewhere down the road, when you're married to him."

I nodded, and took a sip of the tea, which tasted more like brown water with a saccharine tang. I felt bad for not telling Miko the whole truth—that Daniel had been more than unfaithful; his loose ways had been hazardous to my health. The timing just didn't feel right, with all that she was dealing with in her own life.

"The funny thing is," I said, trying not to be completely evasive, "I still care for Daniel. We did share a lot together, and I know him about as well as he knows me. With him, I don't have to explain myself." I caught myself and tried to clean up that statement as quickly as possible. "I guess what I'm saying is, I'm afraid of starting over."

"That's only natural, Jazz. I can't tell you what to do. Hell, I'm just as confused when it comes to my love life. I'm telling you now, Jasmine," she said, interrupting my thoughts, "if Elliott tried to come back into my life, I wouldn't hesitate to take him back. He is the father of my baby, and we were in love. We were supposed to get married, start a family. We've already conquered one out of two. Now the only thing remaining is for him to come to his senses. I don't know why, Jazz, but it's hard for me to get him out of my system. Deep down, I hope, sometimes even pray, for him to come back—a changed man, of course, despite all he's put me through."

"But Miko, my feelings are so strange because, at the same time, I feel hatred toward Daniel. I can't explain it."

"It's called love. I have the same type thoughts about Elliott. Sometimes I get so angry. Especially when I think about all the sacrifices I've made for him. Like how, when we were in school, I supported him in every way possible, even though I couldn't afford to. I was the one who nearly dropped out of college, trying to help him out. And here I am, years later, struggling, trying to take care of our son, while he's moved on with his life. Don't get me wrong. I'm proud to be a mother. I love Christopher more than anything. He brings me so much joy and I'm happy to have him. But it does hurt to know I went through all this—the pregnancy, giving birth, and the two-timing—and Elliott still walked out of my life. Here I am left behind to carry the load, while he's moving on, just as happy and strong as ever."

"I don't see how they do it, girl. They do their damage and move on. Don't you know sometimes I wish I could be more like white women. When their men mess up, they write them off, move on, and don't waste any time doing it either."

"Sure don't," Miko agreed. "They can get divorced, and the next week they're in the arms of someone new. But you know, I think it's because they're not strong enough to take things like we are. Moving on for them is really just a cover-up most times."

"Another reason," I interrupted, "I believe we hold on is because we want to give our men the benefit of the doubt. We want to stand by our black men as much as possible. I guess we feel if we don't, who will? They already have to deal with the pain inflicted by society through the years, and we don't want to add to their burdens, so, oftentimes, we sacrifice for them. Unfortunately, in many instances, we get burned."

"That may be true, but I'll admit, after all I've been through with black men, I've come to the conclusion that dating outside of my race might not be such a bad thing," Miko said, making more than my eyebrows raise. "Shit, white men hit on me all the time, and although I've never given in to their advances, sometimes I'm tempted."

"You're serious, aren't you?" I was shocked to hear Miko talk that way because just a year or so ago, she seemed adamant about sticking with her own.

I don't care how much black men have hurt me, I've never seriously thought of giving up on them.

"Jazz, maybe it isn't meant for me to end up with a brother. If past experience is any indication, it's not."

"But Miko, you aren't giving up on our men just yet, are you?"

"No, not completely. But I am leaving the door open to others. White, Puerto Rican, Italian. I'm looking for whoever's gonna love and treat me right."

"I hear you, girl. But I want you to hear me out, too. If I can still have hope, you should, too. That's not to say I haven't had thoughts of drifting, especially when I'm most vulnerable and hurting like I am right now. You know what hurts the most, Miko? Not the fact that Daniel cheated. It's just there were some warning signs before that even happened. Like the phone calls, and the women who always seemed to just pop up, and those letters. But I ignored them all. I ignored my inner voice. I thought he loved me enough to change. Now I'm left with one hard-learned lesson. I know everything happens for a reason. In this case, I can already see what that reason is. But the pain is still there."

"'This too shall pass,' remember? You just have to keep telling yourself that, Jazz. And most importantly, you have to believe it."

But for some reason, I didn't. Not this soon. Although Miko's encouragement made me feel somewhat better, the trip to see her didn't prove to be as therapeutic as I'd hoped. This was my best friend. I couldn't even tell her my darkest secret. I never did buy into that trite expression, *misery loves company.* What was it that two miserable people could accomplish together besides more of the same?

I was more than convinced that Miko was in no position to offer me advice about men right now. She said it herself; love had turned her into one confused individual as of late. That made two of us. If I had anything to do with it, it wouldn't be that way for long.

Chapter Eleven

"Jasmine, are you here?"

I'd picked up the phone without even realizing it. Hadn't even heard it ring. I had no idea how long this person sounding like Monique had been on the other end.

"Hello? Jazz?"

"Monique?"

"Yeah, it's me. Did I wake you?"

"No, I'm sorry." I was far from asleep. I'd spent much of this Saturday morning mulling over the recent turn of events. "I didn't realize you were on the line. I was getting ready to dial a number, and I guess you were already here," I lied.

"That explains why you didn't say anything. Not even hello. So, how are you?"

"I'm okay. How about you?"

"No complaints here. That's why I'm calling. Marcus and I may have found a baby."

"Wonderful." I inched up a bit. "Congratulations."

"We really are grateful to you for introducing us to Katherine. She found a teenager who wants to have her baby, but doesn't feel she's able to take care of it."

"I knew things would work out," I said, thinking how I never really expected Monique to call. I'd given her my number at the fair two months ago as a contact while she was going through her search. Still, this call caught me off guard, especially at this time.

"Well, it's not over yet, but we're keeping the faith. Anyway, I'm not gon' keep you, but I actually called for two reasons. We'd be honored if you could come to our wedding. It's three months away in January and I can get you an invitation in the mail soon."

"Thanks for the invite. I'd love to come but..."

I wasn't sure if I was safe telling her about the breakup. How close were they? What had he told her, if anything.

"I know you and Daniel aren't together anymore. But that shouldn't keep you from coming, Jasmine." She said it so matter-of-factly.

Now I really wondered what his side of the story was.

"Don't worry," she said, as if reading my mind, "he didn't go into details. You know how men, especially our men, are about puttin' their business in the street."

It was true: Daniel was one of those men.

"I don't think I'd feel comfortable being there, Monique, but I appreciate your interest."

"So, it's that serious? You don't see the two of you getting back together between now and then?"

"No." I gave her nothing extra. She wasn't my friend. She was his.

"I would say 'I'm sorry,' but I don't wanna get in your business and maybe sympathy isn't appropriate right now. You know what's best for you."

"This is best, trust me." I did all I could to keep from breaking down. Monique sounded sincere, making it easy for me to let my guard down some. She also sounded like she knew a thing or two about this love stuff. She was, after all, about to wed her soul mate.

The longer I talked to her, the more I realized she couldn't have called at a more vulnerable time. I'd been holding all this in for well over a month. Couldn't even spill my guts to Miko just yesterday. It was time I confided in someone. As unlikely as it seemed, maybe she was that someone.

"Well, like I said, I'm not going to get in your business. If you ever need to talk, I'm here."

"Could I ask you something before you go?"

"Sure, what is it?"

"Please don't think I'm crazy, but I kind of got this feeling every time I came in the store that you were giving me this look. I can't really describe it, but it was one that made me feel I was dropping by too much."

"Not at all. You didn't come in there that often, Jasmine."

"Well, I've been doing some thinking over the past few days and I think I figured it out. Was it because I wasn't Daniel's only visitor—female visitor—is that why?"

"I really didn't think it was that obvious, but at the same time, I was hoping it was. I wanted to come out and tell you but..."

"You worked with Daniel, and you knew him better than you knew me?"

"Right. Until I got up the nerve, I figured that was the best I could do. You know how perceptive we women are."

"Yeah, but if you're like me, you still ignore your gut, and, in some cases, the evidence staring you in the face."

"Daniel's a good guy, Jasmine. He just hasn't grown out of that phase. I think he wants to, but he's fighting with himself."

I sat up in bed. "Phase? Do you mean—"

"Running the streets. Chasin' tail. Sowing his wild oats. Unfortunately, most men have to go through it. The good thing about it, though, is that at least you can be fairly certain once they get past it, they're past it. I think Daniel's gonna grow out of it. The question is when?"

"When he does, it'll be too late. He's messed up too bad this time."

"You wanna talk about it? If you're concerned about me telling him, don't worry. I'm on your side. We sistuhs have got to stick together."

I couldn't hold back the tears any longer.

"Jasmine, why are you crying? Do you need me to come over or anything?" The questions sounded more firm than commiserative.

"No, thank you." I switched the phone from my right to left ear.

"Okay, well if you need me to, I will definitely come. All you have to do is say the word."

"Thanks for the offer."

"So, what's wrong, sweetie?"

"Well, I've been keeping quiet about this since October, Monique. I haven't felt comfortable talking about it to anyone. Not even my best friend."

"What is it? Are you sick?"

"Yes."

"Are you gonna be okay?"

"I hope so."

"You hope so? It's not something life-threatening, is it?"

"Not quite. Just lifelong."

"A disease?"

"Two," I said, sobbing. I was lucky to get any words out. I couldn't believe I was telling this woman my business.

"Sexually transmitted?" I could hear the shared pain in her voice.

"Yes."

"Oh, my word, Jazz. Is herpes one of them?"

How could she know that? I couldn't say anything. Teardrops, almost like tributaries, rushed down my cheeks.

"Oh, Jazz. This is not something you need to be dealing with by yourself."

"I haven't been able to tell anybody. I've been too embarrassed. You're the only one I've opened up to."

"I'm glad you told me. You need someone to talk to, especially in rough times like this. You mentioned there's two. What's the—?"

"Genital warts," I interrupted. "By the way, how did you know about the herpes?"

"Sweetie, I've been down this road before."

"What are you saying? Not *you*, too?"

Daniel *was* right. This was more common than I'd thought.

"Yes. *Me*, too. Right after my ex, J.T., told me he'd fallen in love with his paralegal, I started having complications. Most likely some of the same ones you've experienced. I felt like I had the flu. There were close to a dozen blisters between my legs, which burned whether I was using the bathroom or not. Jasmine, I know exactly what you're going through. I want you to know you can get through this. I thought J.T. was being faithful. I never thought he'd be this careless with me. Trust me. I know all the emotions you're grappling with. Feeling like your life is over. Like you won't find anyone else."

"Yeah. And I worry I won't be able to have children." Wait a minute—was this why Monique couldn't get pregnant?

"Monique, I don't want to pry too much, but is the herpes what's stopping you from having children?"

"No one can say for sure what's going on with me. As you may have discovered by now, many of these infections lead to even bigger problems like pelvic inflammatory disease, which can cause infertility."

"Yeah, I've read about all that."

"But you can't let it beat you down. Right now, I want you to erase any negative thoughts you're having. You're going to be okay. I'll be right here with you to make sure you are."

"That's so kind of you."

"You could use an ally right now, Jazz. Someone who's walked in your shoes."

"Monique, may I ask, do you know *where*—?"

"No, not for sure. As you probably know, the disease can be in your system for a while before you ever realize it. You could spend an eternity trying to trace its root."

"Daniel claims he doesn't have a clue either. I've got a few ideas though. But that doesn't ease my mind any. I don't think it's right for me to be playing the guessing game. Seems like Daniel would know who he's been screwing. If the number was too high for him to keep count, then he should've been considerate enough to keep me from getting caught up in the middle. Don't you agree? Doesn't it bother you to know your ex put you at risk?"

"Of course it does. But like I said, there's no way to know how long, so I can't place all the blame on him. I've been infected for about a year and a half now. I've done a lot of praying and soul-searching. Spirituality works wonders, Jazz."

"I'm hoping to one day become as strong as you. Right now it just hurts. One day I'm doing fine. The next I find this out. I just can't believe it. I had everything going for me. I feel like this is a major setback."

"It doesn't have to be. You can live with it. You can continue doing the same things you do now, Jazz. Believe it or not, I've only had one outbreak in the year-plus that I've been infected. It's all about keeping your stress level down. Also, don't change your eating habits. The combination of a poor diet and stress can trigger a recurrence. I know crying helps. Trust me. I've done more than my share. But it can also upset you. And you don't need anything that can set off more symptoms."

"Yeah, I know. I've read about all that in the pamphlets the doctor gave me. Plus she warned me. Still, it's hard to keep from crying. I've had few dry spells since I found out. I feel so betrayed. I know I'm not perfect. We all have our flaws. But I don't think I deserve this. I don't think anyone does. I definitely don't feel anyone deserves to get something worse, like AIDS. Why would anybody put another person's life at risk?"

"I know. I tell you, some men are just selfish and inconsiderate. They don't care about anyone but themselves. They claim the reason they don't tell you the truth is because they don't want to hurt you. What they need to realize is the truth always comes to the light. When it does, it hurts twice as bad."

"You're so right. I asked Daniel over and over if he was seeing someone else. There were warning signs that crept up occasionally and made me suspicious, but he always insisted he wasn't messing around. He told me he didn't have any reason to because I made him completely happy. He even said he'd be a fool to do that."

"He was right about that part. Jazz, from what I can tell and from all that he's told me about you, you are a wonderful woman. And you *were* good to him, even went out of your way to make sure he was happy. Just like I did for J.T. They will never find any other women like us and they know it."

"Well, why would they do something like this?"

"Because, men can be stupid. Not all of them are, but some can just be plain stupid as hell. Case in point: J.T. Little does he know, he did me a favor by messing up. It opened the door for a *real* black man to walk right on in. Marcus is the best thing that's ever happened to me. In two weeks, we'll be moving out of this apartment into our new house, and the wedding's right around the corner."

I was overwhelmed but impressed with Monique's candor.

"But it wasn't a breeze getting here. I realized I had to go through everything J.T. put me through so I would be able to love someone like Marcus. All the pain and heartache made me stronger. It made me realize what I was no longer willing to take. When I decided to stick to my convictions I found true love. You can have the same thing. Don't give up hope. There *are* some good black men out there. I'm not saying Daniel isn't the one for you. He just may be. But what you need to do first is stop feeling so down about yourself. Don't lose your self-esteem. Make up your mind about what it is you want, and never settle for less than that. Sometimes you have to compromise, but what you shouldn't compromise are your beliefs."

"Monique, was it difficult for you to tell Marcus?"

"It really wasn't. I did have a hard time telling others before him, though. In fact, initially I went through this fuck-it phase. Meaning, I was in a mindset where I thought, 'Hey, I wasn't warned beforehand, so why should I be so damn considerate?' I made the mistake of sleeping with someone, protected of course, without telling him. After that, I just felt so guilty and I had to take a good, hard look at myself. I didn't like the person I'd become because of my pain. From that day on, I knew I'd be up front with anyone I planned to be intimate with."

"But *how* did you tell them and what was the general response?"

"Whenever the subject of sex came up—as it often does if it's left up to a man—I found it easier to disclose certain secrets. One thing I discovered about men is, when they're discussing the subject of intimacy, they can be quite candid, Jazz, and nine times out of ten, many of *them* have skeletons in the closet, too. It actually wasn't as bad as I'd expected. Another reason I didn't have any problems was because of the caliber of men I was dealing with. If you're involved with an asshole, expect a shithead reaction. If you're involved with a quality guy, expect a mature, understanding response. Gauge the individual, and trust me, you'll know exactly what to say."

Just listening to Monique talk made me feel better. I needed to have done this with someone sooner. But as Mama would say, *everything happens exactly when it's supposed to, at the right time and in the right place.*

"Monique, thank you so much. I already feel better. But I don't know how long this feeling will last. Can I call on you when things get unbearable again?" I pressed one of two pillows to my chest.

"Call on me even before then. Call on me anytime you need to, anytime, day or night. If I'm not home, you can always page me. Jazz, you will pull through this. Just like I did. You're a strong woman. You know what they say about us sistuhs. We're survivors."

"Monique, just one more thing before you go."

"Yeah, sweetie, what's that?"

"Please, don't tell anyone."

"I won't be talking to anybody about this. You trusted me enough to share it with me. It would be wrong for me to divulge anything I know. I'm here to help, not to hurt you any more than you already are. I'm committed to you now. I have no choice. After all, remember, I've worn your shoes, and they don't fit me anymore. Now we've just gotta find you a new pair."

Everything Monique said made sense. Having it come from her, someone who had first-hand knowledge, gave it more credence.

When I'd first met Monique, I never would've guessed she'd serve any significant purpose in my life. Our conversation was meant to be. That was why I couldn't open up to Miko yesterday. I may not have gotten this type clarity from her. To my knowledge, she hadn't been down this path before.

They say everybody comes into your life for a reason. Some don't stick around as long as others. But the thing they all share in common is this: Once you determine why, and for how long they're there, you'll know exactly what to do.

Chapter Twelve

"Rock...Skate...Roll...Bounce. Rock...Skate...Roll...Bounce." The minute I heard those words, I took to the floor, with Tiffani a few feet behind.

"This is my song!" I lip-synched and did exactly what the words to Vaughan Mason and Crew's skating anthem said.

"No, this is *my* song!" Tiffani shouted, her pre-adolescent voice practically drowned by the music.

"Okay, so it's *our* song. Deal?"

"Deal," said Tiffani, who was now skating alongside me. Aside from the arcade at Shannon Mall, the Sparkles Skating Rink on GA 85 was one of our favorite hangouts, with my sister, Justice, tagging along a time or two. This time around, though, she'd had to stay behind to study for a test on Monday. But Tiffani and I, along with the remainder of Sparkles' typical Friday night crowd, mostly a younger bunch, packed the house.

"You having fun?" I asked, looking down at Tiffani who nearly reached my shoulder.

"Yes. I always have fun with you, Jazz."

"You're not so bad yourself, little girl." We both laughed, as Tiffani, apparently losing her balance, grabbed onto the right leg of my blue jeans.

"Don't, Tiff—!" Before I could get the words out, just what I expected to happen, did. Tiffani and I both landed flat on our behinds, as another favorite of mine, "Groove Line" by Heatwave was coming on.

"Tiffani, do you realize I haven't fallen while skating since I was about your age?" I stood and tried to maintain my balance, while helping Tiffani back on her feet.

"That fall was no joke; it really hurt," I said. Tiffani, now standing, swayed her arms in a circular motion in an effort to keep from going down again. "Rule number one. Never pull on someone else when you feel you're about to go down. It doesn't work. All it does is land both people on their bottoms."

"I know that now," Tiffani said, dusting the back of her pants. We clasped hands and slowly skated onto the carpet. "So, what's rule number two?" Tiffani asked, as we made it to our seats.

"What's that?"

"I said, what's rule number two?" Tiffani sat on the long, cushioned bench and began to untie her skating shoes.

"Rule number two: Never try to avoid falling by grabbing the person next to you."

"I thought that was rule number one."

"It is," I answered, lifting my feet out of the shoes. "It's also rule number two," I said, smiling.

A little boy and what appeared to be his mother hopped down beside us. I looked at my watch and saw that it was already 9:30.

"Well, we better go. We've had about enough fun for one night, don't you think?"

Tiffani didn't respond, but her eyes said no.

As much as I wanted to spend more time with her, I couldn't. Katherine, who'd called earlier in the day to say Tiffani was dying to see me, had warned me to have her back to the shelter by ten. I now had only a half hour to get there and I definitely didn't want to spoil my chances of spending time with her again.

She gives me that same sad look every time. I feel so guilty.

"Tiffani, you know we've gotta get back. Remember the curfew?"

"Yeah, I know. But I'm not ready to go. I'm having too much fun."

"So am I, sweetie. But there's always next time."

"Next time might not be till next month, Jazz. It's not like I get to see you every day."

For a ten-year-old, she sure made a lot of sense. And she definitely had a way of working on your emotions. I was already feeling bad for not having enough time before because of work, and for not making any time here recently because I'd gotten too wrapped up in my own daily dilemmas. Tiffani needed me. Besides her caseworker, I was about all she had, until someone else came along and decided to take her away from that shelter for good.

"Come on, Tiffani. Let's go get our shoes," I said, standing over her, reaching for her hand.

"I promise you it won't be another month, okay?"

We walked over and, as if in sync, placed our skates on the counter.

"Okay?" I asked again, looking down at Tiffani.

"Okay," she said.

Despite the cliché, time flies whether you're having fun or not. At least a week of my resting period has passed. Physically, I've gotten plenty of rest. Emotionally, I'm barely hanging in there. The time I spent with Tiffani last night helped tremendously, for the both of us. She's already requesting to see me again and I promised her it wouldn't be long. But right now, I really do need to deal with some things, clear my head and heart. No matter how much I tell myself not to think of Daniel, I do. At moments, I miss him. At others, I hate him. Monique's solution to that is this journal. Seeing my emotions in print, she says, will make it easier for me to deal with them. She also suggested writing Daniel a letter whenever he comes to mind. Only I would see it though; afterwards, if I liked, I could very well toss it.

And while Monique was in the advice-giving mood, she even recommended I start dating again, because, in her opinion, it'll help take my mind off things. I don't think I'm quite ready, but I can agree that it doesn't hurt to get out and enjoy myself. Hence, my engagement to an Isley Brothers concert tonight with Dave (the word date wouldn't actually be appropriate). Watching my all-time favorite oldies group in person is something you do with a significant other, which, in this case, would've been Daniel, whom I'd invited two months ago when I first charged the tickets to my MasterCard. Since I don't have a special someone, the most logical second choice should've been a girlfriend, or, in this case, a guy friend. At least with Dave, I was guaranteed to have a good time, rather "cool" time, to borrow from Tiffani. Maybe she was onto something, after all.

I closed the black, acid-free paper journal as I recounted Monique's compelling speech. "Jazz, I think you deserve a good date or two," she'd said. "You should be out having fun, and if it all works out, and does lead to something more, so be it."

"I doubt that'll happen," I'd said. "I always thought Daniel was the one. I can't trust my own judgment anymore."

"You can't think that way. You just got burned, that's all. It happens to the best of us. Trust me. In the end, you'll be stronger. I felt the same way after J.T. I didn't think I could ever love anyone else after him. But the angels changed all that. God sent me Marcus, and I'm happier than I've ever been. I know he's the one. You have to believe there's someone out there for you. But you really shouldn't be worried about that right now. Everyone's not out to get you and life isn't all that bad. You go through the good, the bad and the ugly. It's all necessary to your development. Relax and enjoy yourself for a change. Promise me you'll at least try to do that much."

Monique wouldn't let things go until she received my word that I'd make the most out of the night. She'd made a valid point: *If I didn't get back out there, how would I ever find Mr. Right? Better yet, how would he find me?*

From the shower, I headed straight to my walk-in closet and pulled out the black, ankle-length velvet dress I'd ordered from a Victoria's Secret catalog. I slipped it on over my black bra, undies and tights, followed by a pair of small pearl earrings and three-and-a-half inch black pumps.

"I look good, if I must say so myself," I said aloud, while checking myself out from head to toe in the full-length mirror on the back of the bathroom door. Good thing this dress got here on time. I didn't have any other appropriate attire for the downtown Fox Theatre, a place you couldn't walk into half-stepping. Initially, I'd ordered an extra small, and had to send the first dress back for the next size. Sizes six to eight were considered small, but still sounded a little too big for me, considering I typically managed to get into fours and fives with no problem. As it turned out, in this particular getup, that wasn't the case.

Dave should be here any minute.

The concert started at 8:00 and I'd told him I wanted to leave an hour early so we could get there no later than 7:30. That way, we'd more than likely make it into the Fox parking area before it filled up. Usually when that happened, everybody and their mama would attempt to flag you down, in an effort to sucker you into paying as much as ten dollars to park in their lot.

"Girl," he said, dragging it out, "you look good. Look at you."

Any second now, I'd have to wipe drool from Dave's mouth. I'd never seen him get this excited about my appearance. Then again, he'd never seen me this dressed up.

"Thank you, sir," I said, taking a few steps down my imaginary runway.

"You go, girl. Tyra Banks ain't got nothin' on you!" We both laughed.

"And Tyson Beckford has nothin' on *you*. You're lookin' pretty dapper yourself." Dave wore black, too: a long-sleeve dress shirt, slacks and a sports coat. Though he wasn't the type that made heads turn, he wasn't bad-looking either. Dave had a round face, perfect white teeth (always a plus) and a shining smile as innocent as the one man on Earth I lusted for—the NBA's Chris Webber.

"If Daniel could only see what he's missin' out on."

I grabbed my formal black bag and apartment key from the coffee table.

"Yeah, if only," I muttered, thinking of the day I'd finally filled Dave in on what had happened. He forgave me for postponing sharing the details with him, even made a threat: "He better not let me see his ass out anywhere." Never had I seen him that upset.

We walked into "The Fabulous Fox," passing the Will Call and Box Office windows. Once at the entranceway, I had my small bag lightly searched before handing over my ticket. A guide, holding a tiny flashlight in hand, led us to our orchestra seats, only five rows from the stage.

The Isley Brothers got the crowd rocking with a funky familiar beat, accompanied by a screaming electric guitar, and the lyrics *Choosey Lover. Girl, I'm so proud of you. I'm so glad you chose me, baby.*

They soon pumped things up with their hit, "Who's That Lady?"

"I bet a lot of guys in here are asking themselves that same question." Dave leaned in close, raising his voice to compete with the noise.

I smiled.

It was encouraging to receive so much flattery in one night.

Dave and I laughed, dance and sang for a good hour until the first twenty-minute intermission.

"You want anything?" Dave asked. "We both could use something to drink after all that."

"And an oatmeal cookie wouldn't hurt," I suggested. "Have you ever had one?"

He answered no.

"You don't know what you're missing."

We stepped outside to a vendor selling round, jumbo-size oatmeal cookies for two bucks. The line was long, but the sweets were worth it.

"You were right, Jazz. These are the bomb," Dave said, biting a tiny piece. "What I want to know is how you can afford to eat these and stay as fine as you are."

Fine? That was a word I hadn't heard from him before—not when he was talking about me at least.

Chapter Thirteen

Over a short period, Monique's relationship with me progressed from acquaintance to confidant to matchmaker. In no time, she got busy setting me up. Her first attempt: a guy named Robert Tate. I had to admit, Robert sounded like someone I could dig. Monique said he was attractive, hard-working and kindhearted. Plus, I didn't think she'd get me involved with somebody who wasn't worth my time, considering she knew what I'd been through. So because of that, I took the risk. Only because this Robert guy was a friend of a friend's friend.

According to Monique's description—a secondhand account from her girlfriend, Angela, who knew Robert better than any of us—he was really nice, handsome, well-mannered and educated. Had his own car, his own apartment and no kids or ex-wives hanging around. As with most everything, there was one hang-up, though. He and his last girlfriend broke up eight months ago because she supposedly cheated on him, and as far as Monique knew, they still maintained a strong friendship. If it was anything like mine and Daniel's situation—which, in terms of a breakup, was approaching the two-month mark—it probably meant much of the love was still there, too.

But Monique said Robert insisted he was ready to move on after three years, and was on the lookout for a good woman hoping, like him, to get married soon. I obviously wasn't ready to get that serious right now. It was hard enough convincing myself to go through with tonight's arrangement. I hated blind dates. But Monique's persuasive skills caused most of my usual reservations to dissipate tonight.

The peach shower gel smelled so good it made me hungry. I hoped the aroma would move Robert somehow.

Even though it was our first date, I decided to let Robert pick me up at my apartment. Monique could vouch for him, and, as with all first dates, I'd alerted Miko and Dave. Generally, I'd call anywhere from two to three friends and/or family members and give them as much information about the date as I could. That way if I ended up raped, my mangled body tossed in the back of someone's trunk, they'd know how to find the culprit. I thought I could trust my own vibes, but I'd learned you could never be too safe. Look at the mess I was in now for trusting a member of the opposite sex.

Enough of the negative thinking. There's a new man to concentrate on now. All I can do is give this one the benefit of the doubt and hope he won't let me down.

The doorbell rang at six o'clock sharp.

He's right on time, I thought. *I like that.*

I opened the door to find a gorgeous prize standing before me.

"So you're Jasmine," he said, a look of approval on his face. "Monique has told me so much about you." He smiled.

I was nearly speechless as I examined Robert from head to toe as he entered the living room. It took just one four-letter word to describe him: fine! He was every bit of six feet tall with broad shoulders, a smooth, shiny bald head and clean-shaven face. And, as if that weren't enough, he had some of the smoothest chocolate skin I'd ever seen.

I do love myself a dark-skinned brother.

In fact, that was all I ever dated. Like Daniel for example. Forget those *pretty boys* or *redbones*. Or whatever you'd wanna call them. They were more of Miko's type. *Give me a Wesley or Denzel anytime.*

"So, will Chinese be all right?" Robert asked, standing with his back to the door.

"Sounds good to me," I said, now all caught up in Robert's dimples and straight, white teeth.

I love a man with beautiful teeth, I thought.

"Good. I know a first-rate restaurant—at least in my tastes—downtown near International. Have you ever eaten at the Imperial Palace?"

"No, but I've passed by it a few times. I've always wondered what it was like."

"Wonder no more. I'm ready if you are."

So far, so good. But that was to be expected during what I considered the first impression stage. Robert scored his first two points when he unlocked the door to his 5.0 on my side, and helped me inside. Although his car was hooked up with what appeared to be an Alpine sound system, he didn't blast music in my ears. Two more points for that. And another pair for helping me into my seat at the restaurant table.

The restaurant's decor was impressive. It had the feel of most upscale eateries. A beautiful, hunter green marble fountain gurgled in the middle of the dining area, seeming to relax us both. Two candles, in the center of our table, set the mood for romance.

"So, what do you recommend?"

"Well, I like their seafood dinners myself. I usually order one of the shrimp combinations," Robert said, pointing at the menu.

"Okay, I'll trust your recommendation. I'll try number four, the garlic shrimp."

"Good choice. Especially if you like lots of mushrooms and carrots in your fried rice."

"I love mushrooms." That was about all I could think of to say. I was too busy checking Robert out.

"So, I'm actually sitting here with Ms. Jasmine Brown, the writer?"

"The one and only. Does that mean you're familiar with *Amsha?*"

"I'll let you be the judge of that. Let's see now. It features articles on relationships, entrepreneurs, movers and shakers, and health concerns in the black community. It's black- owned, operated and staffed, and targets the same audience."

"You've done your research. So, do you subscribe?"

"Sure do. And I've read your work. You're an excellent writer."

"Thank you." I blushed.

"I also love that smile. You're a beautiful woman, Jasmine. I'm sure you hear that all the time." Robert sounded as if he were asking a question, as his hazel eyes gazed deeply into mine.

"Thanks."

Okay, now I know my cheeks are about as red as the sweet and sour sauce sitting on this table. Good thing our waiter's coming to the rescue. But he's not just loaded down with food. What's that in his other hand?

As he approached, I noticed a vase with a single red rose inside.

"This for lovely lady, courtesy of the gentleman," he said in his thick, native accent.

Robert stood, took the vase from the waiter, and placed it between the flickering candles.

"Robert! This is so sweet of you." I was blushing uncontrollably. "Thank you."

"There's that beautiful smile again."

Stop complimenting me, I wanted to say. Not that I wasn't enjoying all the flattery, but I also wasn't used to this much, at least not with Daniel.

As Robert adored my smile, I inconspicuously looked off to the side, and silently thanked Monique. She was so right. Robert was sweet and thoughtful.

"So, how do you like it?" Robert asked as I crumbled a couple of wontons into my egg drop soup, hoping I wouldn't be disappointed with it.

Everyone wasn't good at making egg drop soup. But when it was done right—not too much of a yolk taste, with just enough scallions sprinkled on top—I was a happy camper.

"By *it,* do you mean the food, the surprise or the date?"

"Good question," Robert said. "I'd have to go with all of the above."

"Well, the food is great. The surprise was just that—a surprise, a charming one, I might add, and I'd have to say the date is just as delightful."

"Whew," Robert sighed, pressing his right hand against his chest. "I was getting worried that maybe I was the only one having a wonderful time."

"What gave you that impression?"

"Nothing really. You're just a little hard to read; that's all. You also seem to be preoccupied with something."

Robert was right. My body was here with him, but my mind kept drifting off to thoughts of Daniel.

I wouldn't even be going through this whole dating again drama if it weren't for him. Sure, everything's going well so far, but this is just the first date.

"You're not totally off-target," I said, before biting down on a shrimp.

"You wanna talk about it?"

"No, not really. It's nothing really."

I can't tell him the truth. After all, what would I say? I've got another man on my mind? If he'd had his act together, I'd be with him, and not you, right now?

"Thank you for asking, Robert, but, trust me, I'm okay."

"Okay, I'll take your word. But my ears are open if you ever need to talk."

What's wrong with me? This guy is giving me every reason to like him and here I am thinking about someone who's not worth my time. Why is it we women always fall for the bad guy, the most trifling Negro who puts us through living hell? But we won't give the good ones, the ones on the straight and narrow, the time of day.

"So, tell me a little about yourself, Jasmine." Robert sipped on sweet tea through a straw. "What do you like to do for fun?"

"As you know, I love to write. I also enjoy reading, traveling, tennis and pool."

"*You* play pool?"

"Yes, why is that so shocking?"

"Oh, I don't know, you don't find too many women who list playing pool as one of their favorite pastimes. You like sports?"

I wasn't sure how to take these questions. Robert was almost sounding like a sexist.

He's starting to slip, I thought. *I knew it wouldn't be long.*

"Yeah, I love football and basketball," I answered. "Baseball, on the other hand, is a different story."

"That's cool." He bit into an egg roll. "Those two are my favorites, also."

"Really?"

"I'm not pulling your leg," Robert said.

"So what else tickles your fancy besides sports?"

"I enjoy reading, too. I'm usually more partial to nonfiction, like motivational and self-help books."

Interesting. Daniel always thought reading was boring.

"I also like lifting weights," Robert added. "Do you work out, Jasmine?"

"Not routinely, no. Some days I'll wake up to an aerobics workout on TV or I'll do stomach crunches to a CD."

"Exercise is therapeutic. Physically and mentally. Especially if your job is as stressful as mine."

"For the most part, I don't really find my work stressful, although I do have some tense moments. Things get crazy from time to time, but I manage, probably because I'm doing what I love."

"That's good. I really can't say the same. I like my job, but I damn sure don't love it. It pays the bills."

"Monique tells me you're a pharmaceutical rep. What exactly do you do from day to day?"

"I do a lot of traveling, locally and out of town," Robert responded. "Most times I have to drive around to doctor's offices in the city to try to interest them in different medications. Meetings and training seminars take me away quite frequently."

"Sounds interesting." By now, Robert and I had both finished our meals.

"It was in the beginning. Then the challenge of it all fizzled away. I'm not really doing what I want to be doing, Jasmine. This is definitely not my calling."

Red flag. He's not happy and that type happiness I simply can't give him. Hope he doesn't turn out to be another Patrick.

"What is?" I asked, wondering if I'd truly learned to pay more attention to the initial signs or if I was really just searching for something wrong.

"I want to be a doctor. I got into this young, about three years ago, fresh out of college. This was really just supposed to be a stepping stone, but I got trapped and stuck with it longer than I'd planned."

"So, you looking to go to medical school?"

"I'd like to, but at the same time, I'm scared. Sometimes I feel like I'm still trying to find myself. How's that sound? A twenty-nine-year-old man still soul-searching?"

Join the club, I wanted to say.

"Anyway, I don't wanna bore you talking about my problems. Sometimes I can get so worked up."

"That's okay. We all have problems, Robert, and it helps to be able to talk about them to someone."

"You're right. Thanks for the ears."

"Everyting okay over here?" The waiter, who'd pretty much disappeared since he made his delivery, checked on us one final time.

"Yes, everything's perfect," Robert answered, sounding as if he were correcting the server's pronunciation. "I'll take the check."

"Okay, sure," he said, reaching into his apron pocket for the leather receipt holder. "I'll take this when you're ready, sir."

I invited Robert in for a few minutes after he drove me home and somehow a few minutes turned into a few hours. Although we'd both seen the movie *Jason's Lyric* two or three times each, we ended up viewing it again on HBO. *Allen Payne is too fine*, I thought to myself, as I watched the gorgeous black actor make love to his on-screen love interest, actress Jada Pinkett. The scene apparently did something to Robert, who suddenly began nibbling on my ear.

I don't know if I should kiss him or not. But it has been a while since I had a luscious set of chocolate lips pressed against mine.

I usually didn't kiss on the first date but I couldn't resist the temptation.

Robert ran his finger across my cheek. "That was nice," he said, moving his finger to my chin. *Ditto*, I thought, my eyes focused on his smooth lips, which reminded me of a Hershey's kiss. Dark and sweet.

He can kiss! There's nothing more disappointing than a guy who can't.

"You're a great kisser, Jasmine." Robert was sitting next to me on the sofa and continued to plant smooches on my cheeks and forehead.

He thinks I can kiss, too!

"You're not so bad yourself, Robert," I said while letting out a short, sexy laugh and leaning into his arm. This couldn't be happening. It felt too good. But all good things do come to an end.

We shouldn't be kissing like this, anyway. Don't want to give the wrong impression.

I knew I couldn't let things go any further. I wasn't ready to tell Robert my secret and I believed if we kept kissing as passionately as we were, he'd expect one thing to lead to another.

"So, Jasmine, you mean to tell me you don't have a boyfriend?"

"No, I don't."

"Why is that?"

Why are guys always asking this ridiculous question? If I had the answer to that, I probably wouldn't be single.

"I can't answer that, Robert. I just don't." I lowered the volume on the TV and rested the remote next to my thigh.

"Well, what are you planning to do about it?"

Who said I was planning to do anything?

"I'm letting nature take its course," I said, turning toward Robert. "Que será, será. You know?"

"Good answer."

"What about you?" I was almost afraid to bring up the subject. From what I understood, Robert still hadn't gotten over the fact that his ex had messed around on him. For some reason, it always seemed harder for men to forgive infidelity than women.

"Well," he sighed, leaning forward and placing his elbows on his knees. "I've just been dating over the past few months. Nothing serious, though. Not because I don't want a committed relationship. I'm just taking things slow, getting to really know a person before I dive into something."

"That makes sense."

"Yeah. You know you can never be too careful in today's dating world. Take my last relationship, for example. After three years, I thought she was someone I could trust. But when I came home from work one day and found her in our bed with someone else, I learned what the real deal was."

"You two lived together?"

"During our last six months, yeah. We were planning to get married. So we thought it would be good to go ahead and get used to being together twenty-four/seven. Unfortunately, I was the only one who took the engagement seriously."

"I'm sorry to hear that."

"No need to apologize. Her loss is someone else's gain."

"You're right."

"But, like I was saying, it's hard starting over because there's so much negative stuff out here."

"I know," I said, while nodding in agreement.

"I mean, you know, it's not just the trust factor you're dealing with when somebody messes around. You got so many people out here with

STDs like AIDS, herpes and gonorrhea. It's scary."

I tried to part my lips, but couldn't. I couldn't even offer a consenting nod. Instead, I sat there, trying to register what Robert had said.

Guess that means he's STD-free and is looking for someone who can say the same. Wonder what he'd have to say if I told him I was one of those people. Well, I can definitely say that's something he won't be finding out, at least not anytime soon.

Chapter Fourteen

Robert wasn't out of the picture just yet. I decided to continue dating him because I truly enjoyed his company, which seemed to be the perfect panacea at this time in my life. But that was the extent of it. Nothing serious would come out of this, as far as I was concerned. For one thing, I was still leery about opening up to him completely. I also wasn't convinced that he was over his ex, and, quite frankly, expected them to get back together. I mean, look at all the times I reconciled with Daniel.

Any minute now, Robert should be here, I thought. This morning, we'd made plans to go shopping together to pick out my wedding gift for Monique. Her bridal shower was just six hours away. I picked up the pastel yellow invitation to confirm the time and review the directions to the shower once more. It was taking place in Roswell, a suburb north of Atlanta, at the home of Amanda Frye, one of Monique's bridesmaids and part-time employees.

I went to place the invitation inside my purse, just in case I needed to refer to it while I was driving. As I entered my bedroom, the doorbell rang.

He's early, I thought, as I made a U-turn. The fuzzy view through the peephole revealed an unfamiliar female face.

"Who is it?" I asked, still stepping on my tiptoes.

"Terry," she answered, as I finally relaxed on the balls of my feet. I stared at the white door. "Terry? Terry who?"

"Terry Hall," she answered. "Daniel's ex."

I swallowed hard before peeping through again. I could not believe my ears or my eyes.

*What is she doing here? And how does she know where I live? This has to be pretty serious for her to show up at my doorstep. Uninvited and unannounced at that. Oh, Lord, I hope she hasn't come to tell me something devastating, like she has AIDS and Daniel and I might be infected, too. What **could** she want?*

Before unlocking the deadbolt, I touched my chest to feel the fast rhythmic beats of my heart. The door ajar, I greeted Terry, who was standing less than ten feet away.

"Hi," I heard myself say, unable to mask the shock in my voice or on my face.

"Hello, Jasmine. How are you?" she asked, without moving.

I also stood there frozen, not sure what to say or do next. "I'm fine. How are you? Come in," I said, almost as an afterthought.

"I know this is a surprise."

To say the least, I thought, giving Terry a scrutinizing look. *She's actually attractive, far from what I'd visualized from her letters to Daniel.* Terry had a round, brown face, and didn't seem to be much bigger or taller than I am.

"Well, I must say, you're the last person I ever expected to find on my doorstep."

"I'm sorry for just popping up like this. But I really need to talk to you," Terry said, entering the living room.

"That's okay. By the way..."

"Your co-worker, Jennifer, gave me directions," she interrupted, apparently reading my mind.

Jennifer gave her my address without even calling to get permission from me. That's a company no-no, an etiquette no-no. Doesn't she know that?

I was pissed. I couldn't say a word. At that moment, I wanted Terry out of my apartment so I could call the office and give Jennifer a piece of my mind.

I'll deal with that later, I thought. *It's about her, not me,* I reminded myself of Malik's words. *Still, he's going to know about this, too.*

I forced a half-smile and directed Terry to the sofa.

The sooner we get this over with, whatever this is, the better.

"Again, I apologize," Terry said, crossing her legs. "I hope this doesn't create a problem."

"No, it's okay," I lied. "But I am curious to know how you found out where I worked and what it was you said to Jennifer that made her feel free to give you such personal information."

"I guess you could say I put two and two together," she said in a rather bland tone. "One day I was at Daniel's and noticed a copy of your magazine lying around. I thumbed through it and saw your name on a couple of articles. I eventually wrote down the address listed in the front and have kept it stashed away in my purse all this time."

"So Daniel told you about me?" I interrupted.

"Yeah, at that time, he told me you two were friends but had once been in a relationship that just didn't work out."

What a lie! I thought, refraining from interrupting her again.

"To answer your question about Jennifer," Terry continued, "I have to admit, I didn't exactly tell her the truth. I told her we were former college classmates who'd lost touch and I'd been trying for months to track you down."

I guess I can't be completely upset with Jennifer, but I still feel she should've called.

My thoughts drifted as I focused on Terry's shiny jet black hair, styled in a well-maintained French roll, with a thick bang resting on her forehead.

She really is cute, almost Daniel's complexion. Good thing I'm dressed okay and looking decent, thanks to my appointment at the mall to find Monique's present.

"Obviously, this is pretty important, for you to resort to such measures."

"Yeah, I think it is," she said, causing my heart to pound even more.

"Do you care for anything to drink—juice, a Coke," I offered, trying to lighten the mood in the room.

"No, thanks," Terry said, biting down on her bottom lip. "Well, I won't delay this any longer," she began.

This was one of the strangest things I'd ever experienced, a first indeed. I was curious, but at the same time, antsy about hearing what Terry had to say.

"I don't even know where to start, or how to say this. Excuse me if

I sound a little nervous."

"Trust me, you're not alone."

"Jasmine, have you been experiencing any health problems?" she asked.

Talk about to the point.

"Before I answer that, may I ask why you're asking?"

"Because I have. I guess there's no way to avoid being frank about all this. I went to the doctor a couple of weeks ago for a routine exam and got the shock of my life a week later. I have a sexually transmitted disease. Chlamydia."

I felt a knot in my throat.

*Did she just say **chlamydia**. That's something entirely different from what I have.*

"I'm sorry to hear that, Terry." I broke eye contact, turning my attention to the two goldfish inside my aquarium. "I've also been to the doctor. Twice. My diagnosis wasn't anything close to yours. I have two infections: herpes and genital warts."

"Oh, my goodness. I'm sorry. I don't know what to say. Are you okay?"

"Are *you* okay? We're both in the same boat, you know," I said, again looking Terry in the eyes.

Except yours is curable, at least.

"I'm making it, mostly trying to deal with the emotional pain. I have no doubt I got this from Daniel. He's the last person I slept with. Before I met him, I'd never had any problems."

"Neither had I."

"The doctor says there's no way to tell how long I've been infected. All I know is I haven't been with anybody since Daniel."

"May I ask—when was the last time you were together?"

"It's been a little while. Three, four months maybe."

"Three, four months ago, we were in a relationship," I said.

"You know," Terry said, "since I found out about this, I've been fishing for answers, mainly trying to figure out how Daniel was able to get away with seeing us both, without either one of us ever finding out. Like I said, he told me you guys were no longer involved, outside of friendship. But apparently, he was lying. I admit, I had my doubts. I mean, we weren't in a *relationship* but we definitely were a lot more than just buddies. I think it's hard for two people who were once committed to truly just be friends."

"So, when *were* you seeing Daniel? He practically lived over here in my apartment."

"Well I should've known something wasn't right, because of the time of day I did get to see him." She uncrossed her legs and folded her arms. "It was usually real late at night. Like around midnight. He would always say he was on his way to the club or something, but decided he'd rather be with me instead."

"I guess those were the nights when Daniel was working late and I'd already be sleep by the time he got home," I explained, more for my sake than hers.

"But there were a couple of times when Daniel and I actually were together in public places. Like at the movies or the mall. Sometimes even on the weekends."

"Those were probably the weekends when I was out of town visiting my parents or my best friend in Birmingham," I said, recalling instances of Daniel's odd behavior when I'd return.

I listened even more intently as Terry went on to talk about the first time she met Daniel and their first date.

"I wasn't attracted to him physically," she said. "But he was so charming. When things didn't work out with the guy I was seeing, we started dating. I remember our first date just like it was yesterday. Daniel showed up at my door with a white rose behind his back. He always said white roses were his favorite. But I probably don't have to tell you that."

White roses, huh? Just like the ones from our anniversary night I bet.

The more I listened to Terry talk, the more I realized how familiar her voice sounded. It was almost as if I'd heard it somewhere before.

"Terry, I'm sorry for interrupting, but I have to ask you something. Have you ever called Daniel's, and a female voice answered?"

"Yes, I sure did. But it only happened once, and it really caught me off guard."

"Guess what? That was me."

"No! I asked Daniel who it was, since you know, his rule was no woman could ever answer his phone unless he was married to them.

He told me you were one of his friends' girlfriends."

"Did he really? I remember exactly what month that happened. Daniel and I had been together for almost a year at that point."

"Well, I had no idea. Daniel told me he was seeing only me. We were pretty hot and heavy during that time. But I'll be honest, I never felt like I had him all to myself. I just made myself believe I did."

"I guess in some ways we were thinking the same things."

"What do you mean?"

"Well, one day I stumbled across two of your letters to Daniel, even asked him about one. But I didn't leave him. I wanted to believe if he was doing anything, he'd stop and concentrate on me, on us."

"Did you ever catch him stepping out, though?" Terry asked, almost defensively.

"No."

"Then I can see why you bought his story," she said, carefully scratching the back of her head.

"When you two were a couple, did *you* ever catch him in the act?" I returned the question.

"No, not exactly. One night I made plans to sleep over," she started explaining. "I called before leaving, and Daniel sounded distant on the other end. I jumped in my car and drove over to his apartment. He came out to the living room in nothing but his boxers, then I saw a shadow creep up behind him. It was this girl named Wanda." She sounded almost as if she were asking a question. "Yeah, I think that's what her name was."

"You gotta be kidding."

"No, why do you say that?"

"Unless he knows a dozen Wandas, that's more than likely the same chick who popped up one night we were together. Do you remember what she looked like?"

After Terry finished describing Wanda to a tee, I had no doubt we were talking about the same woman.

"That's her. I'll never forget that look in her eyes. She looked and sounded like they were some sort of item and she wanted to know where *I* fit in."

"Well, with me things got kinda ugly," she said. "While she stood half-naked in her nightie, I walked over and introduced myself. Daniel stayed there in the same spot, frozen, as I worked to get as good of a look at her as I could. I asked her who the hell she was and told her I was Daniel's girlfriend. This bitch had the nerve to say, 'must not be too much of a girlfriend.'"

"What! Sounds like something she said the night she popped up on us. She asked Daniel *which* girlfriend I was."

"And I'm sure he had that same dumb ass look on his face," Terry said, slightly raising her voice. "With me, he let her go as far as asking, 'So does he go down on you, too?' I didn't feel like actin' a fool, so I left. And Daniel didn't stop me. He didn't make any moves to put her out either."

"Is that when you two broke up?"

"Things started changing, and finally the relationship did end. But I was a fool and kept the intimacy with him going."

Which explains how we'd both been sleeping with the same man for months. Maybe even all three of us. There was no telling how many more there were.

"What is it?" I asked. "We both seem to be fairly intelligent women. We aren't ugly," I said, causing us both to laugh. "Were we both obsessed fools? Or did Daniel just know how to run the games?"

"I'd say both," Terry responded. "Like I said, there were small signs. For both of us actually." I nodded in agreement. "I think in my case," she said, "I *wanted* to believe Daniel, but I also wanted to see what I wanted to see. I'm not defending him, 'cause he definitely was wrong. But I can't point the finger his way completely."

"How is it you can think so reasonably at this time, when I feel like a total wreck."

"Girl, don't think it's easy. I'm hurting, too. And I'm worried. I don't know what I'm gonna do when someone else comes along. How do I tell them without running them away? What about having children? All of this bothers me, but what good is blaming going to do?"

Before Terry left, we exchanged numbers and vowed to keep in touch. But I wasn't so sure I'd hold up my end of the bargain. I actually feared getting close to her, knowing how vindictive women can be. For all I knew, despite what she said, she may not have honestly cut all ties with Daniel. Besides, I'd gained quite a bit from this one encounter. Our discussion validated the fact that I'd made the right choice by finally letting things go with Daniel. Her apparent strength was encouraging, just the motivation I needed right now to help me pick up the pieces and start over.

I was reaching for the cordless to call Robert when the phone rang. *What is it now? More bad news?*

"Yes!" I answered, snatching the receiver off its base.

"Hey sweetheart, what's wrong?"

"Oh, hi Robert. It's nothing. I've been trying to get ready, but have had a few disruptions."

"You need some more time?"

"Well, to be honest, I'm not sure if I want to go now."

"What are you gonna do about Monique's gift?"

"I'll probably just wait until closer to her wedding day to get something."

"Are you sure there's nothing wrong, Jazz?"

"Yes, I'm fine. I'll call you a little later, okay?"

"Promise?"

"I promise."

I couldn't move. I was frozen in my tracks, the phone still in my hand. I couldn't believe what had just happened. Couldn't believe the conversation that had just taken place minutes earlier. Probably the most shocking part of it all was when Terry revealed what she had contracted from Daniel. It was like he was a walking time bomb or something. He already had three sexually transmitted diseases we knew of. Two of which were non-curable. Could it get any worse? I had to get out of there. Although I'd told Robert I'd changed my mind about shopping, I had to get some air or else I'd go crazy. I decided to go ahead to the mall.

They say shopping is good for pulling yourself up out of the dumps. Besides, I refused to let Daniel, and our past, continue to get the best of me.

On the way to the mall, I decided to stop at a detail shop up the street from my apartment. It was right near the ramp to 285, which I got on to head out to Marietta. I had the Integra vacuumed and washed, even got the tires and rims scrubbed and buffed. Unfortunately, the clean car didn't do much to improve my mood. One of my favorite songs, Chante Moore's "Old School Lovin'," played on the radio, and I hardly even noticed. I did pay a little more attention to the song that followed. It was one I hadn't heard before. Sounded like my girl Karyn. Superwoman Karyn White. Whoever it was, it sounded good. Easy lyrics to catch on to.

"Can I stay with you baby, for the rest of the night? Can I stay with you baby, for the rest of my life?" As off-key as I sounded, I forced myself to get caught up in the words, so I wouldn't have to think about Terry, or Daniel.

"You mother—!" I slammed on the brake, and pressed on the horn and the button to roll down the window, simultaneously. "I know you saw my signal! I've sat here almost five minutes waiting for this space!" I yelled, as I sped away from the spot stolen by an obviously discourteous driver. Luckily, there was an even better space waiting for me up closer to the mall. I couldn't believe I'd actually gotten that upset about that one.

That white man could've pulled out a gun and blown my head off.

After all, he did have a license plate with the Georgia state, better known as the Confederate, flag and the words "Welcome to the South. Now go home!" hanging on the front of his truck.

Home, I'd thought. *What the hell does he mean by* **home?**

With a bold symbol like that, I wouldn't be surprised to find a rifle hanging in his back window. But none of that crossed my mind before I opened my mouth. I guess my thoughts just turned into anger, part of which was vented at Daniel, who was nowhere around.

Once inside Cumberland Mall, I was able to calm down, temporarily. Thanks to the carolers, who were circling the 20-foot tall Christmas tree and all the other beautiful decorations. I loved Christmastime. The spirit of the season. The holiday carols. The ornaments and the trimmings. It usually put me in a rather festive, joyous mood. At that moment, I felt like greeting everyone I saw with a smile and a wish for a "Meeee-ry Christmas." The way Jolly Ol' Saint Nick bellowed it out.

It took me no time to round up all the gifts on my list for Monique. In an effort to get away from the standard wedding presents—towels, sheets, dishes, et cetera—I decided to be creative. Mine wound up being a combination of things: a wedding album, frames, candles, some smell-good lotion and bath gel from Bath & Body Works, and some sexy underwear from Victoria's Secret. All to dress up with decorative tissue paper, inside the wicker basket I'd bought a week ago. There had to be something in the bunch that she'd be able to use.

After taking care of the business at hand, I decided to make stops at my three favorite stores. The first one I reached was Gap. All I could find in there was a sweatshirt with a hood. I'd always loved sweats, particularly hooded ones. A few stores up was Casual Corner.

"Hello there. Is there anything I can help you find today?"

Why are salespeople always so happy? Is their commission that high? Or is this one just reveling the holiday season like me?

"No, actually I'm just looking right now," I answered, my eyes focused on the navy suit display above the store clerk's head.

"Okay, Hon'. Well, if you need anything, just let me know. My name's Nell, and I'll be happy to serve you."

Hon'? What makes Nell think she has the right to call me that? I don't know her and she doesn't know me. Plus I find the southern "term of endearment" condescending in some ways.

I wanted to say something, but I realized this lady had to be at least sixty years old. Even though it bothered me that she called me that, I gave her the same amount of respect as I would all my elders. Besides, I didn't need anything else to upset me. I was here to have fun, to treat myself to a good time.

In half an hour, I tried on three business suits and a baggy-legged pair of black pants. I thought they'd go good with this solid black jacket I had at home. But even though black worked well with everything, it was one of the hardest colors to try to match to itself. Still, I decided to go ahead and take the pants.

Even if they don't match the jacket, chances are I'll be able to find something in my closet to dress them up with.

I also picked a red suit. Red was not only my favorite color, but when I wore it I felt in control. And right about now, I needed all the help I could get to make me feel powerful and good about myself.

"Is this gonna be all for you, Hon'?"

I could not believe it. This time, it wasn't Grandma Nell calling me the annoying epithet. But *Frances*. Someone half her age, and no more than a handful of years older than me.

"Yes, Hon'!" I sharply responded. "That will be all."

Her slight smile faded. "Okay, well your total is eighty-nine dollars and forty-seven cents."

I was ecstatic to know I'd caught this two-piece suit on sale, and had gotten it, along with a pair of pants and pantyhose, for under a hundred bucks. But you couldn't tell it by looking at my face, which was still wearing a frown. One first brought on by Terry's visit and news of Jennifer's role in that, then the man in the parking lot, and now revived by these two clerks. After Frances ran my check through the register, I snatched the receipt and merchandise and stormed out of the store.

Why did that word bother me so much, when, for all I knew, both of those women likely used that term with all female customers. My moods had been changing faster than the weather here lately. This back-and-forth stuff certainly wasn't like me. But these days, it was indicative of how I was feeling.

I was one of the first to arrive at Amanda's. She, along with the three other bridesmaids and the maid of honor, was responsible for giving Monique's shower. They'd spent a couple of hours in the kitchen preparing Swedish meatballs, finger sandwiches, veggie, cheese and fruit trays and punch. Amanda's living room was decorated with emerald green balloons—one of the colors in Monique's wedding—and a beautiful array of fresh flowers. Before long, the sound of the doorbell was as frequent as that of the wind chimes dancing on the front porch.

"Hey girl!"

"How have you been?"

"It's so good to see you."

"Everyone, this is..." Amanda would say whenever a stranger walked into the room. Then, each woman, forming a circle, would introduce herself to the lucky one. Some were Monique's former high school classmates, which none of us had ever met.

At the start, Monique's bridal shower seemed like more of a mini family reunion. Old friends reunited, while others made new acquaintances. Meanwhile, I felt out of place. I didn't know anyone but Monique and had only chatted with Amanda a couple of times at the store. But Monique did her best to make me feel right at home.

"Okay, Jazz, it's your turn to pin the lips on the hunk," Monique shouted across the room, all the while pointing at a poster of a handsome dark-skinned brotha that hung above the mantel.

I sighed, then stood for Amanda to blindfold me with the paper mask. Everyone cheered, chants like "Go Jazz. You can do it girl!" as Amanda placed a sticker, shaped like a pair of red lips, on the end of my index finger, then spun me around three times. I nearly stumbled as I walked toward the fireplace. I reached toward the model with the lips and pressed them wherever my fingers rested. I missed his lips, but came pretty close, placing them on his mustache, which was a much better range than one of the other players, whose lips landed on Mr. Chocolate's crotch.

The amusement boosted my spirits a little bit, enough to keep me cheerful while I was still in the presence of all those women. By the time I made it home, however, I was back to square one. Exactly where I was before I headed out to the mall. I decided to take a bath and get ready for bed.

As the hot water filled the tub, I poured bubble bath and bath salts under the rushing flow. Before stepping in, I took the peach-scented candle down from the rack hanging over the toilet and lit it, putting on that new Karyn White CD I'd picked up at the mall. As I reached for the light switch, I caught a glimpse of my naked body in the full-length mirror on the back of the door. I could feel the wetness on my cheeks. I wiped away some of the tears, then ran my hands across my shoulders. My breasts. My stomach. My waist. My hips. I wrapped my arms around myself, now drowned in tears. *Look at me. A beautiful body. A precious body. One already afflicted with a pair of permanent problems and haunted by another: the threat of AIDS.*

You've put off an AIDS test long enough, don't you think? I asked myself aloud.

Stretched out in the warm water, I ruminated what could be the worst case scenario. Being diagnosed with a death sentence: HIV. Human immunodeficiency virus. And after about a five- to ten-year battle with frequent doctors' visits, all sorts of medication, night sweats and constant fatigue, I'd test positive for full-blown acquired immunodeficiency syndrome. AIDS.

The stories showed that women like me, ages fifteen to forty-four, were at risk. And the countless testimonies proved that it didn't matter how smart, attractive, spiritual or monogamous you were, when it came to getting AIDS, or any other sexually transmitted disease. All that did count was whether or not you used protection and how many partners you'd had. The greater the number, the greater the risk. But you know, I had to admit, sometimes I just didn't buy that. In some ways I didn't think it mattered how many people you'd been intimate with. Meaning, you could be with fifty different lovers and get infected, or you could wind up in the same situation after just one. That was so distressing. One out of three landed me in trouble.

The note hanging toward the middle of the freezer door was the first thing I saw when I woke up the next morning and went to grab a bottle of Welch's grape juice out of the fridge. A magnet containing the number for Pizza Hut delivery held it up. It was next to the note reminding me to buy a gallon of milk. The milk could wait. But this memo, with the words *Call Dr. Smith*, in black ink, was one I could not ignore. I snatched it down, crumpled it up, and tossed it toward the wastebasket. I missed.

I'll pick it up later, I thought. *Right now, I better just get this out of the way.*

By the second ring, I could already feel the butterflies in my stomach.

Come on, somebody answer the phone please, before I chicken out.

"Thank you for calling," a female voice said. "The office will open in ten minutes. You may leave a message or call back then."

I hadn't even checked to see what time it was before calling. Ten before the hour. Dr. Smith and her assistants got started at nine on the dot, but not a second before then. I left a message with the answering service and decided to go back to bed. Sitting around waiting for the phone to ring would only make me more nervous. If I were feeling this way now, I couldn't imagine how I'd be feeling the day I actually went to get the test done. Or how torturous my days and nights would be while waiting for the results. Hopefully not a repeat of the way things were last month.

A half-hour later, the phone rang. I finally picked up the third time.

"Ms. Brown, this is Dr. Cynthia Smith. I'm returning your call."

"Hi, Dr. Smith, thank you for getting back with me. I was calling to make an appointment."

"Well, it can't be for your yearly. Your file shows you just had a Pap smear back in July. Are you having any problems? Are you *expecting?*"

The question hit me like a bolt of lightning.

Could I be pregnant? I hadn't thought about the possibility before now. I looked at the calendar hanging near my bed. My period was late by about four or five days. It usually came on at the middle of the month, around the 15th or 16th. Thanks to the recent turn of events, I hadn't even realized it was late. This couldn't be. I couldn't afford to be pregnant. For reasons other than financial. *What would that mean for the baby? I could end up infecting the innocent child.*

Even if all went well with the delivery, I couldn't see myself having Daniel's baby, not with things the way they were between us. On the other hand, I knew I couldn't go through that horrible experience again.

"Jasmine, dear, you think you might be pregnant?" The doctor asked again.

"I'm not sure," I hesitatingly answered. "How likely is it when I haven't had sex in two months and my period came on in November? I'm four or five days late."

"Have you been under any stress lately?"

"Yes."

"Then you may not be pregnant, after all. Stress can throw your cycle off schedule. Let's not jump to any conclusions. Let's just get you in here for an exam."

"I also need to come in for something else, Dr. Smith. I'd like to have an AIDS test done."

"Okay, we can arrange for both pregnancy and AIDS tests. You sound a little nervous. Is there some reason for you to be worried?"

"Well, I was about to get to that part. Last month I went to Temple's QuikCare Center. They did some testing there, and—I was wondering if you could call them and request a copy of the results."

"I understand. You don't have to say anything more, Jasmine. I'll get on that as soon as we're done talking. If you'd like, we can set you up for a counseling session to discuss those before we do the test for HIV where you can talk about whatever you'd like and I can answer any questions you might have. Is that something you'd be interested in?"

"Sure."

"Okay, well I'll make someone at the front desk aware of that. I'm going to transfer you up there to one of the receptionists, so you can get everything squared away. Nice talking to you. Like I said, I'll call Temple right now. You and I will talk more in-depth when you get here. You take care of yourself."

"Thank you."

It was over. At least that part. Now I'd just have to make it through the next day. I didn't expect to get an appointment *that* early, especially with it being the holiday season. I figured everyone would be trying to get in to see Dr. Smith, now that they had time off from work and school. But someone had already called in and cancelled. I guess it was better that way. The longer I'd have to wait to get in, the more I'd agonize. At least now, I was one-third of the way there.

Chapter Fifteen

"Jasmine, come on in and have a seat." Dr. Smith ordered as I followed her into the small office. "How are you doing today?"

"I'm okay. How are you?"

"Just fine, thank you."

This was only the second time I'd been inside the gynecologist's cubbyhole. The first being the day of my new patient consultation. Five years later, Dr. Cynthia Smith had not changed at all. She was still the very gracious, very compassionate physician I'd grown to love back then. To this day, getting a Pap smear was an act I didn't feel comfortable going through. But Dr. Smith had a way of making all the peering and prodding endurable.

Just as she settled into her seat, reality hit me about as powerfully as a tornado in mid-July, reminding me of the threefold reason why I was sitting there in the first place. Not only could I be pregnant, but my recent conversation with Terry came as a caveat of the need to have another culture taken, to check for the possibility of more infections. The scariest and most serious reason: to have an *AIDS* test. My first one. Something I hadn't even had to worry about before in my life. I noticed a manila folder on Dr. Smith's desk. I wondered whether it was my file. If so, had she looked over it? Even worse, what did she think of me now? I didn't think I had to worry about that. After all, she hadn't given me any reason before now to feel she was looking down on me. Besides, she was a sistuh, too, one old enough to be my mother.

"Jasmine, I've looked over your test results from Temple." She picked up the folder I'd been eyeballing and opened it. "First, I need to know if you have any questions or concerns."

"The only thing I'm really concerned about now is having children. I've run across some pretty bleak facts and statistics about giving birth, Dr. Smith. Tell me, are they all true?"

"I don't know what you've read, Jasmine. But I imagine what you're talking about are the chances of the baby being at risk?" She wore a serious look on her face.

"That, and if I'll even be able to have children. What are the chances I could actually be pregnant now, with the virus in my body?" My eyes briefly focused on Dr. Smith's medical degrees and certificates hammered on the wall behind her.

"First of all, let me address any worries you may have. Number one, you *can* get pregnant, and you can have a healthy baby, but I'm sure you've read somewhere, there are potential dangers to a baby when the mother has herpes. That's because, after the sores crust over and heal, the virus lies dormant in a nerve root in the base of your spine. It's usually triggered by things like menstruation, stress, illness, and pregnancy. If you have an outbreak of herpes during delivery, the disease can be passed on to your newborn. That could mean anything from brain or eye damage to death. The only way to avoid that is through a caesarean section. But that type delivery usually isn't necessary when there's a flare-up of genital warts. With those, a C-section is required *only* if the warts are blocking the birth canal. The key thing with both is that you notify your doctor if you notice any signs of an outbreak while you're pregnant. Speaking of which, *are* you pregnant? Over the phone, you mentioned your cycle's late by at least four days?"

"Right. I don't know if I am or not, but I've never been this late before, Dr. Smith," I said, catching a glimpse of a vanilla-colored clay figurine on the stand parallel to the doctor's desk. For a moment, the image of a mother holding her newborn in her arms reminded me of the abortion.

"Well, that's not too irregular. As I said yesterday, it all could just be stress-related, but we'll give you a test to make sure." She scribbled something on a white chart. "If you are pregnant, don't panic. We'll keep a close watch on you and the baby. By the way, have you heard about the medication on the market that helps reduce the number of herpes outbreaks?"

"No, I haven't. I haven't read anything like that in any of the pamphlets I have, and no one at Temple told me about it. In fact, they weren't very helpful at all. They were actually rude."

"A lot of people don't quite know how to tackle this issue sensitively. Unfortunately, some people develop stereotypes. But we all know pigeonholing usually brings about the same results as assuming."

"Right. I truly felt uncomfortable the day I visited their hospital. It was like the people there were saying to themselves somehow I deserved this. Like I'm some slut or something. And I'm not." I hadn't had any intentions of turning into a whimpering baby in this woman's office.

"I know. How long have I been your doctor? You don't have to explain yourself to me, dear. Here, clean yourself up."

I pulled a couple of sheets of Kleenex out of the red-and-white-colored tissueholder Dr. Smith held in her hand. On each side were the Greek letters for Delta Sigma Theta, the sorority she'd pledged in college.

"You're going to be okay. This over-the-counter medicine should help. I have patients who take it every day, and they haven't had an outbreak in years. It's called L-Lysine. You can find it at stores like Wal-Mart, Kmart, Eckerd Drugs or anywhere that vitamins are sold. Again, it's L-Lysine," she reiterated, while removing a pen from the right pocket of her sunflower-designed smock. She then began scribbling on a Post-It. "I'll write the name of it down for you, so you won't forget."

"Trust me. I won't have any trouble remembering something that's going to help me fight this."

"Well, just in case, I'll put the note inside this information packet I've prepared for you. It has some brochures on STDs." She handed me a gray 8 1/2" by 11" envelope, with about a dozen pamphlets inside. "I'm sure you've read something similar to most of what you'll find here, but I wanna make sure you're well informed when it comes to your health. You have to take care of yourself. If you do that, you may not have to worry about any more outbreaks. Right now, do you have any other questions or concerns?"

"Just one more. How strong are my chances for getting cancer?"

"Well, any time you contract an STD, you stand a greater risk of developing cervical cancer. That's why getting your Pap smear, at least once a year, is important. It's your best safeguard. Any atypical cells will show up. You'll also find information on that in your pamphlets."

"Okay. Dr. Smith, I really appreciate this."

"Jazz, it's no problem. It's my job. If we doctors can't help our patients, then what are we here for?" She placed the pair of wire-rimmed reading glasses, which were draping her neck, on her nose. "So, are we ready?"

"I suppose," I responded with a smidgen of anxiety in my voice.

"Okay, well, what I plan to do after we get a urine sample and draw your blood, is examine you and make sure everything's cleared up. I see here where you were given prescriptions for Zovirax to treat the lesions and Condylox for the warts. Has the medication helped?"

"It has. I haven't noticed any more warts or blisters."

"Good. But I want to be certain. There could still be some hidden inside your vagina. Sometimes traces of the virus can be present on the skin and you won't even know it. It's called 'asymptomatic shedding.'"

I nodded and raised my eyebrows.

"Well, if you'll follow me. Lisa's going to take your blood and urine sample. Once she's done, you can come back to exam room three. And we'll wrap this visit up."

I made a fist as tight as I could. One I wanted to use to knock the nurse out after she stuck that needle in my arm. Twice. She said she was having trouble finding a good vein, because *they're all so tiny*. What she didn't know was, I was the wrong person for her to be poking more than once. I hated needles. No way you'd get one in my arm unless it was absolutely necessary. Not even for a blood drive. My conscience would eat me up so bad, but I just couldn't do it. I never met the 110-pound weight requirement, anyway.

I used three of my left fingers to press on the cotton ball, which covered my right arm. Applying pressure to the sore spot and tightening the muscles in my thighs and legs helped reduce the pain between them. Dr. Smith probed my vaginal area for about three minutes with the cold, metal speculum. It was a brief moment of torturous déjà vu.

But at least this time, the end result was better. The doctor said she didn't see a trace of any remaining symptoms or new developments. Even better news—the pregnancy test was negative. Before leaving, I breathed a short sigh of relief that it was all over. Until I realized, this ending only marked the beginning of something new. The waiting game I'd now have to play.

Chapter Sixteen

"Jazz, are you there? Pick up. Jazz, pick up the phone! I've left you five messages already! What's going on? Give me a call as soon as you get *this* one."

Out of the three messages left on my answering machine while I was away at the grocery store, Daniel's was the last one I wanted to hear. It was also the last voice I wanted to play back with Dave in the room.

"Why does he keep calling you?" Dave asked. "Seems like he would've gotten the hint by now."

"I have no idea. I haven't talked to Daniel since Thanksgiving. I'm just as surprised as you."

The two of us relieved our arms, placing the plastic Cub Foods bags on the kitchen countertop. We'd just returned from our biweekly grocery shopping excursion; at least that was what Dave considered it. An avid cook, he got a kick out of walking up and down the aisles, in search of ingredients for the week's trial, and, in some cases, error meals. I, on the other hand, hated making the trip alone. Dave's remarkable good nature made the difference between whether I'd be eating home-cooked or fast food.

"I told you this would happen, didn't I?" He asked, giving me a look to match what he was saying. "I knew he'd be coming back. Like I've said before, when the woman's worth it, we don't give up without a fight."

"But why is the timing always off? Y'all usually don't open your eyes until it's too late."

"That's not it at all. Some guys know all along. They just don't wanna admit it, not even to themselves."

"And that's why they end up losing out."

"A lot of times, yeah," Dave said, helping remove the groceries from the bags.

"Are you planning to call him back?"

"I'm not sure. I have to admit he has me a little worried. He sounded like something was wrong."

"Something is wrong. He fucked up and now he wants everything back the way it was. After all he's done, Jazz, why should you even care what's up with him? You still love him, don't you?"

I wasn't at all prepared for that question, although I knew one day I'd find myself trying to answer it for my own satisfaction. I opened the door to the food pantry and began to stock the shelves with whole kernel corn, French-style green beans and other canned goods.

"I'm not *in love* with Daniel. But I guess to a certain degree I'll always have some type of feelings for him. I think that's only natural, Dave." I paused and looked at him, hoping he'd agree.

"I'm sorry I'm being so hard on you. We've all been there. There's no right or wrong to love. What works for one person may not work for another." He walked up alongside me and held his long arms out. "I just want you to be happy, Jazz," he said while hugging me. "I don't wanna see you get hurt again."

"I know you don't. I don't wanna see me hurt again, either." We released the embrace.

Sticking to our plans following this morning's nine o'clock church services, Dave and I began preparing Sunday dinner together. We figured it would give us a chance to catch up on each other's lives. I grabbed the manual can opener from the drawer closest to the kitchen sink and began to remove the top from a can of Campbell's Cream of Mushroom soup. But my mind was far from on domestic affairs. Instead, I couldn't help but wonder what Daniel so urgently needed to speak to me about. At that moment, I made up my mind to put an end to all the guessing, by finally returning his calls. After all, like Dave said, there's no perfect formula.

As the chicken breast-and-rice dish baked in the oven, I filled Dave in on the Robert situation, among other things.

"I have no plans to stop seeing him, Dave," I said, pressing the power button on the TV remote. "But I am being cautious. My gut feeling tells me things aren't exactly over between him and his ex. Plus, the closer we got, I'd feel an obligation to tell him about you-know-what, especially if we decided to become intimate." The television was on the NBC channel, which is where I left it.

"Follow your heart. I've always told you that," he said, gripping one of the cream throw pillows from my sofa. "Look, Jazz, I've listened to you over the past few years, talking about your struggles with Daniel, before him, Patrick, and men in general. As a friend, I want you to know, you're beautiful, loving and intelligent, and one day, someone who truly deserves you will come into your life. Don't ever feel you have to short-change yourself."

"That applies to both of us, actually," I said.

"Right. You're right," Dave said, sounding as if he had to let the thought sink in. "But like you, Jazz, I've had doubts that I'd ever be able to find someone who appreciates me. Some of my most recent dating experiences have more than convinced me that finding a good woman is equally as difficult as finding a good man."

"Really?" I fluffed the pillow behind my back.

"Yes, really. Case in point: About two weeks ago, I went out on my third date with this female I'd met in the grocery store one day...."

"But of course," I interrupted and laughed.

"Watch it, now." Dave brushed his fist up against my left thigh. "Anyway, as I was saying, I was on date three with her, right?" he asked, holding up three fingers. "And it was looking pretty good. Kim—that's her name—is a good-looking, smart and sweet girl. But that was the extent of it. That particular night I decided to try to engage in a deep conversation with her, you know, try to see where her head was." He nodded. "Jazz, she couldn't even tell me what her goals in life were, not even five years from now." He leaned back into the sofa, stretching his five-eleven, near-two-hundred-pound frame. "I mean, I was expecting her to at least have something to say, something about professional, spiritual or financial goals."

"What *did* she say?"

"She said something like, 'I'm just going with the flow.' Can you believe that?" he asked, gesturing.

"Well, is she young?"

"She's twenty-five, your age. Maybe that's my fault. I just see how together you are, Jazz, and I'll be honest, I look for many of your qualities in the people I go out with."

"I'm flattered, Dave. I now find myself measuring guys up against you, too, something I should've been doing all along. I mean, look at you, you can cook."

We both laughed.

"No, but more seriously," I continued. "You are in a class by yourself. I don't know any other guy who does the things you do for others. Like the way you devote time to listening to my sorrows and offering a shoulder to cry on. Or the way you are with Xavier. How much time is it you spend with him each month?"

"I see him every weekend."

"You're well-involved in his life," I said.

"Yeah, he has kinda grown on me." Dave turned up the left side of his lip a little bit.

"That's an understatement, don't you think? I believe if you could, you'd adopt that little boy."

"You're probably right. 'Cause he sure as hell doesn't need to be with his damn mama. She spends too much of her time trying to figure out how she can get with *me*."

"What?" I got up and went to check on the food.

"Yeah," Dave yelled into the kitchen. "Her no-good behind throws herself at me every time I pick Xavier up or whenever I go over to tutor him. It's gotten so bad, I hate going to their place. And speaking of that, she never really keeps it clean."

I returned to the living room and plopped back down in the same spot.

"It just pisses me off, Jazz," Dave said, leaning forward, his eyes focused on the TV screen ahead. I could tell how much the subject bothered him by his foul language. Like me, Dave didn't believe in using too many curse words.

"I never told you this before, but I grew up in the projects, which is why I relate so well to Xavier and wanna do so much for him."

I raised my eyebrows and nodded.

"Jazz, I don't remember a day our home ever looked like theirs. My mom was a single parent, working two, sometimes three jobs, but she still managed to take good care of me. Luckily, I was the only child. I wouldn't have wanted her to have the burden of caring for more than that."

"So, I imagine that has a lot to do with the reason why Mrs. Williams today heads the AHA?" I asked of Dave's mother, who'd since remarried, and had recently taken on the role of executive director of the Atlanta Housing Authority.

"Oh, yeah. We lived in Perry Homes for about a year-and-a-half after my dad decided he'd be happier elsewhere. Mom believes if that was long enough for a divorced mother to get her act together, it's long enough for anybody. She realizes comparing a single mother of five to a single mother of one is like comparing apples and oranges. But her philosophy is, no matter how hard you fall, you can always get back up. Public housing to her is a temporary solution and that's how she wants everyone who has to spend some time there to see it."

"That's definitely a good way to look at it, especially when you have some people staying there for as long as fifteen and twenty years."

"See, that makes no sense. That's why Mama's trying to turn public housing around. She doesn't even want it to be called that anymore. She would like to see it develop into a mixed-income community, where public housing recipients and non-recipients alike can live. Five years from now, you won't be able to look at Perry Homes and know that it was once "the projects." It, along with all the other AHA units, will look no different from any other apartment complex."

"That's great and it sounds like a good story for the magazine."

"You're right. I hadn't even thought about that." Excitement reflected in Dave's voice.

"I'd love to talk to your mom; after all, we're talking about revolutionary changes here."

"She'd be more than happy to talk to you, too. I'll run the idea by her the minute I leave here. I was planning to drop by to see her today, anyway."

This time, Dave walked into the kitchen to check on dinner. "Looks like it's about ready," he said, using a sunflower pot holder to slide out the middle rack. "Sure smells good." He placed the casserole dish on top of the stove.

"By the way, Jazz, how's Tiffani?" he yelled over the noisy oven fan.

"She's fine. I talked to her Friday and we just went skating about three weeks ago. Wanna see the pictures we took?"

"Sure, after dinner. Right now, let's dig in."

Not long after Dave left, I picked up the cordless phone and began dialing Daniel's number, but only got as far as the prefix. For some reason, I couldn't get my fingers to work. A twinge of anger and fear shot through my body. Anger because I couldn't believe I was actually thinking of going back on my word by calling Daniel. Fear because I was worried the call would only bring more bad news. Maybe I wouldn't have to wait to hear from the doctor. Perhaps Daniel already knew the results of my AIDS test because he'd also been tested. I didn't want to know. I couldn't call him back. But I realized I had to. Sooner or later, I was going to find out what he wanted. My hands trembled as I dialed the number. As usual, it took two rings for Daniel to pick up, long enough for him to screen the number on his caller ID box.

"Yeah!"

"Hello Daniel. So what is it?"

"Jazz? Hey. Why haven't you been returning my calls?"

"You should be able to answer that question yourself. Anyway, now that I have called back, tell me what you want." I sounded as rude as I possibly could.

"So, how you been?"

"Just fine, and yourself?"

"I've been okay. How 'bout your folks?" Daniel asked.

"Daniel, is this why you called? Why don't you just get to the point. My family's fine. How's your mom?"

"About the same. She's still sick with the diabetes and all. It's gotten worse; she now goes to dialysis three times a week. After they get through pokin' her with needles and shit for about three hours each time, she's usually real weak."

"I'm sorry to hear that. I'll definitely be praying for her."

"Thank you. I'd appreciate that."

Here he was again, playing on my emotions. For half a minute, there was nothing but silence, almost as if Daniel were in deep thought. Once out of a trance, he quickly changed the subject.

"So, Jazz, have you thought about me any?"

How cocky can he be? This man breaks my heart, rips it out of my chest and tramples all over it. Then he goes an entire month or two without calling and now he wants to know if he's been in my thoughts the whole time. Remember, no hard feelings.

"Yeah, I suppose you have crossed my mind a time or two."

"Good thoughts, I hope."

I didn't respond.

"Well, I can definitely say you've been on my mind, Jazz. Day and night. I'm not gon' lie. Baby, I miss you. I really do. I've thought about you a lot."

Don't even try it. Your sweet talking is not going to work this time.

"Jazz, did you hear me? I said I miss you, baby."

Now that did it. How dare he call me "baby." He knew that was the one pet name sure to make me weak every time.

"Yes, I heard you, Daniel." A gush of tears saturated my face. But I didn't let Daniel know he was starting to get to me.

"Jazz, you don't have to say anything. You don't have to tell me how you feel; that's if you even have any feelings left. I called because I wanted you to know what my feelings are for you. Hell, I don't even know what's happened in your life since we last talked. For all I know, you could be in love with someone else by now. It don't matter. I still want you to know how I feel about you. Even if you was to tell me you're about to walk down the aisle with another man, I'd still want you to know. I've done a lot of thinking over the past month. And more than anything, I've realized one thing. I love you. More than you'll ever know. More than I've ever loved anyone else. I've been in love before, but never anything like this. Jazz, you're a beautiful person, and you're a damn good woman. I'm no fool. I know that. I know I took you for granted when I had you, but that doesn't mean I haven't realized my mistakes. I just hope it's not too late. But if it is, I'll understand. Like I said, I just wanted you to know."

Dave was right. Now, what do I do?

"Well wasn't that thoughtful of you?" I couldn't believe I'd actually said it. It was almost as if someone else was talking for me. "By the way, you are too late. I have started seeing someone else," I added.

"Oh really?"

"Yes, really."

Amazingly, I was feeling rather strong and doing a good job at keeping my guard up.

"So, does he treat you right?"

"Yes, he does. But why would you care? You don't even have any right to be asking about that."

"You're right. You're right. I had my chance and I blew it."

I wanted to say *you sure did* but decided it wouldn't do any good. I'd already made my point. Besides, I'd never believed in hurting people, even if they had done me wrong. I knew eventually they'd get what they deserved because what goes around comes around.

"Jazz, one more thing before you go."

"What?"

"Are you two serious?"

"Daniel, did you hear anything I just said? What is it you're getting at?"

"Okay, I'll get straight to the point, Jazz. I want you back. I want you, and need you in my life. I know I've hurt you. And I know I've done some fucked-up shit in the past. But I'm a new person now. I've changed for the better, and I'm ready to spend the rest of my days proving it to you. Jazz, you're the one for me. You're it, baby. You're all I need. I know that. I've always known it. But now, more than ever, I know I wanna spend my life with you. I'm not making anything official just yet, baby. But I want you to know I want you to be my wife."

By now, it was impossible to fight off the tears.

"Oh, baby, I wish I had you in my arms right now. I'd wipe away those tears, and kiss you all over that beautiful face of yours. Jazz, I love you. I love you. I love you."

"I love you, too," I said, with a slight break in my voice, not sure exactly where the words had come from.

"You just don't know how good it makes me feel to hear you say that. Baby, you've made my day, my year, my lifetime. Damn, I can't wait to see you again. I'd love to be able to repeat everything I've just said to you, face to face. When I can touch you, and look into your pretty brown eyes. Do you think that'll ever be possible?"

Suddenly I thought of Robert. I realized how that wouldn't be fair to him. How this whole conversation wasn't fair to him.

Then again, we don't have a commitment, I silently reminded myself.

"I don't know, Daniel. I'll have to think about it."

"Jazz, all I'm asking for is a few minutes alone with you. I just wanna see your beautiful face and smile and those pretty brown eyes again."

"When?"

Okay, so I broke down. Big deal. What else was I supposed to do? After all, the man did just pour his heart out to me. It wouldn't hurt anything to meet with him. For all I knew, Robert and his ex were still involved in some fashion, even if only through phone conversations.

"How 'bout tomorrow night after you get home from work and wind down? If you don't feel comfortable with me coming over there, you can come here."

I couldn't let Daniel know about my situation at work. I didn't want him to know about just how many changes he'd actually put me through over the past month and a half.

"That's fine. I'll call you before I leave."

"That won't be necessary. Just come over when you get ready to."

That was something new. Daniel never believed in company just dropping over. Maybe he was turning over a new leaf, I thought. I was just twenty-four hours away from finding out.

If you love something, set it free. If it comes back to you, it's yours. If it doesn't, it never was. Those illustrious words, oftentimes dubbed "the rules of love," had been ringing in my head ever since I hung up the phone with Daniel. They were the first thing that crossed my mind when I rose out of bed this morning. It was hard not to wonder, or even question whether they were applicable to our situation. I couldn't understand what had caused Daniel to have a sudden change of heart. Was he really sincere? Or did he say it all just to get a reaction out of me? To see if he still had his hooks in me? After all, he had said things like that before. He'd even proposed once, and made thousands of promises.

And what about the infections? Plenty of unanswered questions regarding those still lingered. I'd often wondered whether Daniel *de-*

liberately did this. I knew it was possible for a person to have hidden symptoms. But the fact that Daniel was roaming the streets was no secret. At least not to him. He knew what he was doing. Knew who he was screwing. Knew when he was wearing a condom and when he wasn't. But he chose not to tell me. Yet he didn't see anything wrong with having unprotected sex with me either. Maybe tonight's meeting would bring answers to some of those questions. If nothing more, I was hoping for the ultimate apology that could provide some closure to whatever we had. If I planned to close the door on Daniel, I needed to do it once and for all. No turning back. Tonight's visit would give me the push I needed to do just that.

Chapter Seventeen

Forty-five minutes had passed since Daniel called and said he'd be over in an hour (the one change in last night's plan). The minute we finished our conversation, I dropped everything I was doing and scurried to the bathroom. I'd been glued to the same spot ever since I got out of the shower. Staring at myself in the full-length mirror.

Looking good, girl.

Looking good was crucial, since Daniel hadn't seen me in over two months.

He'll be here in ten minutes.

I quickly removed the silk robe I was wearing, and was careful not to brush against my hair, when bringing the navy turtleneck down over my head. Then I pulled on a short corduroy jumper, which showed off my petite shape.

Where are those ribbed navy tights?

I never could find what I needed when I was rushing. There. I slid the tights on, slightly above my waist line, and put on a pair of my favorite pumps. Before leaving the bathroom, I teased the front of my hair with my fingers again, and made sure my bangs were draping over my forehead, just the way I liked them to. It wouldn't hurt to dab on another touch of lipstick, either. Okay, all ready. Except now I could use a nerve pill to help me calm down.

The doorbell rang. I inhaled and exhaled as I gave myself the once-over a final time. Then I grabbed the can of vanilla air freshener from the back of the toilet and sprayed it all over the apartment. Daniel pressed on the button again. This time, relentlessly.

"All right! All right! I hear you!" I yelled as I put the spray back in place and sprinted toward the door.

Here we go.

I stopped in front of the door and exhaled again before finally opening it for Daniel.

"Hey baby," the tenor voice on the other side of the door said.

I already felt weak in the knees. Daniel's footsteps ceased in the foyer, while he gazed at me in a way I'd never noticed before.

"Jazz, you look great. You're beautiful, as always." He smiled.

"Thank you. You look good."

At least five minutes passed, with neither one of us moving an inch. I wanted to ask Daniel to stop ogling me, but decided against it. It was actually kind of cute.

"So, are you going to come in?" I finally asked. "Or are we going to stand here in awe all day?"

"I'm sorry. I'm just so happy to see you, baby. You just don't know how much I've missed you. Can I have a hug?"

I nodded, and wrapped my arms around Daniel's neck, as he pressed my head deep into his chest.

"Ooh, Jazz. You feel good. It feels so natural holding you in my arms." He placed his index finger on my chin, and raised my head. "Could we just go sit, and hold each other like this for a few minutes? We don't have to say a word. I just wanna hold you." I followed Daniel, as he led me to the living room sofa. He rocked me back and forth like a baby, until he finally broke the silence again.

"Jasmine, I want to apologize to you for anything I've done to hurt you. I know I've put you through hell at times. I just wanna say I'm sorry. I never meant to hurt you, and I promise you, I never will again. Look at me, baby. I'll *never* hurt you again. Okay? You forgive me?" He placed a quick kiss on my forehead, and two fingers over my lips. "On second thought, don't answer that just yet. I know it'll take a while before you'll be able to. And even when you do, I know it'll be almost impossible for you to forget."

I hadn't realized how long Daniel had been dominating the conversation until I thought about the many burning questions racing through my head, which couldn't afford to go unanswered any longer.

"Daniel, there's something I have to ask you."

"What is it?" He asked it in the most gentle voice.

"Why did you just disappear the way that you did? What stopped you from picking up the phone? Even if it were just to call to see how I was doing. Where were you when I needed you the most?" I tried to refrain from sounding accusatorial. I worked even harder to keep my eyes from watering.

"I know, I know." Daniel brushed his hand against my face and hair. His all-too-familiar touch gave me goose bumps. "I'm sure you feel like I abandoned you. Like I just hurt you, and walked away with no regrets. That's not true at all. Baby, to be honest, I was scared. The last time we talked, you sounded like I was the last person you wanted to hear from. So I didn't want to be rejected by you twice. More than that, I was ashamed. I know I acted like more of a wimp than a man. But I couldn't get up the nerve to face you after what I'd done. Hearing your voice, or seeing you meant I'd have to face the truth, head-on. And I just wasn't ready for that before."

"Well, what makes you think you're ready now? Exactly what made you change your mind?"

"I *didn't* change my mind about anything. My mind was already made up. It just took me a while to get around to listening to my heart. It's really hard to explain, Jazz. Sometimes, I don't understand it myself. The answer was right in front of my face the whole time. But I couldn't see it, or maybe I just didn't want to. So I fucked things up, and took the chance at losing a jewel like you. And it wasn't even worth it. You're one in a million, baby. And don't you ever forget it."

Eventually I got up enough courage to ask Daniel about Terry. He confessed to everything, and apologized for not telling me about their affair, or her diagnosis.

"Now, I have a question for you, Jazz. Why did you agree to see me tonight?"

Just like a man, always had to feed his ego. He asked to see me. I was kind enough to agree to it. Case closed. He had some nerve asking me why I gave in.

"I guess I wanted to, Daniel. I wanted to hear what you had to say. Most of all, I wanted to hear you say those things in person. I figured that way I'd be able to verify if the feelings are still here."

"So, what did you find out?"

"Feels like they are."

"That's music to my ears. And that's all I need to know."

"How do I know you won't hurt me again?" I abruptly asked.

"I wouldn't, baby. You have my word. I know it'll be hard, but you'll just have to trust me."

"I *can't* trust you, Daniel. I may as well be honest. I just can't." Tears began cascading down my cheeks. I quickly brushed them away with my fingertips. "I lost that a long time ago. And I don't know if I'll ever be able to trust you again. Or what it'll take for you to regain my trust."

"Well, I can say I'm ready and willing to do anything it takes to win it back, Jazz. I want you to trust me. I want you to feel comfortable with me. And I don't want you to have to worry. Let me show you, Jazz. Please, baby. Just give me the chance to love you again. To love you better this time, the way you deserve to be loved. I'm not asking for a commitment right now. I don't wanna rush you. But I would like for you to take some time and think about it. In the meantime, let's work on rekindling our friendship. You know what they say about being friends before lovers."

After about thirty minutes of talking, Daniel convinced me to go with him back to his apartment where I spent the night.

Daniel was sleeping so hard when I woke up the following morning, he didn't even hear me climb out of bed or take a shower. Matter of fact, he didn't hear the alarm that got me out of bed in the first place—his telephone. I let it ring four times before the machine picked up. I even tried to wake Daniel, but the man who could sleep through an earthquake wouldn't budge. As I heard the female voice leaving a message, I turned up the volume on the machine.

"Daniel, it's me," she said. "Where are *you* this time of morning? Give me a call. You know the number."

I got out of bed and walked over to the caller ID box to review the name. It read anonymous call.

Good thing. Otherwise, I would've found myself resorting to something I'd stooped to doing time and time again in the past—calling the number.

I can't go there anymore. I made a promise to myself.

That was the final straw. That and finding two Midnight Desire condom wrappers in the garbage can beside Daniel's bed. I decided it was time for me to go.

I never should've come here anyway. It was stupid of me to believe Daniel had changed. I thought of something I'd heard my mom say before: "Old habits never die." Thank God I didn't sleep with him last night; I really would've felt like a fool.

By the time I'd finished dressing, Daniel finally woke up.

"Jazz, what are you doing up so early? It's not even seven o'clock yet. I thought you were gonna get dressed for work over here and I'd just drop you off at your car."

"Your girlfriend woke me up, Daniel."

"What are you talking about?"

"Play your answering machine and you'll see what I mean."

"I don't have a girlfriend so I don't know what you're talkin' about, Jazz. Come back to bed."

"Daniel, I'm ready to go. Take me home."

"Jazz, I know you're not getting upset over a phone call. Come on now, baby."

"I'm not your baby."

Daniel sat up in bed. "What's wrong with you?"

I picked up the small wicker basket next to his bed.

"Here's what's wrong with me. You wanna tell me what these are doing here?"

Daniel's usual "oh shit!" look appeared on his face.

What clever lie is he going to try to think of this time?

"Jazz, what are you doin' diggin' in my trash?"

"I wasn't digging in your trash. I was putting something in the garbage when I saw these." I looked down into the wastebasket. "It's not like they were buried in here or anything. You had them right up on top," I said, dropping it to the floor.

"What's the problem? So you found some condom wrappers in my garbage. Is that supposed to mean something?"

"It means once again you've lied. Last night you told me you had not been with anyone since our last time. You said you'd been out on a few dates, but nothing serious, definitely not intimate ones. What am I supposed to think when I find something like this?"

"I understand how you're thinking, Jazz. But you're not giving me the benefit of the doubt."

"The benefit of the doubt? Daniel, you have two condom wrappers inside your trash can. They were here before last night. They're in *your* apartment. In *your* bedroom. Who else am I supposed to assume they belong to?"

"They're not mine."

"What?"

"I said they're not mine. Last weekend Miles was here. We went out to a club; he met this girl. Need I say more?" Daniel gave a confident look with the words, "I'm off the hook" written all over it.

"So you're telling me Miles met a girl at some club, brought her here, they had sex in your bed and used the two condoms that were inside these wrappers?"

"That's exactly what I'm saying."

"And I'm saying you're a liar. First of all, Miles is married. Plus, if this happened a week ago, why are these still here. You mean to tell me you haven't taken the trash out in at least a week?"

"I just hadn't gotten around to doing it."

"I can see why. This basket isn't even halfway full, Daniel. If a week has passed since Miles supposedly left these wrappers here, why isn't there more trash than this?" I reached in and grabbed the wrappers and threw them at him. "Why were these still on top?"

"Jazz, I can't believe you. You're going on and on about a trash can. I already told you the deal. Why don't you just squash it?"

He jumped out of bed, picked his pair of Joe Boxers up off the floor and put them on.

"Naw, see this is the same type shit we went through before. All this arguing and accusing bullshit. If this is what it's gon' be like if we get back together, I'm not interested. We can just be friends before I go through all that again. Now I've told you you don't have anything to be worried about. I wish you'd just take my word."

Take his word? That's what's gotten me in trouble enough times already. Taking Daniel's words over his actions.

I refused to play the victim again, in other words, overlook the obvious. I'd done it too many times before all because I had this unrelenting, and now I realized, unrealistic belief that people change. But, once again, experience taught me what Mama had advised me a time or two: *People only change if they want to.*

Chapter Eighteen

I'd get so nervous every time the phone would ring, I'd practically jump out of my seat. In no time, I was back to where I was before my heart-to-heart with Daniel. Dodging him. I just couldn't afford any more confusion in my life right now. I definitely couldn't stand to hear any more bad news. Not any coming from Daniel and especially not any from a doctor.

"Hi, Jasmine. This is..."

The minute I heard Robert's voice coming across my answering machine, I leaped out of the dining room chair, where I'd spent the last hour sorting through my bills, wondering which ones were going to get paid this time around and which ones would have to wait, perhaps even until I returned to work. I reached for the phone, knocking its base onto the floor.

"Hello," I answered, panting. "Robert, hang on! Let me turn off the machine."

I laid the receiver on the coffee table before rushing into my bedroom to press the stop button.

"Okay, I'm back." I took a deep breath and exhaled.

"You need me to give you a second or two to catch your breath?"

"No, I'm okay."

"So, besides being out of breath, how are you doing?"

"Wonderful." *Now that you've called.* "How about you?"

"Okay, I guess." Robert sounded significantly different, almost as if he'd lost his best friend.

"Look, are you busy. I really need to see you."

"Robert, are you okay. You don't sound like yourself at all."

"Yeah, I'm fine. I just need to talk to you."

"Okay, when?"

"As soon as possible."

"About what?"

"I'd rather discuss it in person, Jazz. Could you just meet me somewhere?"

"What's wrong with meeting at your place or over here?"

"I'd just rather meet you in a public place."

That's bizarre. Robert's never acted like this before.

"Any public place in particular?" I asked sarcastically.

"How about downtown at Piedmont Park?"

"I'll see you in thirty minutes."

It didn't take long for me to spot Robert sitting in solitude at a picnic table, all bundled up. He was one of only two people crazy enough to be in the park in thirty degree weather. His counterpart had no choice. For him, one of the plaza's many benches or tree stumps more than likely served as bunking quarters at least one or two nights out of each week.

"Robert, what was so urgent we had to meet immediately, in a public place, and in the cold for that matter?" Instead of taking a seat directly across the table from Robert, which was what his vibes made me feel like doing, I plopped down next to him.

"I'm fine, thank you Jasmine. And how are you?"

"I'm sorry for being so forward. But Robert, it's freezing out here."

"I know. I apologize. This wasn't the best choice. I really wasn't thinking."

"Robert, are you sure you're all right? This behavior is so unlike you."

He took my left hand into his.

"I just have a few things to get off my chest."

I couldn't completely determine what kind of look Robert had on his face. It was one that could go one of two ways. Either he was getting ready to proclaim his newfound love for me. Or he was about to tell me he'd lost his very best friend in the whole world.

"Jazz, I don't know how to say this. First of all, I want you to know you are a wonderful person. You're a special woman. Magnificent. Loving. Attractive. Damn." He nodded. "You're very attractive. Intelligent and fun to be around."

Okay, so I can see where this is going. Prepare yourself Jasmine Brown, you're about to be dumped.

"I truly have enjoyed the time we've spent together the past few weeks. You've taught me how to laugh again, how to cherish the simple pleasures in life. You're truly remarkable."

"So, what's the bad news, Robert?"

I felt the tears begin to well up in my eyes.

"Melanie and I have decided to give things a try again. We want to make it work. We shared too much—three years, Jazz—to just give up like that. You understand, don't you?"

I knew it. I knew it wouldn't be long before this would come. Still, it didn't feel good.

"Of course I do, Robert." I almost choked on my words. "That's wonderful. You both want to work at restoring what you once had." Like Daniel and I did more than enough times, I thought. "I can't hate you for that. I'm happy for you. Congratulations."

"I don't want you to feel I've been lying to you. Melanie and I didn't have anything going while I was seeing you. I also don't want you to feel I was just using you, Jazz, until things worked out with us. That's not at all what happened. I really was interested in you. I developed feelings for you, and I believe things could've happened between us. It just turns out all of my love for Mel wasn't exactly dead. Some of the conversations I had with you made me realize that. I'm sorry."

"I understand. Trust me, I do. You shouldn't feel bad about the decision you've made. At least you were man enough to tell me early on, and didn't try to string us both along until you could figure out how to break the news. I can do nothing but respect you for that. I hope Melanie realizes she's a lucky woman."

"Thank you and you are an extraordinary woman. Don't ever forget that. One day someone will come along and love you the way you deserve to be loved, Jasmine. It'll happen when you least expect it, if you believe."

Robert kissed me on the lips one last time, before leaving me behind in the chill. One brought on more by our conversation than the brisk winds fighting a winning battle with my coat and gloves. I sat there motionless, and watched him walk away. Watched him walk right out of my life, about as quickly as he'd strolled into it. Although I'd prepared myself for the letdown, it still hurt slightly.

What else can go wrong in my life? I've contracted two venereal diseases, lost the man I thought I'd spend the rest of my days and nights with, nearly fallen for another, and lost him, too. Not only that, I've crossed paths with one of my ex-lover's former lovers. How much more complicated can my life get? I don't even want to know.

Seven-thirty! I'd better get going. If I wasn't on the road within the next half-hour, I'd never make it to work on time.

These past few weeks spoiled me; I'd gotten used to waking up whenever I felt like it. Now it was time to get back into the swing of things. I was actually excited to be going back to work, my second home as I sometimes called it. The time off had been refreshing. And the visit to Miko's helped me realize I really didn't have it as bad as I'd led myself to believe.

I took a quick shower, and threw on the first thing I saw in the closet: a solid navy widelegged pant suit, with a cream turtleneck. Once in the car, I finished teasing the front of my hair and began applying my makeup. I managed to get the foundation, blush, lipliner and color in place with no problem. But the eyeliner presented somewhat of a challenge. I nearly poked myself in the eye with the charcoal pencil as I turned the corner about a half-mile from my apartment. Temporarily seizing my attention was the answer to all my problems. Nine life-changing words posted on the marquee outside of the Presbyterian church right up the street: *When actions and words agree, the message is clear.* Those words forced me to put away my makeup bag, delaying the job until I'd made it to work. They continued to weigh heavily on my mind some five minutes later when I turned onto the interstate.

As expected, early morning traffic from Decatur to downtown was a nightmare. The bumper-to-bumper cars guaranteed at least a half-hour delay.

That's okay, though. They're not expecting me anyway. So, technically I won't be late at all.

"Jazz, what are you doing back?" Jennifer stood from her desk and started toward me with a frown on her face so big you would've thought she'd just lost her job or something. "You've been gone so long, I was beginning to think you'd forgotten you had a job!"

You mean you were hoping I'd forgotten?

"Anyway, I could never forget this place. I missed being here."

"We missed you, too. I know I did. I've had to do all your work plus mine."

Knowing you, you were happy to have the opportunity to shine.

Jennifer, standing halfway between her desk and mine, took a stack of papers and dumped them into my arms. "Since you're back, I guess I can give these to you. Right?"

"I suppose. Hey, where's Malik?" I asked, anxious to end this conversation as quickly as possible. "He doesn't even know I'm back yet."

"He should be in his office. He's been swamped with work, too. We've all been wearing all sorts of hats around here for the past couple of weeks."

"Kinda like it was before I left, huh?" That was my way of letting her know I didn't *create* the problem. "Well, I'm gonna go track down Malik." I placed the armful of papers on my desk and turned to walk away.

"Wait a sec, Jazz." Jennifer stretched out her arms and started walking toward me. "Welcome back. By the way, are you better?"

"I'm fine, Jennifer," I said, hesitantly returning the hug.

"Good, I was beginning to worry about you."

Sure you were.

I wasn't clear on what she meant by that and what all she knew about my time off.

What exactly could Malik have told her and why her *of all people?*

"Thanks for your concern," I said, turning to walk away.

"No problem," Jennifer responded. "Anytime."

I knocked, and poked my head through the door to Malik's office but he was nowhere to be found. In the meantime, I decided to go ahead and tackle my mailbox and telephone. Both my box and desk were flooded with mail. With everything from letters from avid readers, press releases from contacts, and nearly a dozen belated Christmas greetings from both. About a handful were from friends or people who wanted to thank me for the *good job* I'd done on a particular article about them.

The red light on my phone was incessantly blinking. A sure sign I had messages. About as many of those as the packages I could look forward to opening. It would take me at least a couple of hours to break into them all, and just as long to return these calls. No biggie.

I'd stay here all night if that's what it took. I was just glad to be back.

When I opened my fourth card, I could not believe my eyes. It wasn't the words inside that caught me off guard, rather the signature at the bottom. *Hope your holidays are nice. Thank you for the interview, Joseph and Shelly.* Unbelievable. When I'd gone to this man's house in October, I'd made it clear I didn't want to be there, despite my small attempt at being cordial. Still, they found it in their hearts to forgive me and send me a card expressing their gratitude. To think, the only reason I'd behaved that way was because of my first-hand run-in with jungle fever. That still didn't mean I condoned interracial dating. The point was, once again, I'd let another person—in this case, Daniel—influence Jasmine's actions.

This card was definitely going up. Right here with the others.

I opened the rest of the mail and stacked more cards wherever I could fit them on the shelf above my desk. I also thumbtacked a couple alongside Joseph's and Shelly's, careful not to cover it or the letter from DFACS, which I'd never taken down. After I sorted through all the invitations to parties I'd missed, I was ready to check my voice mail messages. A busy week undoubtedly lay ahead. Thanks to stacks of mail, scores of phone messages, and enough paperwork to last me a lifetime.

"Jazz, Jennifer told me you were looking for me," I heard Malik's voice say from above my head. "What are you doing back? I wasn't expecting you."

Is that it? No "welcome back" or anything? You'd think Malik would be happy to see me. Especially if what Jennifer said about the workload is true.

I looked up to find him standing over my desk, staring down at me.

"I know you weren't expecting me, but I figured you could use the help, Malik," I said, sounding sincere, yet surprised.

"Well, you're right about that part." Malik broke his eye contact, looking off to the side temporarily. "Jasmine, could I see you in my office for a moment?"

In his office. What have I done now? Or worse, what bad news does he have to share with me?

I followed behind, feeling like an elementary student headed to the principal's office to be punished, i.e., paddled.

"Have a seat, Jazz." Malik walked behind his cherry-finish desk.

"Malik, will this take long? I was kinda anxious to get started on that pile of work on my desk."

"That's what I need to talk to you about."

I reluctantly took a seat in the cushioned chair facing him.

"I don't know quite how to put this," he started to say.

Why is that everybody's favorite introductory line when they're the messenger of bad news?

"Jazz, the truth is, I can't afford your salary anymore. Regrettably, I've had to cut back on this year's budget. I hate it had to come to this. I did everything within my power to avoid having to make this decision. But, unfortunately, this is the way it goes sometimes with small businesses, particularly black-owned."

What decision? Stop beating around the bush, man!

My stomach turned sour.

"So what are you saying?" I asked, wearing the most disappointed look.

Malik paused before he said a word. Then he inhaled. "I'm saying that the best I can afford to offer you right now is an independent contractor position. Of course, the choice is up to you. You can either take it or leave it."

Independent contractor? I don't even know what that means. Do I have a job or don't I?

"What exactly does that mean for me, and when does all this take place, Malik?" I asked, trying not to sound too ignorant. But the heavy look on my face, I imagined, had the word *unenlightened* written all over it.

"It takes effect immediately. Tomorrow, actually," Malik said, tapping the eraser end of a pencil on his desk. "What it means is, you'd perform certain services, just as you do now, either here in the office or in the comfort of your own home."

Why is he sounding like he's practicing for a part in a commercial or something? Does he realize what he's saying?

"You could continue coming into the office as you have in the past. Or you may take your computer, printer, and whatever else you need home and do the work from there. You'd set your own hours." On that note, he looked as if he were thinking, "bet you'd like that, wouldn't you?" "For example, if you wanted to do your work at eight-thirty at night, as opposed to eight-thirty in the morning, you could."

Malik's disposition suddenly changed. "As far as pay's concerned, you'd be compensated per individual project. Also, no taxes would be taken out, so you'd be responsible for filing those on your own. Some people prefer to do that quarterly," he added. "The company would no longer be able to match anything." Malik paused again, as if to warn me that the true bombshell was coming. "It also means you'll lose your vacation time, Jazz, and company-matched benefits like medical and dental insurance."

I swallowed hard.

Did he just say I'd lose my benefits, including health and dental? I've never had to worry about not having insurance, from the time I was covered through Daddy's job when living at home.

"Jazz, I know this is a lot to take in all at once," he said, as if sensing my thoughts. "I'm sorry. Unfortunately, I can't say how long this will last. All I can promise is, as long as the money is here, so are you. I've said it before and I'll say it again. You're one of the best editors around. I hate to have to make such a drastic change as this, even though it may only be temporary. I want you to know when things improve—and I do expect them to—you'll be the first person to know. I'll be calling and begging you to come back full-time. That's if you'd still like to work with us."

"Malik, I'd love to work for you again. I'm just sorry it can't be sooner than later." I hesitated before asking my next question, but figured I had every right to know. "What's going on?" I asked, spitting out the words. "Is the company having financial problems?"

"Well, in comparison to as little as six months ago, we haven't made much in terms of ad revenue. As you well know, advertising dollars are what keep us alive."

Six months, I thought. *That's not a very long time to use as a barometer, in my opinion. Then again, I've never run a business.*

I felt a headache coming on. I'd never suspected the company of having money troubles. This was all such a shock.

"I can tell you have some things on your mind, Jazz. Is there anything else you'd like to ask?"

Yeah. For starters, what about all that overtime put in here and at home? I borrowed a line from Jennifer: *You'd think [that] would count for something.*

"Well, Malik, what about the time off you gave me? Was *Amsha* heading into trouble then?"

"At that point in time, I didn't see it coming," he said. But, again, with small businesses, anything can change, almost overnight."

"That's about the only part of this that makes sense. Probably the least understandable is why I have to go, instead of someone else, like Jennifer."

"I figured that one was coming. This is not a Jasmine versus Jennifer thing. I don't want you thinking that. Jennifer won't be affected by this because, unlike you, she's part-time. Right now, it's more economically feasible for *Amsha* to have her around because she serves in a number of unrelated capacities: administrative and editorial assistant, writer, even graphic designer. I know you also wear many hats around here, but see, on those days when I need Jennifer to do nothing but man the phones—" He shrugged his shoulders. "This wasn't an easy decision for me and Sandy. You have to realize, for us, this means things will go back to the way they were before we found you. This move defeats our whole purpose for bringing you on board. The two of us will again have just as many editorial as managerial responsibilities."

I hadn't given much thought to what this meant for anyone else.

"I promise you, Jasmine, there's no need to worry. When things start looking brighter, your job will be here waiting on you. In the meantime, you still have work."

"Does that mean I can wait to clean my desk out later?"

"You shouldn't have to clean it out at all, but if you'd like to take some of your things with you, you're welcome to. Like I said, you have the option of coming in here at anytime to work in that space. And again, when things improve," he said, crossing two of his right fingers, "you'll be back to full-time. You have my word."

"Thanks Malik." I walked away, feeling as if I'd been given the pink slip, which, in essence, was exactly what had happened.

Briefly, I thought of Daniel and of what he'd think of my career crisis, considering how I'd looked down on his job when we first met. At least he still had one.

I didn't know much about this independent contractor business, but this suddenness didn't sound legal to me. I didn't want to get Malik into any trouble though. That was funny—when I shouldn't have cared anymore about him than I felt he did about me right now.

What a way to start the new year.

My first day back at work was over in a flash. Two years of dedication and hard work over—just like that. Just like my career. And my so-called love life.

The ironic thing about it all is I should've seen everything coming, I thought as I dragged myself out of Malik's office.

I'd ignored all the warning signs from Daniel and turned around and did the same with Jennifer.

Maybe I shouldn't have spent what amounted to two extra weeks away from work, outside of the Christmas and New Year's holidays.

Over the past year, Jennifer's made it clear how badly she wants to trade places with me. Why, I didn't know. For the first time, I understood what she meant when she said, "You'd think loyalty would count for something." But what had happened, before me, to make her think that way?

This was all so unbelievable, I almost wanted to laugh. But it hurt so much, I couldn't help but cry. I found myself in the same boat I was struggling to paddle a day ago.

Here's to a lonely apartment, nothing to do and nowhere to go.

Chapter Nineteen

First thing the next morning I got busy burning up the phone line. I called the U.S. Department of Labor, its Pension and Welfare Benefits Administration and the Internal Revenue Service. In the past, I'd always had to do research for someone else. It felt odd making investigative calls for myself.

"In the state of Georgia, all the laws are in the employer's favor," one lady with the Department of Labor told me. "This is a right-to-work state. The employer can change his or her policy at will," she said, sounding like one of my great-aunts.

"It may not be fair, but the state of Georgia supports them in all of this," she went on to say. "You came out better than a lot of folks. They could've let you go that very day."

"Just like that?"

"That's what I'm trying to tell you," she said in a firm, yet empathetic voice. "An employer has the right to change pay, cut hours, and fire you without giving any reason at all."

The news concerning my insurance was slightly better. Thanks to Georgia's continuation coverage laws, I'd be covered throughout the rest of January and for the next three months. However, Malik had the option of continuing to match the premium or of not paying any portion whatsoever. Unfortunately, for the same reasons he made me an independent contractor, he decided to go with the latter, which meant I'd be footing the bill alone.

There's no way I can manage this coverage alone, was what I thought as I reviewed Blue Cross' individual packages. *It's expensive enough as it is, even with the company doing its share.*

But I also couldn't afford to go without coverage, thanks to all the doctors' visits I'd been making. Lately, it seemed life sure had a funny way of kicking me where it hurt. And to think, someone, whose name escaped me at this moment, had the nerve to say that maybe all this was "a blessing in disguise." I sure didn't see it that way. It actually felt like a stab in the back. I felt as if Malik, whom I'd always considered to be more than just a boss, had turned on me. I wasn't convinced that he was *really* saving that much money by changing my status. I was only one person. I also questioned Malik's sincerity, although he'd never given me a reason to doubt him in the past, but things were getting to the point where I didn't think I could trust anyone.

I went into the office the next few days as normal, dressing down like never before. I wasn't quite ready to move everything into my home. Wasn't at all prepared for the adjustment. So I carried on with business as usual. The mail I hadn't gotten a chance to get around to on Monday, along with a new batch, was waiting on me. I figured I should lower the stack as much as possible before doing anything else.

I started from the top, with the cream envelope with a familiar black logo in the top left-hand corner.

What's this from the Atlanta Association of Journalists' nominating committee? I sure could stand some good news. Hopefully, they're writing to let me know I've been selected as a candidate for this year's journalism awards program at the end of January.

I'd submitted the article on Tiffani to be considered for AAJ's annual awards ceremony. A representative from the selection committee had advised it would take them about a month to choose the finalists.

I sliced open the envelope with the silver doodad resembling a butter knife. There were two pages enclosed. I put the cover letter to the side and went straight to page two, the list of honorees. I skimmed the list twice but didn't see my name anywhere.

How could this be? Surely, that story was good enough to qualify.

I picked up the two-paragraph letter and began reading. *Dear Jasmine Brown, we're sorry to inform you that you have been disqualified from the list of nominees for this year's Atlanta Association of Journalists' Pioneer Awards.*

Disqualified? Why? How?

I continued to read. *As you well know, in order to be considered for an award, you must meet certain criteria. Those requirements are as follows:*

1) You must work full-time in an editorial position for a well-established Atlanta magazine or newspaper.

2) You must be a resident of Fulton or a surrounding county for at least one year.

3) You must demonstrate excellent leadership skills, while playing a positive role in the community.

I'd been nailed by number one. But, to be honest, the thought to inform them of my employment status had never crossed my mind, nor did I expect them to find out about it. Besides, I was working full-time at the time I submitted my story for consideration, a factor that most other journalistic organizations generally took into consideration.

But how did they find out? Oh, silly me. Of course, from Jennifer! This is ridiculous! Hasn't she gotten what she wants by now? I mean, really. Why won't this chick leave me alone? I'm tired. Tired of Jennifer's crap. Tired of Daniel's lies. Tired of people, period.

"Jennifer, it's time we talked. I mean *really* talked."

She was on the phone but I didn't care.

"I'll call you back," she told the person on the other end.

A personal call—maybe I should've been in here to eavesdrop on her.

Jennifer slowly turned my way, remaining at her desk. I continued to stand. She wasn't too happy with my intrusion.

"I just got this," I said, holding the letter up so she could at least make out who it was from. "I'm not even gonna ask if you did it. I already know that answer. I also won't limit my question to *why* you did it." I never dropped my hand—the letter was still staring her in the face. "I wanna know why you've done *everything* you've done. Why have you been so out to get me?"

Jennifer cut her eyes toward the floor.

"I know I haven't done anything to you, Jennifer," I threw in, while awaiting her response.

"All I ever wanted was a chance," she finally said, her voice cracking. "I know what I can do. I'm tired of trying to prove it to people. Mama. Malik. You."

She stormed out toward the bathroom. This was the first time I'd seen Jennifer cry. I wasn't sure if I wanted to go after her or leave it alone. *If you had any sense, you'd go on about your business,* a voice said. But the weak, nice side of me took over.

Jennifer was looking into the mirror, rubbing her face with a wet paper towel when I walked in. She snickered upon seeing my reflection. "Bet I was the last person you thought you'd see cry. Not hard, mean, spiteful Jennifer."

I didn't speak.

"I'm not that person, Jazz. That's just the side you see."

"Why?"

"It's a defense." She wet more towels. "When I was a teenager, my parents divorced after eighteen years of marriage. My mom became a bitter woman, Jazz. Nothing I did was right." She patted her face. "Nothing still is. It's been ten years and her heart hasn't healed yet."

I patiently listened, as a feeling of relief came over me.

"I don't know, when it happened, I told myself I could replace the happiness my dad had taken away. I would become Mama's joy. I was all she had. Step by step, I'd do whatever I could to make her proud."

I could relate to that. I'd spent a lifetime trying to convince my daddy that I could manage taking a route unlike the one he saw fit for me.

"...slowly, but surely, filling the void," Jennifer added.

"Jennifer, I know what it feels like to live for somebody else," I said, referring to my father and Daniel. "But I don't go around hurting or stepping on people in the process."

"The more I tried, the less progress I saw. Eventually, I felt dejected, too, and my heart started to harden." She tossed the paper in the trash. "It's no excuse, but it's the truth."

Finally, I had the truth. As Malik had told me, it had nothing to do with me. It was, indeed, all about Jennifer. And her past.

After I finished talking to Jennifer, I headed home. Being an independent contractor allowed me such freedom, which, at this point, appeared to be the only advantage. One I wasn't used to and didn't care to get used to because I planned to work full-time again for somebody at some point. For the first time, I decided to follow my mother's advice about putting people's names in the Bible. I added a unique flair to her suggestion though. Besides just writing names on a blank sheet of paper and folding it up, I wrote a mini-letter to God. I started out talking about my problems, particularly most recently, with Jennifer. I also asked for clarity concerning the work situation and the drama with Daniel. By the time I was done, I'd covered the entire front side of a white, legal-size piece of paper.

Noonday Saturday. For me, that meant one of three things: I could either tune in to *Soul Train* as I usually did when I wanted a good laugh, thanks to the show's exotic dancers. Or I could sit here and channel-surf, until I settled on one of the five hundred cartoons on the tube. Even worse, I could get up and do a few household chores, beginning with cleaning up this pigsty.

I'm sure we could all agree, more than anything, I could use a little dose of laughter right about now.

I turned to Don Cornelius' brainchild, just as it was fading to a commercial break. A beautiful mocha-complected sistuh's face appeared across the screen, followed by an assortment of cosmetics. Fashion Fair. My favorite. Next on, an advertisement for Dark & Lovely no-lye relaxers. Pathetic. For the first time, I realized this was one of the few occasions you got to see commercials with black people. But of course, it was during the *off-peak hours.* That was what I called the opposite of *prime time,* the time when advertisers, and television as a whole, maintained their biggest audience and when ratings counted the most. Suddenly infuriated, I changed the channel.

"She has survived countless days of low pay and low self-esteem," a very attractive tan-colored sistuh with a headful of dreads and a thick northwestern accent spoke into a microphone. "As she herself will tell you, that low self-esteem stemmed from a number of things. An abusive marriage that ended in divorce, difficult days of single parenthood accompanied by her share of financial struggles, and the internal struggle of facing a new job with nothing more than a high school diploma."

A wide-angle camera view revealed a sea of African American women, spread out at dinner tables. Many nodded their heads in unison following the speaker's words.

"Well, as most of you know, this extraordinary woman went on to become one of New York's most popular female columnists in her twenties, and one of the country's most renowned orators."

The audience applauded.

Patrice Powers, I thought. *I adore her.*

Ever since my college days, when I'd first been introduced to Powers' nationally syndicated columns, I'd looked forward to them each month. Oftentimes, the spirituality pieces were like a good sermon on a Sunday morning. Just the right words to help you get through whatever was troubling you at that moment.

I couldn't believe I'd forgotten she was going to be in town this particular weekend, for an annual event dubbed "African American Women: Movers and Shakers," taking place at the Ritz-Carlton Hotel downtown. The "empowerment" seminar was being hosted by a group called Sisters Wanting A Change, or SWAC, a local organization, which had been around for only about three years. Its main focus: to uplift our race. One way SWAC tried to do that was by bringing in renowned speakers such as Patrice Powers. Other than her, they'd hosted an appearance by author and lecturer, bell hooks. I was there for that one, on the campus of Morris Brown College last year. Like Powers' appearance, hooks' was broadcast on C-Span. Getting such national publicity undoubtedly helped build up the group's membership. It also let people see just how serious the sisters involved were.

On a more regular basis, SWAC held monthly meetings, and offered weekend seminars that taught women how to love themselves, how to set goals and reach them, and how to operate a successful business. It also encouraged black women to support our men. Annual membership was only fifty dollars, and was open to anyone who was down with the cause, anyone wanting to improve her life, or help make a difference in someone else's. I'd been planning to join ever since I ran across the application in the mail at work about a month ago. I just hadn't gotten around to it. But I realized even though money was tight right about now, it was time to put that at the top of my list.

"I could stand up here all day and rave about this remarkable African queen," continued the sistuh—her hair adorned by cream-colored Afrocentric shells, with a matching choker around her neck. "But I don't wanna give away her whole success story, or there'll be no need for her to come up to the mike!"

Dozens of the ladies laughed.

"Without further delay, Ms. Patrice Powers."

More applause.

I should go down there, I thought, realizing I'd miss the first half of Powers' speech, but at least I'd get to hear some of it in person. Not only that, something was telling me I needed to be there, that somehow, being amongst such a diverse crowd would be somewhat therapeutic. I searched for a usable VHS tape so that I could set my VCR to record the entire event. That way, once I returned home, I'd be able to see the portions I'd missed and would always have the tape to refer back to whenever I needed a little inspiration.

I coughed up ten dollars for the hotel's valet parking to save time. As it was, I'd already missed much of Powers' speech.

"One thing I've learned ladies, is life is like a classroom," I heard a rather soft-spoken, relaxed voice say as I walked through the ballroom door. "With each passing day, come lessons and tests to help us grow and develop."

Good, she's still on.

I turned toward the podium to find a stunning, tall, slim, brown-skinned Patrice Powers, wearing a sparkling gold knee-length dress, which perfectly complemented her skin. I quickly scanned the room for an empty seat—to no avail. Realizing it wouldn't be long before she was done, I decided to stay put, standing near the double doors. I remained focused on the front of the room, listening intently as she talked about how "every crisis, or moment of truth in our lives, draws us closer to God." As she articulated, the camera slowly panned across the room, a room distinctly filled with harmony, and overflowing with a diverse congregation of beautiful African American women. Women of all shades. Chocolate. Cafe au lait. "Redbone." "High yellow." Ladies of all shapes, sizes and ages. About as many sporting naturals as those with perms. Young sistuhs, some who appeared to be around my age. Middle-aged women, who, through their appearance and aura, still seemed to be clinging to some of their youthful years. And the oldies, but goodies bunch: first-generation mothers, grandmothers, and great-grandmothers.

By now, Powers was holding a purple book, from which she was paraphrasing some of her most inspirational words. She told the women how they'd find most of what she'd talked about in her first work—a compilation of her columns—which was for sale outside at the registration desk. Then the room echoed with accolades, and a simultaneous standing ovation, signifying the end of the workshop. I felt chills run through my body as I beat the crowd in exiting. Right around the corner were two tables: one for purchasing the book; the other set up for Powers to sign copies of it. I joined about two dozen others in line and pulled out my checkbook to purchase something that, financially, I knew I couldn't afford, but emotionally, I felt I couldn't do without.

Hundreds of people, who'd apparently purchased their books beforehand, were already awaiting Powers' signature. Still, I didn't mind the wait. In my opinion, it was well worth it. I was not only gaining a valuable read, I was finally able to meet and talk with an awe-inspiring role model such as Patrice Powers.

"Isn't she wonderful?" the sistuh in front of me turned to say.

"She sure is," I responded, glancing over at Powers, who was shaking hands with an apparent fan.

"I mean, to go through all she did, it's amazing she's so strong," said the heavyset woman who appeared to be a few years younger than me.

"Well, all of the bad stuff just made way for something better," I said, somewhat shocked that the words had come from my mouth. "Her first marriage may not have worked out, but this second one apparently makes her extremely happy."

"Yeah, and I'm really impressed with her professional track record. It gives me hope," she added.

"Are you in school?" The line moved slightly forward. "By the way, I'm Jasmine."

"I'm sorry, I'm Joan. And yes, I am. I'm a junior at Morris Brown. But I work full-time at the airport, too, sometimes as many as fifty hours a week." The tone in her voice lowered. "My mom's real sick." Her voice cracked. "She has AIDS." My body shivered. "She doesn't have any medical insurance." We stepped forward a few feet more. "And she's not able to work anywhere. On top of that, my dad is no longer around, so that leaves me no choice but to work full-time to help keep the bills paid."

"I'm so sorry to hear that," I said, feeling bad that I couldn't think of anything better to say; nor could I do anything to help.

"Thank you," Joan said. "It's hard, I tell you. That's why I had to come down here today. I never have any extra money to go out and do anything I enjoy. So being able to come here at a student rate really helps." She looked down at the front cover of her book, which contained an image of a Nigerian garment. "I'm really looking forward to reading more about how Ms. Powers made it."

"So am I," I said. "And I'm sure you and I both will soon have similar stories of survival to tell. I realize no matter what I say, it won't change things. But I will say this, I'll be praying for you and your mom."

"Thank you. That's so sweet, when you don't even know me."

The minute I got home, I did exactly what I'd promised Joan, before writing in my journal.

Today has been remarkable. I met two extraordinary women who will forever touch my heart. One is named Joan Harmon. The other, Patrice Powers. I've just finished saying a prayer for Joan, a Morris Brown student whose mother is dying of AIDS. She's a strong young woman I could learn a thing or two about survival from.

Patrice Powers, of course, needs no introduction. But what I can say about her that most people probably didn't know is that she, too, has suffered. You see, a lot of times, we (including myself) have a tendency to think no one else has ever gone through or will ever have to endure the trials and tribulations we face. But what we soon realize, by talking to and meeting others, is that we're not alone. I'm not alone. I could even go as far as saying I haven't suffered nearly as much as a lot of other people. Matter of fact, I haven't suffered at all. If anything, I've grown. After all, that's what life is all about. As I'm now fully realizing, life is indeed a journey. A journey in self-discovery. Each blessed day we should look forward to creating our circumstances, rather than aimlessly discovering what the next twenty-four hours hold for us.

Since I'd discovered the meaning of quiet time, I'd begun to spend pensive moments in a candlelit living room, during which I meditated and admired the incense coming from my burning scented candles. At other times, I'd stretch out on the sofa, snuggled up to my new book.

Ever since I picked up the hardcover copy, I felt like a new person. It was such an inspiring piece of work, tackling issues such as forgiveness and "emotional baggage," a term I'd, ironically, been introduced to by Joseph White. The latest chapter I was reading dealt with spirituality and self-love, something I was just now learning about, at age twenty-five. For so long, I ignored my wants and needs, and went out of my way to please Daniel. Now, as I reflected back on things, I realized I wasn't completely happy nor secure in our relationship. There were times when I'd get depressed and cry for no apparent reason at all. I'd just sit and think about Daniel, and out of nowhere I'd get this nervous feeling, like a knife jabbing me in my stomach. Almost like a warning. Sure enough, shortly afterwards, something would happen to cause me pain and tears.

One of those things I'd never forget was the night I pulled up to see Daniel and his white companion entering his back door. Nor would I let that surprise visit by Wanda slip my mind. And it would be almost impossible not to think about his little fling with Terry. I never caught the two together, but having mental knowledge of their rendezvous was painful enough. To think, I took the blame for all that went wrong. I led myself to believe that Daniel strayed because I wasn't on the job. Because I wasn't a good lover. Because I wasn't a good woman. I was brainwashed into believing I was the problem. When in actuality, the problem was one we both could accept the blame for. Daniel, for taking me and my love for him for granted, all because he hadn't yet learned how to love and respect himself. Which meant I never should've expected him to be able to love and respect me. Along those same lines, I never should have tried to give my heart to anyone, until I'd learned how to first take care of Jasmine. I was just now realizing how wrong I was for loving someone else more than I loved myself. No more.

No more falling in love again until I know the true meaning of self-love. No more falling for anyone who hasn't made the same discovery.

"This is the day that burdens will be removed. I pray to you Lord that no individual will walk out of here feeling the way he did when he walked in."

Hundreds of "Amens" reverberated across a packed Transformation Ministries. Some of the older attendees even waved their hands above their heads, in attestation of Reverend Paul Washington's sermon. The six-foot-four, two hundred sixty-five pound "gentle giant" was good for getting the congregation all roused up. Thanks to his booming Barry White-like bass.

"People, ahh, have you ever noticed how soon we turn to God when we experience hardship in our lives? Ahh. Can I get an amen?" Pastor Washington shouted into the wireless mike attached to the lapel of his jacket. He then stepped away from the podium—adorned by a beautiful arrangement of flowers and live green plants and two floor speakers by its side.

"Amen!"

"Amen, Reverend."

"Praise the Lord!" Several members of the congregation shouted as a handful of video cameras panned the dome-shaped, stadium-seating room.

I looked over at Tiffani, who sat beside me, and smiled. This was our first church experience together, the first time I'd ever seen her in a dress.

"You notice how quick we are to call His name, when we're down and out?" He continued in his theatrical voice that made you pay attention. "When we're down to our last dime? When we've reached that all-time low? When we're all out of solutions, and we have no one else to turn to for advice or help? We're all guilty of it. Amen?"

I feel like he's talking to me.

Apparently much of the congregation did, too.

Throughout the sermon, there were many ovations, some standing, from the mass of people.

Tiffani seemed to be taking it all in as much as the next person.

"Well, what we learn from all this is that God should be first and foremost in our lives at all times," he said, gesturing. " 'Cause people, just as sho' as we're alive, we're going to experience deep trials and suffering. There's just no way to get around it. When we go through these trials and tribulations, God is working purposefully in our lives to draw us closer to Him. He uses these tests of faith to build us up, not to tear us down. And He's careful to select exactly what each one of us needs for our individual spiritual growth. Our hardships are not the result of fate. We go through everything in life for a reason. And God never lets us go through more than we can handle."

Guess you could say I was guilty of exactly what Pastor Washington was preaching about this Sunday morning. Now that I'd hit rock-bottom, I found myself turning to the altar. But it wasn't always like this. As a young child, around Tiffani's age, I read my Bible every day. I also used to attend services twice a month when I was back in Smithsville, which were held only on the first and fourth Sundays at the Baptist church I'd joined years ago. I was very active back then, participating in any and every church program, even singing in the choir (never mind that I couldn't carry a note).

In Atlanta, I was still in search of a church to call home. So I became more open to houses of worship such as Transformation, which was non-denominational, and attracted anywhere from five to seven thousand visitors.

After the sermon, I felt so much better, as though I were developing into a much happier, more spiritual person. One who had learned some valuable lessons from everything she'd been through. I felt exactly the way Monique said I one day would. No longer would I look back with regret. Instead, I'd look back on my experiences—both good and bad—to see how each one helped me to grow. Not only that, I'd give thanks for my afflictions and work at being stronger and better prepared for what was to come.

I've been through a lot over this past year, I thought, while walking to my car. *All for a good reason, I'm sure. But I've survived and I've come too far to give up. If Joan and Patrice (and Tiffani) haven't, why should I?*

I prayed Daniel would soon feel the joy I was feeling right now. I hoped he, too, could develop into a new individual who'd learn to love himself, and most of all, God.

In fact, from this day on, I'll make it my duty to avoid holding any hard feelings against him. I have to let go, as Joseph suggested. Unpack my baggage. I'll start by replacing any malice I have for Daniel with wishful thoughts and prayers. After all, this is the new me we're talking about.

Chapter Twenty

The blinking red light on my answering machine was the first thing I noticed when I walked through the door. I was returning from Waldenbooks, where I'd picked up my last belated, inexpensive Christmas gifts, a couple of their bargain cookbooks for Dave. I was a little reluctant at first, but finally gave in and played the message.

"Ms. Brown, this is Lisa at Dr. Smith's office, calling with your lab results. Please give us a call when you get in."

I got this nauseating feeling. I'd waited on this phone call for almost a month. Now I was almost afraid to hear the news.

It's more than likely bad news. Otherwise, she would've left the results on the machine.

I picked up the phone and anxiously dialed the number. After three rings, one of the office's midwives picked up.

"Hello, I'm calling for Lisa."

"May I tell her who's calling?" she asked.

"Sure, it's Jasmine Brown."

"Okay Jasmine, hang on a second. I'll let her know you're on the line."

I was on hold long enough to hear the ending to Whitney Houston's soulful rendition of Dolly Parton's "I Will Always Love You" playing in my ear before the nurse picked up.

"Jasmine?"

"Yes."

"Hi, it's Lisa. I've got some news for you." Her southern accent sounded a little too chipper. "Remember how I told you, once we got the results back, for confidentiality reasons, I'd call and say one of two things? I'd either tell you 'it's good news,' or I'd say, 'we need you to come back into the office'?"

"Right." My heart was beating fast.

"Well, you'll be happy to know part of it is good news. Your AIDS test was negative."

I sighed.

"But we will need you to come back in for a repeat Pap. This one turned up some abnormal cells."

"Abnormal? What does that mean?"

"We're not sure exactly. But in most cases it's nothing to worry about. A lot of women have at least one or two Pap smears in their lifetime turn out this way. We always suggest a re-test within two to three months to see if we get the same results. Nine times out of ten we don't."

"Okay, so I guess I should make an appointment for March?"

"March will be perfect. You wanna go ahead and pick a date now?"

"Sure."

"How about the 15th?"

"That's fine."

Who knows what I'll be doing by then? Hopefully, I'll be out of this rut and will again have reasonable, full-coverage medical benefits.

"Morning or evening?"

"Morning."

"Okay, Jasmine. We'll see you on the 15th at 9:30. You take care of yourself now. If there's anything we can help you with, don't hesitate to give us a call."

"I won't."

Once off the phone, I dropped the two packages I still held in my arms, and fell straight to my knees.

Thank you, Lord. Thank you, I said, looking toward the ceiling.

I thanked the Lord a million times over for sparing my life, because that was exactly what He had done. I had no idea what I would have done if I'd learned I had AIDS.

I wouldn't even want to live anymore. I would've wanted my life to end the instant I found out.

I realized this AIDS test probably wasn't the last; but I couldn't let future exams trouble me just yet. Still, even with that good news, I wasn't completely happy. I'd never had a negative Pap smear in my life. And although Lisa tried to explain what it all meant, I still didn't understand. It made me wonder if it was all a domino effect of my other health problems. Sure, the nurse said chances were there was nothing to worry about. But that was no guarantee, especially considering the way my luck had been going.

My flight from Atlanta to Orlando International, the nearest airport to my hometown, took only a couple of hours. Justice and my mom were waiting for me at the wrong Delta gate. But, even through the hundreds of other bystanders, I was able to find them in no time.

"Hey, baby. Lord, I'm so glad you made it okay." My mother greeted me with a bear hug out of this world. "How was your flight?" she asked, still clinging to me. "You know how much I don't like you flying on these things," she said, finally letting go.

"Everything was just fine, Mama. I read a little, and slept through most of the flight."

"Hey sis." Justice's embrace felt about as tight as my mom's. This was the first time I'd seen her in about three weeks, the last time I'd gone to her dorm to visit.

"Hey, where's Marlo?" I pulled away and looked around. "Where's Daddy?"

"Girl, where do you think? Daddy is at home, stretched out in front of the tube. And as usual, 'Megamouth' is stretched out on her bed, with the phone pressed up to one side of her face."

"You mean they couldn't give up their favorite pastimes long enough to come out and greet me?"

"Oh, Jazz, don't start now, your father was tired," my mother quickly defended. "He's worked hard lately, and he's trying to catch up on some rest."

"So, what are we gonna do tonight, Jazz?" Justice chimed in.

I was so glad Justice changed the subject. "*I'm* going to get some rest, and relax with the most important people in my life. What else is there to do on a Friday night in Smithsville?"

Besides, I made this trip for one reason and one reason only. If I do nothing else while I'm here this weekend, I plan to come clean with my mama.

I'd put this conversation off at Christmastime because I didn't want to kill the spirit.

"You just had two weeks to do nothing but rest. How much more time do you need?" Justice asked in her smart-alecky tone. "I tell you, sometimes you can be so boring. You need to start getting out more. You may be older than me, but you're still young, Jazz, even though you don't always act like it."

"Justice, leave your sister alone. She deserves a break from that big city and her stressful job."

My conscience was eating me alive for letting my family believe I had work to return to. But I didn't consider the airport an appropriate place to tell them the supposedly exemplary daughter/sister was unemployed, and had become an independent contractor, whose paychecks—when they came—were barely enough to cover her expenses. Just like me, I was sure my mother needed to be schooled on all this, particularly the definition alone. Not only that, knowing her, she'd feel some sense of financial obligation until things got better. I was hoping my "better" was right around the corner; that way, they'd never have to know about the setback.

During the thirty-minute drive to Smithsville, I mostly kept quiet. The ride was interesting, to say the least, as always. Within Smithsville's city limits, we passed farms, cow pasture after cow pasture and several small, older, "built-to-last" homes, as my great-grandmama would call them. I even noticed, still standing, after all these years, that same small red brick house, which sat alongside South Broad Street, rolling out the red carpet, rather the red flag, to visitors from Orlando and the surrounding cities. For years, it had hoisted a miniature confederate flag on a pole directly in front.

The more things change, the more they stay the same, I thought to myself, nodding.

From South Broad, we turned onto East Main, where the old white courthouse—white Christmas lights still on every corner—sat in the middle of "town," considered the heart of the city.

These very decorations were up weeks ago when I came home for the holidays. When are these backwards people planning to take them down?

Whatever you needed, in the way of doing business, was centered around this area. But that didn't amount to much. The only interesting site was a BP service station, which I noticed still displayed a sign of public humiliation out front: "Frank James and Willie Davis You Owe Me Money!" Within walking distance were two family-owned grocery stores, Allen's Supermarket and Big Red's Grocery; a Family Dollar Store; People's Bank; and McClendon's Drug Store, also family-owned. In addition, a matchbox-size post office, washerette, Electric Power Supply, State Farm Insurance office, video rental store, family-owned floral shop, Big Bertha's Fried Chicken, Dairy Queen and Rally's Burgers.

As the Ford Caravan turned onto Pine Street, I felt as though I were riding through Christmas Island, a small white Edgewood Drive neighborhood of ten to twelve homes, which annually went overboard with its decorating, drawing scores of families from all around, including folks from neighboring Orlando. Every year, one home in particular made sure it kept electric company employees laughing all the way to the bank, with its vast display of decorations, such as a lighted sleigh led by reindeer. It was occupied by the Harper family, which consisted of a husband and wife now that their three kids were all adults. Four houses down Pine, I spotted my family's four-bedroom brick house, apparently the only household that had sense enough to realize when it was time to pack things up until next year.

"Jazz! Guess what? I've made up my mind. I'm gonna be a Panther!" Before I could make my way into the house good, my baby sister, Marlo, greeted me with her good news.

"I've already been accepted to Clark. My first semester there will be next fall."

"That's great, Marlo. I'm glad you've decided to come on up to Hotlanta. I guess that means you and Justice will be roomies again, huh?"

"I guess," she said, turning up her nose.

"And once again, you'll both have to answer to me." Each one of them shot me a look from hell. "I'm just kidding, girls. But you know I wouldn't be doing my job if I didn't look out for you two."

"Yeah, yeah, just give me these bags. How many did you bring anyway? Between your junk and Justice's, I swear, there's not going to be any room left in this house."

The three of us spent the rest of the night watching a movie we'd rented from a Blockbuster in Orlando. Meanwhile, my dad did what he was known best for and my mom camped out in her favorite place: the kitchen. Sweating over meals, she listened to some of her favorite spirituals on the same boom box she blasted the gospel radio station on every Sunday morning beginning around eight.

Once Mama saw that everything was under control—boiling and broiling at just the right pace—she took a break, which I found to be the perfect opportunity to stop keeping secrets from the one person I'd never had any trouble talking to about practically anything.

"Mama, there's something I need to tell you."

I sat at the foot of my parents' queen-size rice bed, where my mother rested on top of a down comforter.

"I haven't said anything about this before now because I didn't want you to worry." I turned to face her, crossing my legs Indian-style. "Before I tell you what it is, I want you to know you still don't have any reason to worry." My voice cracked a little. "I'm okay now. I'm a much stronger person."

"What is it, Jazz?" My mom asked in her usual motherly tone.

"You remember when you all came up to visit for Thanksgiving, I was going through some things but I wouldn't tell you what?"

"Yeah. When my gut feeling told me you were sick, but you insisted you weren't?" She raised her head off the satin pillowcase she'd been sleeping on ever since her beautician advised her it was better on black hair than cotton. "Jazz, what's wrong? What is it, baby?"

"I *was* sick. I still am, but I'm much better now."

She inched her way to the edge of the bed and placed my head on her left shoulder. I began crying uncontrollably.

"I have herpes and...genital warts."

"Oh, Jazz. Oh, baby."

For the next five minutes neither one of us spoke a word. Instead, we cried and held each other tight, rocking back and forth the entire time. For the most part, Mama kept quiet, allowing me to open up to her at my own pace. I told her about everything: the diagnosis, the medication, even Daniel's reaction, which, naturally angered her. I eased her mind a little by telling her about the negative AIDS test. The results of the Pap, on the other hand, didn't sit too well with her.

"You make sure you keep that appointment," she said. "If you want me to, I'll go with you."

"I will. Thanks for the offer, Mama. I just may need to take you up on it."

"Jazz, I have some things I need to share with you, too." She reached for my left hand. "What you've told me today really breaks my heart. Not just because it happened; I actually feel I could've prevented it."

"What do you mean, Mama? You had no idea—"

"Jazz, I could've talked to you. As a mother, I *should've* talked to you."

"Mama, it's not your fault. If it's anybody's, it's mine. I knew what to watch out for, but went into things blindfolded." I said, wiping tears from the corners of my eyes.

"Baby, that's not what I mean."

The only other time I'd seen my mother looking this glum was at my grandfather's funeral a year and a half ago. The two of them were very close, with her being the oldest of three girls and two boys.

"If I hadn't been so damn secretive." She nodded, appearing to regain her strength. "Six years ago, I was diagnosed with gonorrhea. Over the years, I've wanted to tell you and your sisters, in order to keep the three of you from following in my footsteps. But at the same time, I didn't feel my children needed to know those kinds of personal details. I was especially concerned about how the news might affect your relationships with your father."

"So, Daddy *did* mess around?"

"Yes he did, and he brought his nasty shit home to me." This was probably the first time I'd ever heard Mama say anything about Daddy that wasn't in his defense. Maybe the news of a man mistreating one of her daughters had really set her off. She could take it, I assumed she'd reasoned, but nobody better mess with her children.

"It happened while you were away at college," she continued. "For a solid week, I noticed this discharge in the lining of my underwear. At first, I thought it was normal, so I bought a box of pantiliners. Then I started feeling this slight burn every time I went to the bathroom. That's when I went to my OB/GYN. She gave me a shot and some antibiotics. That cured it. I just hate I never told you. I could've saved you from gettin' into this mess." She looked away, as if in deep thought.

"Mama, don't be so hard on yourself. I'm just glad you're okay. You don't have to worry about me. I'll be okay, too."

My mother and I agreed not to disclose the details of our conversation to my siblings. Not until the time was right. After all, what would they think of big sister now? Before leaving, I also updated everyone on my employment status. After much explaining, particularly to Mama, they were finally able to put it all into perspective. "You just can't work for black people," she'd said, frowning. I was even shocked at how understanding—in his own little way, of course—my father was. "There's no security on jobs these days, unless you've been somewhere as long as me," he'd said. "Companies are downsizing all the time. I'm lucky I'll be able to retire soon. Not too many people can say that."

Not one cynical remark during the talk, I'd initially thought. *That is until Daddy opened his mouth again.*

"You tried the post office?" he'd asked out of nowhere. "They have good benefits and pay well. Thirty, forty thousand dollars. That's good money."

"No, I don't want to work at the post office," I'd said. "I want to use my talents somewhere where they're needed. I don't wanna get up and go to a job just for the benefits. I don't wanna dread going to work every day. I want to do what I enjoy most. And I feel I have too many skills not to be able to."

"I'm just saying," he continued. "You'll have pretty much a secure job, with good money, retirement...and you won't be struggling like you are now. Or you can always come back home until you get on your feet again. You could work at one of the papers in Orlando and save all that money you pay in rent by staying in your old room."

His poor advice was suffocating.

What makes him think I want to work in civil service or move back home for that matter. I've worked too hard and enjoy what I do too much to just give up. Plus, I wanna believe I'm good at it. I've got skills and I don't have to trade them in for something I don't desire.

Two days later, I was sad to leave my mother behind, but happy to get away from my father; I was certain if I hung around much longer, my tongue would slip and I'd say some things I'd later regret. My flight back to Atlanta left at 9:55 Tuesday morning. It was my first chance to sit back and try to digest everything. My mother's news was heartbreaking, beyond belief. How could my father do this? What would make him cheat on my mom? A beautiful, educated, professional woman, who gave him three wonderful children and a home stocked with love. She'd always kept herself up, maintaining a dress size of somewhere around an eight or ten. At fifty—four years my father's senior—she could pass for thirty-five. And here he was, a forty-year-old man at the time of his *alleged* affairs some six years prior, running in the streets.

The news really didn't come as much of a surprise. Thanks to all the trashy talk in the hallways back in high school. But, as with Daniel, I'd never wanted to believe the worst.

I couldn't help but wonder why my mother had stuck it out for nearly thirty years. "Why should I leave?" she'd said. "If anybody's moving out, it should be your father. I've been through too much to just walk away." That was my whole point: If you've been through enough pain and heartache to last a lifetime, why stick around? But the longest I'd ever been in a relationship was two years, so I really couldn't try to compare twenty-four months to three hundred and twenty-four. One thing was for sure: I refused to make the same mistake. My mother wouldn't want me to. I now knew what she meant when she'd always say, "I want you to be happy, but don't take no mess from nobody."

If only I'd listened then. I will from now on.

Like Karyn White sang in what had become one of my favorite tunes, *I won't be a fool. A fool for love. 'Cause I know "I'd Rather Be Alone," than be here unhappy. After all, if you're not happy alone, how can you expect to be any better off with someone else? If only I'd known then what I knew now.*

This was one time the cliché "better late than never" proved true to form.

But really all that mattered was that I'd realized my mistakes, and could accept them as invaluable lessons. The biggest thing for me being getting to know Jasmine a little better. Learning what made her happy and how to go about making herself happy without help from anyone. The bottom line: self-love.

"Ladies and gentlemen, the captain has turned on the Fasten Seat Belt sign, indicating our descent to Hartsfield International," a voice overhead said. "At this time, we ask that you return your seats to the upright position. Make sure all trays are back in place. Please keep your seat belts fastened for the remainder of the flight. We'll be on the ground shortly."

At that moment, I realized there was no need to keep looking back and regretting. Something positive had to come out of all this. I just couldn't let what had happened to me or my mom go in vain; these things obviously had taken place for a reason. For me, that reason was to reveal what I needed to be doing a long time ago. Educating others. That was exactly what I made up my mind to do.

Chapter Twenty-one

It took all the energy I could muster to get me out of bed this morning. Going into the office these days was almost as bad as going to the gynecologist for a Pap smear. I hated it, felt as if I were choking the minute I got there.

Malik had dressed up his bad news speech weeks ago when he'd made it sound as if I'd be spending the majority of my time away from 100 Peachtree Street. That wasn't the case at all. In fact, I found myself traveling back and forth a little too frequently. My mileage log was proof of that. Now that I'd become an independent contractor, I was forced to document any and every expense for tax purposes.

How do you just go and make an editing position independent? I thought, as I reached the red light next to the Hardee's on Memorial Drive. That much I'd never figure out. There were still deadlines to be met, stories to be written and edited. I still had to coordinate things with the graphics department, which included Malik's nephew and now, Jennifer.

Still, I surmised, Jennifer wasn't any happier. I believed I could handle the countless darts she'd thrown my way a lot better than I could the kind of internal battle she fought with herself.

The light changed. I was relieved that the day—at least the office-related part—was over.

This is the third time this month, already, I said to myself while passing the Willow Lake apartment complex.

Willow Lake has to be the most evictingest complex on this side of town! I feel sorry for these poor people, I thought, doing my best to drive and watch the two men and one woman gathering their belongings. I caught a glimpse of a headboard, worn mattress, flowery sofa and several pieces of clothing covering the sidewalk.

That could be me. The way my luck is going, I wouldn't be surprised if eviction were the next setback. All it takes in my complex is for you to get behind in the first month. Around the 15th, the warrants start going out.

Images of the trio still reflected in my rearview mirror, some ten yards away.

This is sad. I shouldn't even be having thoughts like this. My career just got off the ground and already it feels like it's crashed.

Never in a million years did I imagine it coming to this.

I'm young. Hard-working. Experienced. Talented. College-educated and unemployed. Referral after referral. Classified ad after classified ad. Interview after interview. It's all turned up nothing. But I refuse to give in to my father's suggestion.

Although I still performed many of my same compensated functions with the magazine, slow pay was more of a problem now than before. That was another reason why I had to give thanks for my freelancing opportunities. I was hoping the payoff for the articles would be twofold. On one end, writing provided true personal gratification as well as helpful advice for others. On the other, I counted on it to help keep me alive. I'd learned that some national publications paid as much as a thousand to five thousand dollars per article, particularly for features.

I definitely could use that to supplement my "survival money."

The money I was getting from Malik sometimes wasn't even enough to buy groceries; it only covered my rent and car note. Meanwhile, neither State Farm, my car insurance company, nor Georgia Power, failed to send me those friendly reminders. Also, my monthly gas and cable expenses, as well as regular statements for the Visa, MasterCard, Discover and Spiegel credit cards I didn't need, continued to roll in. I'd decided, the minute I got in a position to pay all these cards off, I was going to cut them up.

And, of course, I always looked forward to hearing from Ma Bell each month around the 22nd. No matter how hard I tried, I just couldn't seem to get my long distance charges under seventy-five dollars. What, with my parents and Marlo, and a host of friends living out of town.

Then there were the fifty dollars I paid monthly on this bedroom furniture I just had to have six months ago—or so I thought. I mean, it was nice and all. And it *was* a good deal. A queen-size black ironpost bed with matching chest, mirrored dresser and nightstand for nine hundred ninety-nine dollars. With interest, though, the full amount ended up costing me about fifteen hundred dollars, all because I didn't pay it off within ninety days. Needless to say, three months just wasn't enough time for me to come up with an extra thousand bucks. But having to pay an additional amount, as much as six hundred dollars in interest, didn't bother me too much. I managed to handle the payments during my days of steady pay. At least I didn't have to repay the federal government for a freakin' student loan like most of my friends. Miko owed them at least ten thousand dollars and was taking care of that debt by way of fifty dollars a month. But guess what? Not even half of that went toward the principal; the majority applied directly to interest. And, as she'd always put it, it was probably going to take her all her life to reach a zero balance.

Speaking of zero, that was what I'd have once I dropped the only two bills I could afford to keep up in the mail. In order to take care of my smaller bills like the cable and lights, I had to dip into my minuscule savings, which was steadily dwindling. The credit cards and few past-due medical bills were a different story. My parents had to chip in to help with those. I hated receiving financial assistance from them. I hadn't had to since I'd first started out on my own. Whenever I accepted their help, I felt myself sinking to a new all-time low. Every day I was hoping for good news to change all that. If not a call from Malik, some friendly correspondence from *Essence, Woman's Day* or any one of the other five publications I'd submitted to. So every day around two, I'd make my afternoon trek to the mailbox, only to be disappointed. Seemed like the more I looked for good news, the more bad I got.

Even a rejection letter at this point would suffice.

But all I got were more bills. More demands. More threats. Like "this is your third and final notice" or my favorite, the one that came in the mail earlier today for a six-month-old doctor's bill I'd completely forgotten about: "The named creditor has placed this account with our office for collection. It's important that you forward payment in full. If this account is not resolved within thirty days, your credit rating will be adversely affected." Those who weren't harrassing me through the mail enjoyed the convenience of the phone. Some days I sat and screened my calls, oftentimes laughing at their sarcastic and not-so-polite messages, which cleverly never identified where they were calling from. Vague messages such as: "This message is for Ms. Brown." *No, duh. Whose house did you call?* I'd think.

"This is Mrs. Jefferson. Please return the call at..." Of course, it rarely was a toll-free-number. Which meant most would never hear back from me. But that didn't stop them.

I'd never understood bill collectors. What was their beef all about? It wasn't like I owed *them* the money or anything. That thirty-seven dollar overdue medical bill was no loss whatsoever to them. So why all the hassle? I figured it out. Most of them were probably in the same shoes. So they felt it was only right to vent—on some poor person who was struggling as much as they were to get on their feet. But did these pests take any of that into consideration? Of course not. To some degree, I believed they got some sense of pleasure out of it. Or maybe it was that their lives were so miserable. Particularly the ones who'd be lucky enough to trap you on the phone, only to make you feel like a criminal on the lam.

"Ms. Brown, we haven't heard from you," they'd say. "We've called, left messages and even sent you letters. You *are* still obligated to pay this debt, you know? You can't just run from it and pretend it'll go away." At that point, I'd always want to say *why don't you go away?* The worst part about it all was that many of the voices on the other end belonged to sistuhs. And I'm certain, they could tell I was a sistuh, too.

That's not to say a person's voice is a dead giveaway of the color of their skin, although in some cases it is. But that's beside the point. I guess all I'm saying is, looks like you could expect a little compassion from your own.

"Please don't be mad. I know Christmas has come and gone and I'm just now giving you your gift but, as you know, I've been busy."

"That's okay. I'll forgive you this time. Just don't let it happen again!"

A slight smirk appeared on Dave's face, as he removed just enough wrapping paper to reveal what was inside.

"Meatless Meals: 51 Savory Favorites for Vegetarian Lovers," he read aloud. "And *Where's the Beef: You Won't Find it Here.* Jazz, how thoughtful of you." Dave was careful not to tear the paper, which was decorated with tiny black angels, as he unwrapped the two cookbooks. His face lit up like a kid's in a candy store.

"I know how committed you are to becoming a vegetarian, Dave. And when I saw these I couldn't resist."

"I'm glad you didn't. I can't wait to start experimenting with some of these recipes." He walked over and planted a kiss on my left cheek.

"Well, when you get to the point where you can actually burn some of the meals, I wanna be the first to sample."

"You will be. I promise. Matter of fact, you even get to pick the dish. Whatever you want, I'll make just for you."

"Okay, that's a bet. This low-fat veggie lasagna sure sounds good." I thumbed through the pages of one of the cookbooks. "Um, and so do these marinated vegetables on skewers."

"Okay, I'll definitely keep those two in mind." He smiled, and folded back the pages.

"So, what's on your agenda for tonight? What weekend hangout has the honor of your presence?" Dave left the kitchen, returning to his half-bath, where he stopped in front of the mirror. He finished getting dressed—something he was doing when I dropped in—as I reclined in his black leather lounger located in the adjacent living room.

"Writing."

"Writing? Jazz, that's all you ever do now," he said, brushing his hair. "Can't you afford to take a break for at least one night? As a matter of fact, why don't you join me for this party one of my co-workers is giving?"

"I'd better not. Besides, I'm not dressed," I said, looking down at the gray sweats I was wearing. "Look at you, all decked out in your slacks, turtleneck and vest. *You* look good. You don't need me by your side, messing up your image."

"Jazz, you look fine. The attire is casual. Come on. You should get out tonight. You definitely deserve to have some fun." He played with his collar, then the buttons on his vest.

"You're probably right, but I don't have room for slacking right now. Besides, I will be having fun, doing what I enjoy most: writing and helping others."

"Okay, have it your way." Dave patted his cheeks with the Obsession cologne he'd poured in the palm of his hands. "So what are you working on now?"

"Some more safe sex pieces. I'm trying to get the word out there in as many publications as possible—locally and nationally. I recently read somewhere that blacks are most often affected by STDs, yet we're the ones who tend not to heed the warnings. We don't take it as seriously as we should. I think it has a lot to do with who's writing this stuff. If there were more black voices spreading the word, they'd probably listen."

"True. So how's it going?"

"Well, I've pitched at least one of my articles to seven different publications, all on the national level. I just got those query letters off in the mail. So now I'm basically playing the waiting game, and continuing to write at the same time."

"Just be patient. I know you don't have any doubts it'll all work out. I know I don't."

"Why, thank you. You're right, I am pretty optimistic. But this writing thing is so competitive, you know?"

"And what isn't?" he asked.

"You have a point. I guess I hadn't ever thought of it that way."

"Hang in there. I've got your back. I'm proud of you. You're a brave woman."

"Well, I wasn't always, remember? In the beginning, I couldn't talk about my experiences to anyone, not even you, much less a stranger. So I'm proud of myself, too."

"I can't say it enough," Dave said. "You're one of a kind."

Chapter Twenty-two

I pulled into a space on the campus of Grove Park Elementary at 3:00 on the dot. That gave me a good ten minutes to get to Tiffani's school bus before it took off. Katherine had given me the okay to surprise Tiffani and spend a few hours with her as long as I agreed to have her back at the shelter by 7:00.

She's going to love these, I thought as I lifted the two packages from the passenger's seat. In a decorative Tazmanian Devil gift bag, I'd packed a few African American storybooks, including *The People Could Fly.* Tiffani loved reading. She also enjoyed making stuff. So I knew she'd be more than grateful to receive the Beads 'n Things and Friendship Bracelets kits, both wrapped in a medium-size box, covered with Bugs Bunny paper.

I pressed down on the lock with my elbow and used my right foot to push the door to. Walking along the thin sidewalk, I passed several students making their way to the parking lot, some seemingly escorted by their mother, father or another adult.

No Tiffani in the bunch. Guess she's out back already.

I reached bus G4 just as the driver slammed the door. I pressed my nose against the plexiglass while banging on it twice before nabbing his attention.

"Hold your horses, dear!" ordered the driver, who appeared to be in his late fifties, thanks to his mini salt-and-pepper-colored Afro and beard.

"I'm sorry, sir," I said, stepping onto the bus. "I'm just trying to catch someone before you pull off. They're supposed to ride home with me today." I stood at the head of the bus and began looking around the crowd for Tiffani.

"Well, who is it you looking for?" he asked as if I were holding him up.

"Tiffani Powell," I said in my loudest but most pleasing tone, so not to upset him anymore than he apparently already was.

"Tiffni Powell?" the driver asked, simultaneously gripping the wheel and the seat's head rest, in order to boost himself up.

Tiff-a-ni! I wanted to say, but saw that he was already a little testy.

"Well, do you see her anywhere?"

"No, sir. But there are a lot of kids on here," I said, looking at him like a mother in search of her lost child.

"We don't have all day, young lady," he said, giving me no time to respond. "Tiffni Powell! Is there a Tiffni Powell on here?" he asked the mass of juveniles.

Not one soul responded. But I wasn't convinced anyone heard him either. After all, the students continued making a fuss, even as the driver tried to temporarily divert their attention.

"I guess she's not on here." He gave me a look that said, "You're clear to leave now."

But I wasn't giving up that easily. "I don't think anyone heard you," I yelled over the dozens of voices. "Would you mind asking again?"

"Look, young lady," he said, looking down at his watch. "We gotta get goin'. Now, this is *the* last time." He raised his right arm above his head. "Quiet down, young'uns! Quiet down!" he said, waving his long arm. Most everyone followed his orders, while one particular unruly congregation kept doing its thing.

"If there is a Tiffni Powell on this bus, please come up front. This young lady is here to pick you up."

Surely, if Tiffani's on here and she sees me, she'll come forward.

No one moved.

"There's your answer," he looked at me and said.

Knowing I couldn't hold him up anymore, I turned away. As I exited, seemed as if, all at once, every bus in the lot started its engine. I rushed off to the side to avoid being trapped in the middle of the motorcade.

Where is Tiffani? I know Katherine said G4. Maybe she's in the office waiting, but then again, this was supposed to be a surprise.

Inside the small school office, I spotted only the receptionist, a middle-aged, brown-skinned woman whom I didn't recognize right off. *She must be a temp,* I thought, as I approached the counter which shielded her from visitors.

"Hi, I'm Jasmine Brown," I said, unable to extend my right hand since I was still carrying the packages. Seeing that the name apparently didn't ring a bell, I felt a need to explain why I was here. "I've come to pick up Tiffani Powell," I said, looking around, anticipating Tiffani would come from somewhere in the back.

"Tiffani Powell?" she asked as if she'd never heard the name. "I haven't seen Tiffani today. Was she supposed to meet you here?"

"No. I was supposed to pick her up at her bus and take her back to the shelter later on." The combination of disappointment and concern reflected in my voice.

"I'm sorry. I've been sitting in for Rosemary all day and it's been pretty slow," she said, almost dragging her words out. "I haven't had many students come in and out of here, especially this afternoon."

"Well, could you check your records to see if she made it to school today?"

"Oh, sure," she said, reaching for the student ledger. She turned to a particular page and glided her finger up and down. "Shows here that she was in attendance today. Did you check out front?" she asked, sort of as an afterthought.

"Well, I parked out back here," I said, pointing behind her head.

"You should go look. She could be standing out on the sidewalk, maybe even near the school sign."

"Okay, I'll go check. But to my knowledge, she wasn't expecting me. It was supposed to be a surprise." I turned to walk away.

"If she's not there, feel free to come back. I should be here at least until a quarter to four," she said, looking to her left side at the big white clock on the wall.

As I'd suspected, Tiffani wasn't outside either. By now, I had a strong hunch that something was wrong. Back inside, I phoned Katherine, who confirmed my gut instinct.

"Jasmine, I assumed Tiff would be with you by now."

"And I thought she'd be with *you*," I said, sounding worried, "since she's apparently nowhere around here."

"So if she's not back here, she's no longer on campus, and she's not with you, Jazz, where is she?" Katherine asked in her matronly tone.

"I wish I could answer that, Katherine."

Realizing that statement didn't come out quite the way I wanted, I quickly tried to reassure her. "I'm sure she's okay wherever she is, though. It's just a matter of finding her."

"I'll alert everyone here," Katherine said. "I'll make sure I get as many people involved as possible, including the police."

"Could you hold off on calling the police?" I pleaded, feeling secure that Tiffani wasn't in harm's way. "Let's try this on our own first," I suggested.

"Okay, I'm trusting you on this one. But I'm telling you, if my baby hasn't turned up in an hour or two, I have no choice."

What have I just done? What if I can't find Tiffani?

I was flattered that Katherine trusted me enough to come through with my game plan (the specifics of which remained to be seen). But the responsibility now weighing on my shoulders felt as burdensome as climbing to the top of the Empire State Building with a full set of luggage on my back.

I have to find Tiffani, though. She'll listen to me. Besides, if I don't get anything else right this year...

But where on Earth do I start?

"Slow down and think for a minute," I said aloud. Tiffani couldn't be too far. Between school and the shelter, the only other spots she was remotely familiar with and knew how to get to via MARTA were Shannon Mall and Sparkles Skating Rink. Sure, we'd been to tons of other public places—Six Flags, White Water, Chuck E Cheese's and a few movie theatres—but my gut feeling instantly told me I could rule those venues out.

She couldn't be at Sparkles this early in the day. I couldn't imagine anyone would be there at this hour. But at Shannon Mall, I was likely to find her at one of three places: the arcade, candy shop or pet store.

Perfect timing, I thought as I pulled into the parking lot next to

Shannon's food court entrance. I waited for a space as a mother placed her baby inside a car seat. No sooner than her Honda Accord was in drive, did my Integra move in.

Please be here, Tiffani. There's only one other place I can count on if you're not.

Through the double glass doors, the arcade was situated to the left in the center of the food court. A small, after-school crowd was just starting to form when I walked in. But, unfortunately, Tiffani wasn't part of the pack.

The food court traffic was fairly heavy in comparison to any other Wednesday afternoon.

The Valentine's Day crowd out in full force. There was a time that I was part of it.

Everyone who passed me probably felt like a criminal, thanks to the scrutinizing expression covering my face.

Not one lone child. I quickly headed toward Morrison's Cafeteria and hung a left in the direction leading to Pampered Pets. Before long, I realized my luck apparently had run out in the parking lot. Tiffani wasn't in any of the places I suspected nor did she respond to any of the three pages made from the information desk.

This is not looking good, I thought, while nearly running a traffic light on Jonesboro Road. *Sparkles is the last place I'd expect to find Tiffani. But I don't suppose it'll hurt to try there.*

I wanted to cry and scream as I exited the rink in the same state. Tiffaniless.

I don't know where else to try. I collapsed against the driver's side of my car, literally pulling my hair out. *I don't have much time. Katherine said two hours, tops, and I've already used up more than half of that.*

I felt a huge obligation to find Tiffani, as much as I'd felt responsible for her fate months ago. Not quite ready to update Katherine on my search, I decided to call home to retrieve my messages, just in case she'd left one letting me know our worries were over.

Short of change, I went back inside to use the phone near the register.

When will people learn to hang up before the announcement plays out if they have no intention on leaving a message?

By pressing one, I deleted the first two hangups, making way for message number three, which I wanted to skip, upon realizing who'd left it. Jennifer.

"Jasmine, the minute you get this message, could you call the office? It's very important," she said.

Hope they don't think I'm coming into that office today. I refuse to be at their beck and call.

I couldn't think of any other reason why Jennifer would be calling me. Since our talk, we hadn't bonded anymore than before, nor had I seen a drastic difference in her personality.

Jennifer's message was my last. Katherine had not called, but I knew, in this case, no news definitely did not mean it was good news. Before continuing my search, I reluctantly returned Jennifer's call. "This had better be important," I mumbled to myself, while dialing the number.

"*Amsha,*" she curtly answered by speakerphone on the first ring.

How lazy. She was about as professional as that Laura character on "Dr. Katz," a weekly Comedy Central cartoon about the rude receptionist, her "professional therapist" boss, his comic patients and his loafing son.

"Yes, Jennifer, it's Jasmine. I'm returning your call."

"Jazz! Great!" She said, picking up the receiver. "Girl, you need to get yourself a beeper. I've been trying to reach you for over an hour."

Care to pay the monthly charges for me, since you do still have a steady income? I wanted to ask.

"I don't have time for small talk, Jennifer. What is it, already?"

"You need to get down here. That little girl, Tiffani, has been looking for you," she said, rather excitedly, while apparently chewing a piece of gum.

"Tiffani?" I shouted. "Did she call there? Did she say where she was?"

"Calm down, woman. She's right here."

"Tiffani's *there*—at the office?"

"Yeah, she's been here waiting. Ever since she got here, I've been trying to reach you."

"Well, where is she? What's she doing now? Is she okay?"

"She's fine. What are you panicking for?"

"Because no one knew where she was. Anyway, could you stay right there with her for me, please? I'll be there in no more than twenty minutes."

"Will do," Jennifer said, before hanging up.

Before taking off, I called to let Katherine know Tiffani was safe and sound and that I'd provide her with full details once I'd had a chance to sit down and talk with her.

"Jasmine!" Tiffani sprinted in my direction with the same vigor as the day she was scheduled to move into her new home.

I reached down and wrapped my arms around her.

"Tiffani, you have no idea how happy I am to see you."

"I'm happy to see you, too," she said, still clinging to me.

"Are you okay? Why didn't you get on the bus like you were supposed to?"

"Because I wanted to see you, Jazz," she said, gripping my hand.

"How'd you get here, Tiffani?"

"MARTA," she said with a sense of certainty. "I called the number on the back of a bus schedule I'd found around the shelter and they told me which bus to get on."

"Where did you get the money?"

"I saved up my lunch money from one day this week."

"Well, what's wrong? Nothing has happened, has it?"

"No," she answered, looking up at me with a stare poignantly comparable to that of the set of brown and white basset hound puppies trapped inside the cage back at Shannon.

"Come on, let's go somewhere where we can talk," I suggested, leading Tiffani into the nearby conference room.

Tiffani pulled out one of the highback chairs and hopped into it.

"Are you sure everything's okay, Tiffani?" I asked as I took a seat at the head of the glass top-covered, cherry wood table.

"Yes," she said, kicking her feet in the air.

"Well, why didn't you go back to the shelter? You've never done anything like this before. You had us all worried."

"I just didn't want to go back there, Jazz. And I really wanted to see you. We haven't spent any time together since we went to church."

She's right, I thought. *And for a ten-year-old, she has a pretty good memory and sense of time.*

"I'm sorry, Tiffani. Things have been so crazy for me, lately; I just haven't had a lot of free time. I know you've wanted to see me, but that doesn't mean it's okay for you to just run away like this. We all thought something bad had happened to you."

"Something bad *is* happening," she said, folding her arms.

"What do you mean?" I placed my elbows on the table, leaning in closer to her.

"I can't take it there, anymore. I want a mommy, a daddy, a little sister or brother."

I felt a teardrop roll down my right cheek.

"You will have all that one day. I know it. Katherine knows it. We just don't know *when.*"

"I want it now," she said, sniffling.

What do I say? What do I do?

"I can't go back to the shelter, Jasmine. Please don't make me go back. Let me come home with you."

"I wish you could. But even if I took you home for a few days, you couldn't stay there forever."

"Why not?" she asked. "Wouldn't you want to be my mommy?"

"I'd love to, sweetie. I'd love to. But right now, Jasmine's having enough trouble trying to take care of herself."

I only wished I had my act together a little better. Then, and only then, could I seriously consider caring for a child, especially one Tiffani's age.

"Well, I'll just stay with you as long as I can. Just don't send me back. Please."

"You *have* to go back, Tiffani. At least long enough for Katherine to give you the okay to spend some days with me."

"I don't wanna go," she contended. "If you take me back, I'll just leave again," she threatened.

"You can't keep running away from problems. Be patient, in no time, things will work out just fine."

I felt like a hypocrite. Here I was, giving this little girl advice I had trouble following myself not too long ago.

"That's not true!" For the first time since I'd known her, Tiffani raised her voice, almost as if she were at a breaking point.

I struggled to keep my voice from cracking. "Trust me, Tiffani. They will. They always do, if you just believe. If I can have enough faith they will, you can, too. I'll do whatever I can to make sure they do. Even it if means letting you come home with me for some time. That's if Katherine allows it."

"You promise?"

"Yes, I do," I said, "and it won't take a month this time. As a matter of fact, let's head back; Katherine's waiting. When we get there, I'll talk to her about what we need to do in order to make this happen."

"Greetings, sisters. How are we doing today?" SWAC President Daphne Lewis-Lawson looked around the crowded boardroom of her workplace, a consulting firm located on the fifth floor of the Georgia Pacific Center building downtown. It was standing-room only, packed with sistuhs from wall to wall. At least three dozen. Most answered with a simple "fine." About half just put on a smile and nodded as a form of acknowledgment. After she called the meeting to order, the secretary read the minutes from last month's gathering. That took a while, considering they were about three pages long. I couldn't believe how much I'd been missing out on. These sistuhs really had been on the move. They'd already accomplished quite a bit during the first quarter alone of the new year. Like sponsoring weekend mini-camps for our youth, in order to get them off the streets. And providing scholarships to college-bound juniors and seniors. I loved working with our children. It made me feel like a big sister, even a mentor of sorts.

"Okay ladies, any suggestions for who will serve as our keynote speaker at this year's empowerment seminar?" Daphne asked, looking all around. "Believe it or not, it's that time of year again. Time to start planning for the annual African American Women: Movers and Shakers conference."

Everyone began to shout at once. Names like Rosa Parks. Oprah Winfrey. Angela Davis. Alice Walker. Maya Angelou.

"Those are all great suggestions, ladies," Daphne said, "but we can't get any of them if we don't get on the ball. Most of those 'super sisters' would cost us an arm and a leg."

"Not necessarily," someone near the back shouted. "Once they see that it's for a good cause, I think they'll be willing to do it for little or nothing, maybe even for free."

"That may be so, sister," Daphne replied. "But we don't want to assume that. We need to make sure the money is available, and if we don't use all of it, that's all well and good. We can use what's left over for something else. After all, we do have a full calendar of events scheduled for this year."

"Why not raffle off some tickets?" I suggested from my seat near the front. "Everybody likes to try their luck at winning something. Since I have access to printing materials, I'd be happy to volunteer on that end."

"That's not a bad idea," Daphne said. She placed her right index finger against her cheek, as if she were in deep thought. "We've raffled tickets before, and the results were well worth the effort. We don't have to give away anything extravagant. A weekend getaway. Color TV. Braves or Hawks tickets. Anything. How do you ladies feel about that?"

By a show of hands, my proposal was unanimously accepted.

I'm making strides. The old me is returning.

Thanks to my renewed involvement with SWAC and the recent rescue of Tiffani, I suddenly felt needed, and more in charge of my life than ever before. That following week, I spent every free moment at *Amsha* getting the tickets ready and devoted quite a bit of my time on the phone planning and updating Daphne on my progress.

It's so ironic how the minute your life starts to get on track, running just the way you want it to, someone or something does their damnedest to screw things up for you. Enter Daniel, whom I'd have to admit, has been in my thoughts a lot less lately.

It was bad enough that I'd have to see him at Monique's wedding, which had been pushed up to April. But he'd turned to calling me a lot more frequently. The majority of the time I'd let the machine catch his calls. His desperate messages had the same rhythm:

"Jazz, I love you. I need you. Come on baby, I just wanna talk to you." I didn't want to talk to him though, and made every effort not to. He forced me to continue screening my incoming calls. I figured if anyone really needed to talk to me, they'd leave a message, or call back.

"Jasmine, girl, what are you doing? Screening your calls?" The minute I recognized Miko's voice, I picked up.

"Hey, girl. Hang on, let me turn off the machine."

I walked into the bedroom, and pressed the stop button. The cassette rewound to its proper place as I reached for the cordless and started back toward the living room.

"Okay, what's up?" I asked, hanging up the phone I'd first answered.

"Girl, I've been calling you for a couple of days now. I just haven't left a message. You know how much I hate talking to machines."

"I'm sorry, Miko. But I have no choice. It's the only way to get around talking to Daniel."

"Well, how are you?"

"I'm fine. As a matter of fact, each passing day I feel better."

"That's great. It's good that you're avoiding Daniel. But realize you may have to face him again one day."

"Make that *will*." I rested on the floor, my back against the sofa.

"What? When, Jazz?"

"Next month."

"Next month? Okay, what have you been keeping from me? Are you and Daniel back together?"

"No, Miko. You must think I'm crazy."

"I don't and I wouldn't if you told me you had gotten back with him."

"Trust me, that will not be happening."

"So, what's going on next month?"

"I guess I'm going to his supervisor's wedding. I met her last year when we were still together and she invited me to come."

"Daniel's gonna be there?"

"I'm sure. It is his boss, you know. That's why I'm not positive I'll be showing up. Of course, she encouraged me to bring a guest, which might be Dave, but I still don't know."

"Go. I think you should. It might actually make you feel better, Jazz, to get him told once and for all. I'm not saying you have to make him feel he's destroyed your life, or anything. But at least let him realize how badly he hurt you. The guilt alone will tear him apart."

"I guess you're right. I still feel we haven't had any real closure. But I just don't know what I'll say to Daniel, if I ever get the chance to talk to him again."

"Trust me, you'll know exactly what to say. The words will come to you naturally. Just like it did for me with Elliott during our last court proceeding."

"What happened?"

"That's what I've been calling you so much for lately. I won! The judge ordered Elliott to pay eighteen percent of his annual salary to Christopher every month. He also has to maintain certain visitation rights. I couldn't believe it. Girlfriend didn't cut his butt any slack at all, and she wasn't even black."

The good news brought me to my feet.

"That's wonderful, Miko. I'm really happy for you. I just hate he had to be forced to do what he should've been doing all along."

"Me, too. But maybe one day he'll realize that. I think once Elliott starts to spend more time with his son, he'll get to the point where he'll actually *want* to be with Christopher. All he needs is the chance to see what a blessing our baby is."

"I sure hope so. That baby doesn't need to grow up without a male role model in his life. I'm not saying you can't do the job. But I just believe children need both parents in their lives these days. Especially little boys. Times are changing, unfortunately for the worst."

"Don't remind me. That's why it's becoming increasingly more important for families to stay together. I just wish Elliott could open his eyes and see that."

"One day he will. The moment he decides to stop being a boy, and become a man."

"Ditto for Daniel, Jazz. Take my word. When he grows up, he'll realize his mistakes. Every single one of them. From what you're telling me, he's already starting to."

Chapter Twenty-three

What would Tiffani do? I thought, as I walked inside Dr. Smith's Cascade Road office, her new location since leaving her M.L.K. address.

First and foremost, she'd be strong, which is what I had to do. At this point, there was no turning back. Nor was putting off the appointment altogether an option, despite the fact that I had no medical insurance. March 15th, the dreaded day of my repeat Pap, had arrived sooner than I'd expected. Right about now, if I'd managed to keep my continuation medical coverage, it would've been drawing to a close. But because I couldn't maintain the premium alone, I'd had to drop it completely last month. And individual coverage was no more affordable at this point. Good thing I could honestly call Dr. Smith my doctor/friend. There was no doubt in my mind she'd agree to set up a payment plan with me.

More proof that, aside from bringing Tiffani into my life, my experience working for black people had been nothing short of disappointing. As much as I'd wanted to stick it out with my own, demonstrate my talents in a black-owned establishment, I'd had enough.

Malik and Sandy had done an about-face on me. They turned out to be anything but the mentors I expected them to be when I first came to work for them. That thinking came from the fact that they're around my parents' ages. Nevertheless, it seemed all that they'd put me through lately was of little, if any, concern to them. I was well aware that they had a business and all to look after, but they led me to believe that was *all* they thought of. I really wanted to believe their self-serving actions weren't deliberate, and that money was indeed controlling their behavior, but it was hard.

To a small degree, I think I know the disappointment Tiffani felt when Barbara changed her mind at the last minute.

"Jasmine, how are you doing today?" One of Dr. Smith's new nurses asked, while leading the way to one of a handful of examination rooms.

"Oh, just a little nervous," I said, passing a stack of unpacked boxes stashed away in a corner.

"Don't be nervous," she said, sounding like a dental assistant prepping a young child about to have a cavity filled. By this time, I was sitting on the exam table. "Remember, you aren't the first to have to go through this. It happens to women all the time. At least one, sometimes even two, negative Pap smears aren't cause for alarm." She rubbed her hand across my back, really making me feel like a little girl. "You'll be all right," she said, sounding as if she had a slight lisp, thanks to the retainer on her top teeth.

I forced a half smile.

"Go ahead and take everything off and slip into this gown. Dr. Smith will be in to see you in just a minute." She walked out, letting the door close behind her.

I stepped into the adjacent restroom and followed the nurse's orders. After peeing, I took one of the wet wipes from the basket on the back of the toilet and wiped between my legs. As I nervously waited for Dr. Smith, I fought off butterflies in my stomach as well as the negative thoughts running through my head.

What if I have cancer? I thought.

The pamphlets I'd read cited studies showing that women who'd contracted *any* STD were at a greater risk of developing cervical cancer. Maybe that was why the Pap turned up abnormal cells.

"Hi Jasmine. How are you feeling today?" Dr. Smith walked in just in time; my eyes had begun watering and I could feel the tears starting to well up.

"Just a nervous wreck, that's all. I know I shouldn't be. Kenya said I really don't have any reason to worry."

"Rest assured, you don't. She probably told you this, too: Even if this test turns up negative, don't panic. We'll just repeat it in another three months. After that, it becomes a little more serious. That's when it may become necessary for a colposcopy."

"What's that?" I asked, feeling a little wet behind the ears.

"A colposcopy is an examination done by way of a magnifying device. It takes pictures of the vaginal area, giving doctors a clearer view of what the problem is. We don't want it to get to that point though. Those examinations can be quite expensive."

"Are they painful?"

"No, they're actually quick and simple. Because of the technology and lab work, they cost more."

I closed my eyes and held my breath for as long as I could, wishing, in some ways, my mother had come along. I wouldn't have wanted her in the exam room with me. Just feeling her presence from outside the door would have sufficed. But I'd urged Mama—who rarely traveled alone—not to come because I wasn't ready just yet to face my father. She understood and asked me not to hold a grudge against him for what had happened, or let it influence our relationship from that point on. She also reminded me to call her the minute I heard something.

My results were back within a week. That called for yet another consultation with Dr. Smith. The first in her new office.

"Your results are a carbon copy of your last test, Jasmine," Dr. Smith said. "I've decided to forgo another Pap and just go ahead and perform a colposcopy in another six months.

I nodded, looking behind Dr. Smith's head through the nearby window, which offered a view of the busy street.

"There's no reason to worry between now and then," she offered. Before giving her full eye contact, I caught a glimpse of the new artwork on the wall, including a painting of the Phenemonal Woman, three images of an African American woman: one of her working, another of her nurturing her baby and the last of her loving her man.

"Jazz, you're not worried about this, are you?" Dr. Smith asked.

"In a way, yes. But this isn't the only thing bothering me. I feel stressed out, too."

"What's causing your stress?" she asked, a puzzled, yet concerned, look on her face.

"My job, or lack thereof," I answered. "Right before Christmas, my boss decided to *make* me an independent contractor. It's been a struggle trying to adjust to the change."

"Consider it a blessing," she said. "You may not wanna believe it, but they did you a favor."

A favor? It sure doesn't feel like one, I wanted to tell her.

"Now, you're self-employed. There's nothing better," she said. "I wouldn't have it any other way. That's why I left my office on M.L.K. to move here and do my own thing. No, it's not easy, but neither is working for someone else."

"You're right," I said, glancing down at the marble, pyramid-shaped desk clock.

"It just means you have to work a little harder, but at least you're working for yourself. Thank God, I'm able to keep my bills up, pay my small staff and draw a little salary myself. You can handle this, Jasmine, and when it's all said and done, you'll be glad you did. Just get out there and hustle. Start writing for other publications. You have the skill."

"I have been trying," I added. "I'm waiting to hear back from some national magazines."

"Don't just depend on them," Dr. Smith suggested. "Tap into the local ones, too. I'm sure there are some you've never even thought of."

I needed to hear that, I thought as I unlocked the door to my car. Working for myself wasn't a bad idea. But was I ready to step out there on my own right now?

The minute I got to my apartment, I called my mother, as she'd instructed, to give her the news. Naturally, again, she was disappointed but remained hopeful, urging me to do the same. Calling Mama to tell her the news wasn't her only piece of advice I followed. I decided to listen to what she had to say about Daddy. I still wasn't ready to face him, plus it had never been easy for me to talk to him. But I knew I needed to do something to help me deal with the pain. I decided to write a letter.

Dear Daddy:

There are so many things I want to say to you. I just don't feel comfortable saying them in person right now. Perhaps someday I will.

First of all, I want you to know I love you. I've just never really felt we had the best father-daughter relationship. Part of the reason I think has to do with the fact that I never felt I could please you; most of the times when you parted your lips to speak to me, you were criticizing something about me, something I'd done, or not done. I never understood and still don't, what that was all about. What I do know is, it created a small gap in our relationship. Now that gap is widening because of something I just learned. If Mama hasn't told you by now, I know about what happened six years ago. I know about Mama getting sick.

I want you to know I am hurt by all this. It's bothered me so, I didn't want to be around you for a while. I just can't understand why, Daddy. This has hurt me deeply, not to mention, Mama. And I just wanna know why. What was worth turning your back on your family? What was worth the pain you've caused, the damage you've done? There's so much more I want to say. I'll save it for when we are able to talk in person. I'll let you know when I'm ready.

Love you,

Jazz

Chapter Twenty-four

I was becoming a pro at filling out these new patient registration forms. But the latest, for a first-time consultation with Dr. Harriet Watkins, a licensed psychologist, was a challenge. In the twenty minutes it took me to complete the three pages, a handful of women entered A New Day Counseling Center.

Bet they're wondering what I'm doing here, I'd think each time one would take a seat next to me on the terracotta-colored sofa, or across my way in the matching chairs. I was certain at least one of them thought that way because I was guilty of the same thing.

Bet at least one of them has thought of turning back, too.

For one thing, I was taking a chance with this insurance card, knowing my coverage had expired. But, fortunately, as I'd hoped, this was one office where they didn't see a need to call to verify beforehand.

They should know they're going to get paid either way.

How, I didn't know just yet. That was a problem I'd have to tackle later. If I took Mama's classic advice, they wouldn't be getting the total all at once, though.

If you can't send 'em no more than five dollars at a time, send that, she'd say. *If they take it, there's nothing they can say or do about it.*

Besides that concern, there was the obvious one. Outside of high school, I'd never met with a counselor for any reason. Not that I hadn't thought about it from time to time. But one constant fear always stopped me. The idea of being branded as "crazy."

"Jasmine Brown," a voice from my left side said. I looked in the direction to find a sistuh standing with a clipboard in hand. I stood and walked her way, hoping she was indeed Dr. Watkins and not an assistant.

"How are you today?" she asked, leading the way down a short hall and around the corner to a secluded office.

"I'm okay," I responded, a tinge of uncertainty in my voice.

"Have a seat," ordered the walnut-complected doctor, who appeared to be around my mother's age.

I slumped near the edge of her solid maroon-colored loveseat, while she sat in a matching highback chair, a notepad resting on her lap.

"So, what brings you here today?" she asked, crossing her legs.

I clasped my hands and leaned forward.

"Well, this is something I've thought about doing in the past. I just never could get up the nerve to go through with it."

"It's a good thing you did. Many people view counseling as something negative, something only for 'crazy people.' Rarely, do you see us seeking professional help for our problems, Jasmine."

I felt an unexplainable level of comfort with Dr. Watkins. It was as if I were returning for a fourth or fifth visit.

"Well, Dr. Watkins, I have to admit it wasn't easy convincing myself to do this. I unfortunately come from a family background that fits your description. My father, for example, would never support my decision to come here."

"Which brings me back to my earlier question," she said, picking up a solid black mug. "Why *did* you come?"

The aroma of what smelled like an apple-flavored herbal tea drifted my way.

"I've had a lot of things happen in my life over the past year and a half that have really made me wonder *why*. For two years, I was in and out of a dead-end relationship that brought me more pain than happiness. But, up until recently, I couldn't, rather, I should say, *wouldn't* let go. This man cheated on me several times. I never caught him, but I didn't need to. Not only have I gone through an abortion with him, I've been diagnosed with two non-curable STDs."

She nodded, looking at me as if I were one of her own children. "What are they? Herpes and genital warts?"

I shook my head yes, then picked up where I left off, as she placed the mug back on the table and began jotting something on paper. "This whole situation has just been ugly. Daniel—that's his name—has lied to me, humiliated me, talked down to me and made promises he knew he couldn't keep. He's even made me do things I never imagined doing in my entire life. I've made phone calls to females I found numbers for lying around his place or even inside his wallet. I've even followed him before. This is not me. I don't know how I got this way, but I don't like it."

Despite the fact that this was the first time I'd met Dr. Watkins, I couldn't stop talking. Occasionally, she looked over to her right at the mini clock on the small round table beside her chair.

"At first, I did think I was crazy," I continued. "That Daniel had driven me crazy. But something happened recently to make me believe all this may have been unavoidable. I've started questioning whether my fate is actually a direct result of my childhood."

"What exactly do you mean, Jasmine?" She glanced at the clock again.

"Well, more and more, I'm realizing my parents don't necessarily have a happy marriage. They're content, but I'm not convinced they're happy. For one thing, my father has messed around on my mom. Recently, I learned that he also gave her an STD. You know, I heard the rumors when I was younger, but I never really thought much of them."

"Suppressing those thoughts was perhaps intentional, huh?"

"I think so. No one wants to know one of their parents is being unfaithful. More than that, no one—I know I don't—wants to believe it."

"You're right, Jasmine. So, as is generally the case, this has hampered your relationship with your father?"

"It has. Over the years, he's always been so critical. I never could understand why."

"Ahh," she said. "That's a topic for another session."

This time, I looked at the clock and saw that my forty-five minutes were already up.

"Before you leave though," Dr. Watkins continued. "I want to give you something to think about that we'll discuss next time we meet. Think of all the genuinely happy, lasting couples you know. We don't have time to get into that today, but we'll discuss it first thing next week."

I'd never really thought about it before, but I personally couldn't say I knew of too many surviving blissful couples outside of Monique and Marcus, who I really wasn't around that much.

"You see," she started to explain while standing. "We as humans emulate what we see, what we know. You've heard that saying,'You learn by example?'" she asked, tilting her head.

I nodded.

She opened the door. "Again, think about it. Come up with some names. And we'll pick up where we left off next week. You do plan to come back, don't you?"

"Most definitely," I said, a slight smile crawling across my face.

Chapter Twenty-five

Monique sauntered down the aisle of Bethel Baptist Church, looking like a vision of beauty. Decked out in a gown her mother had meticulously sewn with her bare hands: a white, ankle-length wedding dress with a touch of African flair. Her veil resembled a crown, as she, herself, painted the image of a queen. An African queen.

As Monique made her grand entrance, her proud, misty-eyed father by her side, you could feel the happiness radiating within her. Her face lit up, in turn, illuminating the entire church on this gorgeous Saturday eve in April. About a hundred and fifty well-wishers, mostly family and friends, stood with their eyes glistening, their mouths open in astoundment. But it was clear to see the two happiest individuals in this packed church were none other than Marcus and Monique. The lovely couple's day finally had arrived. Three months later than they'd planned, but right on time.

I watched in awe and tried to grapple with two conflicting emotions. On one end, I felt complete joy for my new friend. On the other, a twinge of envy. *Why couldn't this be me,* I thought? Then a sudden sense of peacefulness emerged.

One day this will be you, Jazz, I told myself. *Just you wait and see.*

I looked out into the crowd and spotted Daniel, who, fortunately didn't see me looking.

You knew he'd be here. You can handle this.

After all, I wasn't alone. Dave sat to the right of me with Tiffani to the left. I wasn't sad either. Uneasy maybe, but not sad. Right about now, Tiffani and I both probably shared the same level of happiness as the bride and groom. Finally, she had reason to believe that dreams do come true. Yesterday, I completed all the necessary paperwork to be considered as an adoptive parent for Tiffani. Katherine said she didn't anticipate any problem, but urged me to be patient during what could end up being as long as a nine-month process. Four months would be considered a quick turnaround. In the meantime, Tiffani was free to spend as much time with me as possible. Plus, that gave me plenty of time to get my finances in order.

Ironically, I was the lucky one to catch the bouquet, out of more than a dozen women, who'd nearly scuffled for the beautiful arrangement. I never would have tried my luck had I not been persuaded, rather coerced, by Monique. To celebrate the victory, I took to the dance floor with Dave. I was glad to have him by my side, as a shield of sorts. Hopefully, Daniel was somewhere watching.

"Monique looks stunning, doesn't she?" Dave whispered into my ear, as we slow-danced to one of The O'Jays' all-time hits, "Stairway to Heaven." The reception at the Buckhead Towne Club had just kicked off, and we'd already withstood two fast numbers.

"Yes, she sure does." I glanced over at the two lovebirds, as they stuffed each other's faces with wedding cake.

"You know who else is gonna make a beautiful bride?" he asked.

"Who's that?"

"You, of course."

"Thank you." I blushed. The more we were together, the more Dave had begun to confuse me with his roundabout gestures, which—as with everything else—I tried not to read too much into. Whenever we went out, I worked hard to keep from looking at it as a date. In some ways, I guess I was worried about ruining a perfectly good friendship by becoming lovers. More than that, I was afraid of giving my heart again, and having it broken up into a million little pieces. Nevertheless, I enjoyed his company. He'd proven to be a true friend more so here lately than ever before. To be honest, I didn't know what I would have done without him and friends like Miko and Monique around over these past few months.

Monique and Marcus were on their last dance, when Dave and I walked over to bid farewell and wish them a safe and pleasant trip to their two-week honeymoon in St. Croix. We interrupted the newlyweds as they were slow-dancing to Vanessa Williams' "Save the Best for Last."

"Just wanted to wish you guys a great time on your honeymoon," I said. "Wish I were going with you!"

"Thank you," they both shouted at once.

"Jazz, before we get out of here, could I speak to you for a moment?" Monique asked.

"Sure." I turned to Dave. "Excuse me for a minute."

"Don't stay gone too long," Marcus said, reluctantly releasing Monique from his arms.

The lovebirds kissed before Monique and I left the noisy reception behind, walking right outside the double-door entrance into the hallway.

"Jazz, I just wanna say I'm so happy you were able to come. I really appreciate it. I know how worried you were about bumping into Daniel. It wasn't as bad as you thought, was it?"

"No, but I haven't left yet."

"Don't worry. Daniel knows better than to act up at my wedding. He does wanna keep his job," she said, laughing.

Monique was glowing so. It was clear to see this was, without a doubt, a moment of ascencion in her life. "Thank you for insisting I come and for suggesting that I bring a guest."

"I couldn't resist. Daniel's my sidekick and all, but a little jealousy never killed anybody, now did it."

I shook my head no and gave her a look that let her know I followed her completely.

"Now, for the big news," she said. "I'm pregnant."

"No! You gotta by kidding!"

"Not one bit. We just found out. I'm six weeks."

"Congratulations." I reached to hug her.

"Thank you," she said, squeezing me. "It's a miracle and blessing, all rolled into one."

"It sure is." I was so happy for Monique and Marcus. I always felt good when things turned around like this to work for the best for deserving people like them.

"But I have to tell you, we were all set on adopting that baby. God just had another plan."

"The one you'd wanted—and the one meant to be—all along," I added.

"Amen."

"I'll be praying that all goes well."

"Thank you."

Monique wasted no time changing the subject.

"I also want to apologize to you, Jazz. I haven't had a chance to do this before now, and it's been bothering me," she said.

"Apologize for what?"

"I'm sorry about the way things turned out with Robert. In a way, I wish I had not introduced you guys. I should've known better."

"What happened between us is not your fault. You had no idea Robert would go back to his ex. Neither one of us knew one hundred percent."

"I know, but I still feel bad about the whole thing. I just want you to be happy. I really was hoping things would work out with you two."

"Well they didn't, so don't sweat it. I'll be okay. I've learned survival skills from the best."

"You sure have." She smiled. "I'm proud of you. By the way, Dave's a cutie!"

"Thanks. But we're just friends."

"That's the best way to do it, girl. Friends first, lovers later."

"To be honest, I've never seriously thought about anything more developing between us."

"Well, maybe you should. Did you hear anything Vanessa had to say in that song? *Sometimes the very thing you're looking for is the one thing you can't see*, Jazz. Girl, you better open your eyes. Anyway, we should get back in there before they start freaking out."

Monique held out her arms to offer a hug.

"Thanks again. Don't forget what I said. When I get back, I wanna hear some good news, you hear me?"

For someone who hadn't quite mastered the art of surprise, Daniel sure knew how to drop a bombshell or two every once in a while. Back inside the reception area, he'd managed to draw a crowd, gathered around him and Marcus on the dance floor. Monique made her way through and joined her new hubby up front.

"Ladies and gents, could we have your attention over this way, please?" The DJ trumpeted over the mike, before handing it over to Daniel.

"Today we celebrate the union of two very special people," Daniel began. I stopped in my tracks, not sure where Dave and Tiffani were. A nauseous feeling came over me.

What's he up to?

"In honor of your love and commitment for one another," he said, facing the couple, "I present you with a labor of love." He removed brown wrapping paper from a canvas painting that rested on an easel. In the piece, obviously Daniel's work, Monique and Marcus embraced, scenes of nature serving as their backdrop.

"Ahhh!" several voices echoed. With one finger, I caught a tear in the corner of my right eye.

It's beautiful—and touching.

Monique cried and hugged Daniel as Marcus studied the gift, his hands massaging her shoulders. The spectators drew closer.

Daniel pushed through the still ooh-ing and ahh-ing onlookers. He seemed to be coming toward me.

What could he possibly have to say?

My last conversation with Miko surfaced. *As she said, it just might make me feel good to tell him off.*

"How you been doin'?" Daniel stood about five feet away.

"I've been fine. How have you been?"

"Okay. You haven't returned any of my calls."

"Haven't had any reason to."

Where are Dave and Tiffani? I thought, looking around.

"What—you lookin' for your little family? I saw you out there. Is that the same guy you told me about?"

"No, it's not Robert."

"Oh, so it must be that dude you went shoppin' and shit with?"

"Daniel, what is it you have to say. I've gotta go."

"So, this was going on right up under my nose?"

"Nothing was going on. Just like I told you before when you were acting all suspicious."

"Uh-huh."

"Uh-huh, nothing." I noticed Tiff and Dave 'cuttin' the rug' (another classic line from my great-grandma).

"Well, I admit, I got a little jealous. I was thinkin' I should've been the one dancin' with you. The whole time I painted the picture, I was thinkin' 'this should've been me and Jazz.'"

"It *could've* been, if you'd *really* wanted it to. If you'd done me right."

"I don't know what to say but I'm sorry."

That's nothing new, I thought.

"Jazz, I've done a lot of thinking, and I realize I was a fool. I can't believe I let a woman as good as you get away from me. All you ever did was try to love me, and I took you for granted. But I want you to know I cared deeply for you. I still do, and I still love you. I just should've been honest with myself. I really wasn't ready to settle down. It's not that I don't ever want to. I do, and I'd like it to be with you. But I guess at the same time, I enjoy my freedom."

I noticed my "little family" looking on. I felt bad, in a sense, for even talking to Daniel.

"You're right. You should've been honest with me and yourself. But you know what? This may sound crazy; I'm kinda glad you weren't. Everything you put me through has taught me so much, and it's made me a stronger person. So I thank you for that. No, it wasn't any fun getting my heart crushed time and time again. But I can accept the blame for some of that pain. I didn't have enough self-esteem at the time to realize I deserved and could do much better."

"You're right about that. You're a good woman, and you deserve nothing but the best. I just hope one day I'll be the one to give it to you."

"Your day has come and gone, Daniel. Come and gone," I said, walking away.

A white limo with deep-tinted windows escorted Marcus and Monique from the reception to the airport. Soon as Dave, Tiffani and I saw them off, we left.

"Thanks for a beautiful day," Dave said as he walked us to my apartment door.

"No, thank *you*. I truly enjoyed myself." I turned the lock, opening the door so Tiffani could go inside.

"I did, too. So, we're still on for tomorrow, right?" he asked.

"We most definitely are. Tiffani's all excited about it. In fact, I may have to sedate her so I can get some sleep tonight."

"Yeah, Xavier has talked about it every chance he got, too. I think they're really going to enjoy themselves."

"Me, too. I can't think of two people who deserve it more."

"Three people you mean," Dave said. "Don't leave yourself out."

Sunday morning, the sun beamed through my bedroom window, as if it were smiling down on me. A magical feeling I really couldn't explain rose over my body.

Today is going to be a good day, I thought.

I wasn't exactly sure of why, but intuition told me it would be. And considering all that I'd gone through over the past year and a half, I'd learned to pay a lot more attention to my sixth sense.

Dave and Xavier met us at eight in the morning so we could get an early start on our near two-hour drive to Chattanooga. Destination: Lookout Mountain and the Tennessee Aquarium. In exchange for media passes to the two sites, I'd agreed to write a combination travel piece for *Amsha,* with the possibility of selling it elsewhere. I figured since I wasn't getting the kind of pay I deserved, I might as well take advantage of any perks.

If the parking mania and the sea of individuals waiting in line outside the Tennessee Aquarium were any indication, the much-talked about site was indeed a thriving tourist attraction. Once inside, it was easy to see why.

"Look at that pretty fish over there!" Tiffani shouted, pointing inside the floor-to-ceiling level glass tank at a catfish that appeared to be as long as my legs. According to the identifying marker, the Blue Catfish was sixty inches long and weighed about seventy pounds.

"That's as big as you, Tiffani," Xavier said, excitement in his voice.

"You, too," Tiffani retorted.

"It's bigger than both you guys," Dave jumped in.

"Hey, a couple of inches more and it'll have me beat in size," I said.

"Look at *him!*" Tiffani was now pointing to a bubble-eyed fish, which suddenly seemed to appear out of nowhere.

"Okay, you two," Dave interrupted. "There's much more to see here than fish. Let's move on," he suggested.

Dave was right. The Aquarium's name could be somewhat misleading. Along with fish and other water creatures, it featured turtles, frogs, snakes and birds. The educational portion of our trip complete, we moved on to a spot offering serenity, adventure and beauty. Lookout Mountain. Climbing the winding mountain in Dave's Mitsubishi Eclipse was a challenge in itself. Not only were the lanes filled with curves, they were thin. Thirty miles an hour was perhaps the maximum speed to attempt up this hump. Once we'd made it to the top, we parked the car in a spot within walking distance of Rock City, a Lookout attraction where, through a telescopic instrument resembling a parking meter, you're able to see seven different Southeastern states. After the four of us experienced a mountaintop view of Georgia, Alabama, Kentucky, Virginia, Tennessee, North and South Carolina, we split up. Xavier and Tiffani wandered off to take part in some of the children's activities, including Mother Goose, a storytelling adventure. Dave and I walked around until we found somewhere to rest our bottoms.

"It's beautiful up here, isn't it?" I asked, studying the clouds and magnificent city view from my park bench seat.

"It is," Dave responded.

"This seems like the perfect spot to come to whenever I want to get away to relax, or to meditate. There's just so much about nature to appreciate, you know?"

"Yeah, you're right," Dave said. "Places like this are the tangible signs of the Almighty's existence."

"They're God's gifts, I think."

A couple, hands locked, looks as heavenly as the view upon their faces, walked past.

How sweet, I thought.

"Thank you for suggesting that we come here," I said, looking into Dave's eyes.

"No problem. I knew you needed to get away. Plus, my mom and stepdad couldn't seem to stop raving about Chattanooga and its attractions after they came here for a weekend getaway about a month ago. I figured it was at least worth checking out."

"From the looks of it, it's worth checking out more than once or twice."

"So, you wanna try to come back again later?"

"Oh yeah. That would be great. I'm sure Tiffani and Xavier would think so, too."

For the next ten minutes, we sat in silence. I continued to bask in the moment and soak up the scenery.

"Jazz, may I make a confession? Two, actually." Dave asked, his voice elevating over the consistent chirps of a bird sitting on a nearby tree limb.

"Sure." The bird's song left me mesmerized and in a dreamlike state.

"When I saw you talking to Daniel at the reception, it bothered me a little bit. I guess 'cause I've gotten so used to spending time with you. I enjoy it."

I opened my eyes long enough to see if Dave had more to say, the whole time, fumbling with the rainbow-cording friendship bracelet Tiffani had made me from her kit.

A future artist, for sure.

"I always have," he continued. "But especially now that you've shared so much of yourself with me. It's made us closer. I feel privileged to know you trust me. That says a lot."

I remained focused for good this time. "I feel just as fortunate, Dave, to have a friend like you that I can be open with. You've taken the time to listen to all my problems, and even provided a shoulder for me to cry on from time to time. I know I've said it many times before, but thank you."

"You've said it one time too many. It's not necessary. I'll always be here for you, Jazz. Anytime you need me."

Never before had I looked at Dave in a way outside of friendship. But he was beginning to make it a little hard for me not to.

Maybe Monique knows of what she speaks.

"Jazz, do you remember the first time we met?" he asked.

"I sure do. It was six years ago this coming August."

"I'm impressed." He blushed. "Your memory is better than I thought. I know I'll never forget that day you walked into the financial aid office. You were so frustrated, almost at your wits' end."

"That was a pretty rough time for me. One of my most taxing

quarters. I didn't know if I was going to be able to take classes or not. My grant money was late, for the first time ever. Matter of fact, that was the only time in my entire four years that my check was lagging."

"I remember. I felt so sorry for you. Even partially responsible for the delay, although I had nothing to do with it. But I knew I had to do something to make things right."

"You were a lifesaver from the start. I don't think anyone else would've cared as much as you. You pulled some nearly impossible strings, and the check arrived two days later. Just in the nick of time."

The events of that day were as vivid as yesterday's.

"I felt so proud of myself for being able to come through for you," Dave said, reaching down to pick up a handful of gravel. "I'll admit, at first I felt like a big brother pulling his baby sister out of a distressing situation. Then, almost overnight, you became one of the best friends a guy could ask for."

"You became the same for me. Ever since that day, you've been right there, each time it seemed that I was about to descend into a bottomless pit. I'm truly indebted to you."

"You shouldn't feel that way. Your friendship has been payback enough. Seeing you glow the way you are today is another bonus."

I smiled.

"You know, I never told you this before," Dave said, tossing a couple of the rocks forward. "I'm glad your grant was late."

"What?" I asked, nearly baffled.

"Think about it. If that hadn't happened, I never would have gotten the chance to know you as well as I do. Had the money come on time, any one of the student assistants could've handed that check over to you. But, as the director of financial aid, whenever there was a problem like yours with a student's funds, I had to handle it." Dave looked toward the sky, and placed his hands together in a prayerful fashion. "Thank you. Thank you. Thank you."

A warm feeling crawled through my skin. But I refused to reveal any of my emotions to Dave. *There's plenty of time for that.* After all, there was no rush. Dave's past six years of unremitting friendship and love had spoken for themselves.

"We better get back to the kids," Dave said, appearing a little antsy.

We walked over to Deer Park to find Tiffani and Xavier had made some new friends, other than the live deer. They seemed to be having the time of their lives. As I watched Tiffani, I reflected on the many ways in which she'd influenced me. All along, particularly when Barbara surfaced and when Tiffani turned up missing, I'd led myself to believe I saved her life. For the first time I realized, in actuality, she saved mine. Thanks to her, I was even more inspired to keep writing, and to keep believing in my work. But more important, I learned some valuable life lessons.

You just don't know what you've done for me, I silently said to Tiffani as I remained in the same spot, looking on.

"Tiffani and Xavier, time's up," Dave called out. "Come on," he said waving.

The duo started toward us, moving at a turtle-like pace.

"Aw, poor things," I said, looking down at the pair of sad faces.

"Cheer up, you guys," Dave said, sounding as empathetic as I. "I know you're not ready to leave, but we can't stay here all day and night."

"Why not?" Tiffani stood almost shoulder-to-shoulder with Xavier, facing me and Dave.

"Did we forget? You do have school tomorrow," I said.

"But we didn't spend enough time with the deer," Xavier said, almost as if he were coming to Tiffani's defense.

"Sorry about that," Dave apologized. "But we can't stay any longer. We still have to drive back to Atlanta and you two are gonna have to hit the sack soon as you get home."

"Arrgh," they both growled, looking at each other.

"The good news is, we'll be back," I offered.

"Sooner than you think," Dave added. "Until then, we have enough to keep us busy, right Jazz?"

"Right." Not exactly sure what he meant, I played along.

"We are still on for dinner, aren't we?"

"Oh yeah. I almost forgot. You promised me that dinner months ago."

"Well, I'm not the one who hasn't been able to make the time," he said, giving me a now-what-do-you-have-to-say-for-yourself face, before looking down at Tiffani and Xavier. "So does next weekend sound good?" he asked us all.

"Yeah!" Xavier and Tiffani shouted, simultaneously.

"Sounds like a plan," I said.

"And Xavier, we can watch our *Star Trek* collection again," Dave suggested.

"Cool," Xavier said, barely able to contain his excitement.

"So you guys are trekkies?" I asked.

"Die hard," Dave said. "Captain Benjamin Sisko is the man."

"Well I have to admit, I've never been crazy about *Star Trek*, *Star Wars* or any of that sci-fi stuff."

"You don't know what you're missing," Dave said.

"Sure don't," Xavier added.

Oh yes, I do, I thought, as the four of us drove off. *I'm willing to try most anything. But Star Trek. Now that'll take some getting used to.*

I'm guilty. I know I haven't been writing in my journal as much as I should. I realize the only way to get into the habit is to do it, every chance I get. It's not that I haven't had a reason to write. I've had plenty. What I haven't had a lot of is free time. Later this week, I begin my thirty-hour adoption training session, which paints a realistic picture of foster care. The adoption process, combined with exhaustive job-hunting, pitching my article ideas and finally, selling one to a national publication, have kept me busy, to say the least. Turns out the STD piece I was pushing didn't spark quite the interest as an updated account of Tiffani's heart-wrenching-turned-happy experience. Essence magazine, of all people, picked it up. Proof that persistence and hard work do pay off. The almost 1000-word Interiors piece on the ironic ending to Tiffani's fate won't exactly make me rich. But the thousand dollars' pay will definitely be put to good use. I'm a mom now, or soon-to-be and budgeting is more a part of my vocabulary than ever.

I just took Tiffani back to the shelter after spending a week together here. Until the adoption is a done deal, this is how things have to be—occasional sleepovers here and there. We both cried when our time was up. I really love that little girl. Her presence makes me more grounded, brings both joy and peace into my life. For that reason alone, I know I made the right choice.

I've decided to follow Dr. Smith's advice. Even Dr. Watkins has jumped on the bandwagon. During my second appointment with her, she echoed my gynecologist's sentiments. Looks like they could be right. Between the two of them, I think God's trying to tell me something: All of this may actually have been a blessing in disguise. The more I think about it, working for myself doesn't sound like a bad idea at all. I've been too dependent on Malik for far too long. Sure, this would be a big step, but, as they'd both warned, nothing worth having would be easy getting.

At first, I wasn't completely sold on the notion of giving up full-time work. But I have faith in myself. After all, I did a little freelancing at the start of my career, so I have a fairly good idea of what to expect. Plus I realize most contracts are slanted toward the employer's best interest, anyway. Next week, I'll be meeting with a couple of editors from publications around town. Those freelancing opportunities, combined with Essence, *which I already have my second assignment for, are a start. Just the other day, I overheard someone say, "The best students get the hardest tests." I believe that's true when it comes to me and Tiffani. But what's even more certain, as we've proven up to this point, is we're sure to pass.*